A Darker Dawn

A Darker Dawn

Rohit Gore

NIYOGI
BOOKS

Published by

NIYOGI BOOKS

D-78, Okhla Industrial Area, Phase-I
New Delhi-110 020, India
Tel: 91-11-26816301, 49327000
Fax: 91-11-26810483, 26813830
email: niyogibooks@gmail.com
www.niyogibooks.com

Editor: Gita Rajan
Design: Write Media

ISBN: 978-93-81523-00-1
Year of Publication: 2011

Printed at: Niyogi Offset Pvt. Ltd., New Delhi, India

To all the authors I have grown up reading. Especially Stephen King, who has been a constant source of inspiration

Contents

1989

Dev was in no particular hurry to reach his classroom.

He loved sharing the bench with his best friend Avi, cracking jokes with him and beating him at solving crossword puzzles, but those moments were very rare. There was a routine to his day at school. It started with a vicious beating from the class-teacher Bokade, and ended with a vague sense of pain somewhere in his body. There were many stages in between: the numbness immediately after the beating, the eruption of a bruise, a few uninvited tears sometimes, and a prolonged period of gradually reducing pain.

The first time Bokade had asked the class to write every chapter of the Physics textbook—"Word for word, you little idiots!"—as homework, most of the children didn't do it. It would have taken them at least five hours after going home, which meant no game of cricket in the evening, no *Chitrahaar*, and certainly no comics. The next day, Bokade systematically beat the offenders with his black cane and large, fleshy hands. A terrifying smile, ringed by his unruly beard, never left his face as he battered every single one of them, boy or girl. No one repeated the transgression.

Except Dev. Dev didn't play cricket, didn't have a television to watch *Chitrahaar* on, and couldn't afford to buy comics. But he refused to do the homework. He thought it was ludicrous.

Eventually, Bokade had stopped asking. He just walked up to Dev and performed his daily ritual.

That day, the first slap numbed Dev's cheek and split his lower lip. Bokade's hand was a blur, raining rapid blows on Dev's face, but he didn't feel the pain. His classmates' gasps echoed in his ears after every slap. The beating seemed to go on for eternity. When Bokade stopped, his sweaty palm was red.

"Look down, boy," he said.

His words came out in huffs, reeking of cheap alcohol and cigarettes. Dev felt dizzy and wanted to throw up, but he didn't look down.

Bokade scanned the classroom as though daring anyone to stare back. Dev didn't need to look—he knew that all the children had their chins buried deep in their throats.

The last slap was indeed the hardest. Dev staggered over the bench.

"Don't you ever look at me like that!"

Dev still didn't look down. Bokade grabbed his hair and yanked him towards the exit, throwing him out of the classroom with such force that he crashed into the wall of the corridor. He took a couple of steps as though launching himself into another attack.

Dev stole a glance at the horrified faces of his classmates. They were shaking with fear.

A few dared to look at him, their mouths agape as if screaming silently. He knew that if he did not look down, Bokade would beat many of them just to let off steam. He fixed his eyes on the dusty floor.

Bokade slowed his charge, but only momentarily. He grabbed Dev's ear and savagely twisted it. The excruciating pain made him cry out.

"That's good, Gokhale. Keep staring at your feet."

Bokade pushed him against the outer wall of the classroom. His head hit the rough concrete with a dull thud.

"This is where I want you to stand. You move one step, and I'll thrash you for one hour."

Dev looked at the patches of sweat spreading rapidly on Bokade's shirt, which strained to contain his pot belly.

"What are you all waiting for? Get back to writing the chapters!" Bokade bellowed as he entered the classroom. His command was immediately obeyed.

***

After some time, a familiar pain settled in Dev's body. His split lip bled and tasted salty. Pressing it gingerly, he hoped the tear wasn't too big.

The school was perched on a little hillock on the outskirts of Amrapur. Standing outside the classroom, Dev could see the entire town as it sweltered under the April sun. Engulfed in heat-haze, it looked like a blurred photograph. Thirsty crows hovered over the roads, cawing incessantly. The two big playgrounds had a smattering of barefoot kids playing football.

Inside, the only sound was the tap-tap-tap of Bokade's cane—a relentless reminder of the brutal beatings Dev had endured.

Two hours later, the bell rang, announcing lunchtime. Bokade walked out of the classroom and went up to Dev. Tapping his thigh with the cane, he said, "So have you learnt your lesson, boy?"

Dev said nothing, fixing his eyes on the football game, straining to hear their laughter. Bokade growled like an animal, "You will bow down to me one day."

Dev thought he heard Bokade whisper "bastard" as he walked away.

For a few moments, an unsettling silence reigned as the kids waited to hear Bokade's footsteps fade away. Then they ambled out of the classroom with smiles of relief.

"You're setting new records for standing outside," said Avi.

"You forgot the slapping record."

"Your cheek and lip are badly swollen."

"They don't hurt, though. Let's go to the riverside."

***

The 'riverside' was a little patch of wavy green grass right next to the river—a tributary of the Saraswati—that skirted the town. A thicket of trees hid it from the eyes of passers-by. Sunlight filtered down through the leaves, making beautiful patterns on the ground. The silence was punctuated by the whispering wind and the scurrying of little animals.

"I love it here," Avi said as they sat facing the stream.

"Me too."

"Dev, why the hell don't you do the homework?"

"The homework's stupid. Besides, I don't think the beating will stop even if I do it."

"Aren't you scared of him?"

"It was frightening the first time he beat me last year. Like that movie we watched at your house, remember? *Evil Dead*. We watched it too many times after that, and it doesn't frighten me anymore. It's something like that."

Avi nodded. He had burrowed deep inside his blanket as they watched that movie. Dev smiled at the memory.

"I'm so scared of Bokade," Avi said, his prominent Adam's apple jumping in his throat. "A couple of days back, I had a nightmare about him. It wasn't him really, just his face. And his hand. They were attached to a dragon's body. He...That creature attacked me. And after a lot of running, it caught me. It could've caught me easily, but it was enjoying making me run. You know what it did after that?"

"It slapped you, right? The hand was a giveaway," Dev laughed.

"Hey! Don't laugh at me," Avi smiled. "But then something happened."

"What? You peed in your pants?"

"Oh, shut up! I heard your voice, Dev. You asked it to leave me alone. And you know what? It did. That horrible creature just left me and walked away."

"I wish *I* could have that dream. Bokade scared of me! God, won't that be simply great?" Dev said and they laughed. "Come on, let's go. Lunchtime is over."

Jeet Mehra stood outside class VII-A. His heart was beating rapidly and he was sweating. "Like a fat pig," a teacher in one of his previous schools had said. The kids in the classroom had laughed for a long time. They had christened him *"dukkar"* and hounded him for months.

The schoolbag his father bought the day before was meant for someone thinner. Its straps dug into his shoulders and armpits, and he would have red blisters on his skin by evening. His starched white shirt had balled up between his back and the bag. Its top button dug painfully into his throat.

He stood, not daring to look inside, certain that the kids would receive him just as they did in all the other schools—with roaring laughter followed by day-long mockery. This was to be his sixth school in five years. His sixth city.

Taking a deep breath, he entered the classroom and was relieved to find it empty. It was lunch time. But that posed a new problem: Where was he supposed to sit? The kids in all the previous schools had complained that he blocked their view when he sat in front. It wasn't true, but he had since decided to sit at the back. He looked around the empty classroom and decided to take the last seat in a row that seemed unoccupied.

The kids started to trickle in, initially in ones and twos, and then in larger numbers. Jeet sat holding his breath. At first, the kids didn't notice him. Then they did, and there were whispers—"New boy", "Fatty", "He'll need a whole bench"—followed by suppressed laughter. After a while, the voices became louder and the laughter more pronounced. Everyone was talking about him, but no one looked at him.

Then a voice said, "Hey, fat boy!"

Jeet flinched. His hope—of being left alone, for once, in a new school—was dashed. He looked up with his trusted smile plastered on his face.

"This is my place," the boy said.

Jeet's smile faltered. The boy was reed-thin, buck-toothed and squint-eyed. He sprayed Jeet's shoulder with spit as he spoke.

Jeet stood up, but all the other benches were taken.

"Can I share this bench with you?" he asked, willing the smile to stay.

"No. This is my bench. I sit alone."

Jeet looked around again. All the kids were staring at him, eager to see what he'd do next. Flashing a yellow smile, the boy said, "You can sit with me if you pay me ten rupees."

"What?"

"Are you deaf, rich boy?"

"No."

"Then what did I say just now?"

"That you'd let me sit if I paid you ten rupees."

"See? At least you're not dumb," he said and laughed. A few other boys hovered around him. They laughed too. He seemed to be the leader of the rowdies in class.

"Okay, I won't sit here," Jeet said lifting his schoolbag.

"Just pay me ten rupees. I'll return them to you later."

"I don't have ten rupees."

"You have the money, rich boy. Just look at your costly bag," the boy said, snatching at it.

"I'm not a rich boy. Hey! Don't touch that!"

Jeet was shocked to hear himself shout so loudly. The boy, stunned by the sudden ferocity in Jeet's voice, took a step back. The other boys fell silent.

In that moment, when everything in the classroom stood still, Jeet knew what was going to happen. He broke out into sweat. The boy grabbed his collar and brought his face within an inch of Jeet's. "Don't you ever talk to me like that again! Now give me the ten rupees that you owe me," he snarled. His breath stank.

"I…I…I don't have ten rupees. And I don't owe you any money."

The boy punched Jeet in the stomach. Pain shot through his abdomen and he yelped, stunned by its intensity. He doubled over. Tears filled his eyes. The boy raised his hand to land the next blow.

"Stop it, Jagan!"

Jeet heard a loud voice, but he could not bring himself to look up.

"Don't you dare hit him again, Jagan." The voice was a lot louder this time.

"You want to have it, Gokhale?"

"You leave him alone."

Gokhale was the lanky boy standing at the entrance of the classroom with his hands on his hips. His lips were drawn in a determined line, a look of disgust in his eyes.

"That's enough Jagan!" This was a girl's voice. It suddenly struck Jeet that he had been punched and was crying like a baby in front of so many girls.

"I can see the Principal heading this way. I can go to him right now," Gokhale said.

Jagan let go of Jeet's collar. "Gokhale, you're dead," he said and walked away.

Jeet collapsed on the bench. He held his head in his hands, wishing he was dead or, at least, invisible. His tears would not stop falling. Nobody had ever hit him—not his family, not the thousands of kids in all the previous schools.

"Hey. Are you all right?" Gokhale said.

He nodded without looking up.

"What's your name? Mine is Dev."

"Jeet Mehra."

"You can sit with me, Jeet. Come."

He followed Dev to his bench. There was another boy sitting on it.

"Hey, Avi. Move your fat arse a little. Jeet will be sitting with us from now on."

Avi was perhaps the thinnest boy Jeet had ever seen. He wore thick glasses that made him look owlish.

"Sure, Dev," Avi said and moved over.

"Jeet, you're sitting next to the class topper. Avi has always topped every single exam."

Avi smiled brightly. Jeet sensed the deep familiarity, a friendship taken for granted, between Dev and Avi. He felt he had intruded into their space. Why had Dev saved him from Jagan, he wondered. It was as though Jagan and Dev were two warring giants, and their spectacular confrontations an everyday affair for the class. Today, he had been caught in their never-ending feud. The pain in his stomach was a reminder of what Dev had saved him from. How would Jagan retaliate? And would Dev save him every time? He had been ridiculed and ignored in all his previous schools, but never beaten or rescued. Dev quickly moved his schoolbag to accommodate Jeet's. The space created on the right corner of the bench felt safe and welcoming. Dev smiled at him. Avi had a curious expression on his face, as though he was still trying to make up his mind about the new fat boy who had already grabbed almost half their bench.

Jeet looked at the girls' rows in the classroom, ashamed of his tears but anxious to gauge the level of their contempt. A few girls looked at him and whispered to each other—mocking him, he was certain. One girl was watching him intently. She had a smile on her face, and the most beautiful dimples he had ever seen. Her large eyes were deep blue, He was sure she was the one who had shouted at Jagan.

"Dev," he whispered. "Who's that girl?"

Dev craned his neck swiftly.

"Hey, don't look so suddenly!"

"Oh, come on! That's Anita Kulkarni," Dev said, then loudly asked Anita, "Hey, why are you smiling?"

Jeet glanced at her and noticed that she was blushing hotly. That was the way he would remember her forever. Dev was laughing with his head thrown back, relishing her discomfiture, and Jeet found himself laughing with Dev. Dev's laughter had that effect—it spread amongst the people around him and made them join in. Then Jeet's eyes briefly fell on Jagan, and he ducked behind the bench as though hiding from a vicious dog. Jagan's eyes, focussed on the laughing Dev, shone with such fierce anger that Jeet shuddered.

Just then, a bearded teacher entered. The classroom, which had been humming with conversation, suddenly became silent. Jeet sensed the tautening of Dev's body. All the children looked down. Jeet had, long ago, learned to become invisible by following what the other children did—he did the same.

He could see nothing. He heard the teacher tap his cane, the fearful breathing of his fellow students, the slow, menacing footsteps of the teacher, Dev's nails scraping against the desk, the teacher's growling voice, Dev's silence, the sound of flesh striking flesh as the teacher hit Dev, the teacher's grunts and Dev's suppressed cries of agony. Jeet flinched at every sound, helpless and afraid.

Then the beating stopped. Dev sat down, his body shaking, drenched in sweat.

After the bear-like teacher walked out of the classroom, the entire class let out a big sigh of relief. Jeet asked Dev why the man beat him so much. Dev just shrugged. Jeet had never been afraid of a teacher before. He had always been a teachers' favourite—the only child of the city's Collector was bound to be.

Jeet had heard his parents talking about Amrapur in derisive tones. The town was a "trouble spot" according to his mother. It was "a stupid little pointless place" according to his father. His first day in school made him feel it was far worse—a hostile, malevolent place.

Bokade rotated the paperweight on the table. The stillness of the school was soothing, devoid of the dissonant voices of the little vermin and the pesky teachers. He leaned back in his chair and lit a cigarette, smiling at the thought of Father Cyriat seeing him smoking with his feet on the table. What would the doddering bastard say in his supercilious, holier-than-thou voice? "Bokade sir, you should be a shining example of conduct to the students." Didn't he realise what the little pests were for?

He tapped the wooden cane on his left hand. The vermin shook at the sight of it. The cane made beautiful patterns on their bodies. He played a little game in class while the pests copied the drivel he wrote on the board—that of spotting the patterns on their bodies. "Ah, this was from two days back. That one still looks so beautiful. This one is fading—time to create a new one."

And then he remembered Dev Gokhale. He spat on the dusty floor, his lips contorted in a snarl. He gripped and twisted the cane, imagining it was Dev's neck. After a few seconds, he relaxed. He took a long soothing drag of the cigarette and wondered what made Dev Gokhale defy him. Not a single day in the past year had gone by without the cane sating its thirst with his blood. But that bastard did not fear him. Why? He took another drag of the cigarette, crushed it under his chappal and vowed he would break Dev Gokhale's will one day.

Dev and Avi rode their bicycles on the curving road that went down the hillock.

Dev remembered how, just a few weeks back, they used to try and pedal as fast as the wind. "We're gods descending from the heavens," he used to say as they hurtled down. One day, Avi had taken his hands off the handlebar. "Look, Dev! Look! Gods don't need to hold the handlebar!" he'd said, pedalling hard. The gods had descended that day, but in a mess of scratched and bloody limbs, bicycle wheels, torn clothes and strewn books. Dev was amazed that they'd escaped with just scratches. "They look like long red earthworms," he showed Avi his arm and laughed. Avi had almost cried, but then started laughing too. Since that day, the gods had stopped descending so rapidly.

The road at the bottom of the hillock was bustling with vehicles. It led to Ambedkar Square, the busiest part of town. Rickshaw-pullers and cyclists hogged the road and swore at each other for slowing down the traffic. Scooter-riders expertly navigated past ancient potholes while spraying the road with red betel juice. Hawkers, their carts brimming with mouldy vegetables and fruits, rushed towards their spots in the evening market, already warming their throats up by announcing their wares and prices. A big Ambassador car, the only car on the road, bullied its way through, honking non-stop.

Dev always wondered why Ambedkar Square was called a 'square'. It was actually quite round, with a large statue of Dr Ambedkar standing in the centre on a cylindrical pedestal. Many roads—some tarred, some muddy, some wide enough for a car, some too narrow for even a moped—met at the statue like a confluence of rivers.

Dev saw them first. He braked hard and skidded to a stop. Avi let out a loud yelp and stopped too. Jagan, his elder brother Bappa, and five of Bappa's friends were waiting for them.

"There they are!"

Dev saw Jagan pointing his finger and shouting as if he was unleashing a pack of dogs on them.

"Move, Avi!" Dev shouted.

When he saw the seven older boys turning round Ambedkar's statue, riding their big Hero cycles, Dev pedalled furiously towards the adjoining road. The boys' mouths were twisted into snarls. A couple of them were already panting. He knew that all of them smoked cigarettes and he could out-pedal them, but he was sure they would catch Avi. No matter what happened, Dev vowed he wouldn't let them catch his friend.

He decided to concentrate on riding and looked back only after they had reached the end of the road. "Pedal hard, Avi!" he shouted, hoping he didn't sound afraid. Avi looked back at him, scared to death. "Don't look back!" Dev cried.

Avi quickly turned and pedalled his BSA Street Cat as hard as he could, grunting loudly all the while. The lightweight bicycle was Avi's only advantage over the older boys with their big Hero bicycles. Avi's heavy schoolbag, wedged on his bicycle carrier, was slowing him down. Dev snatched it and hung it on his shoulders. "Faster! Faster!" he urged.

He could also hear the older boys shouting: "Wait, you bastards!" "You are dead, Gokhale!" and "Get Avi! He can't pedal!"

Dev watched his friend cycle as never before. The road was riddled with potholes but Avi didn't stop. They dodged the pedestrians and other vehicles on the street, ignoring their curses. There was a T-junction ahead. Dev quickly looked back. They had put some distance between the older boys and themselves. Bappa was at the front, bent over the handlebar of his bicycle. There were just four boys behind him. Two of them were panting so hard they were frothing. The other two were not as fast as Bappa. Jagan was nowhere to be seen. Dev noted all this in a fraction of a second.

A right turn would take them to the old cemetery, which had lots of open spaces and a high likelihood of Bappa catching up with them. A left turn would take them to the crowded Sarafa Bazaar.

"Turn left!" he shouted to Avi, who gave him an almost imperceptible nod. Dev was surprised he had to pedal so hard to keep up. He brought himself on level with Avi and glanced at him. Avi's eyes were bulging behind his thick glasses and his hair was matted with sweat. He was struggling to breathe. In another fraction of a second, Dev took a decision. "Drop your cycle when you reach Sharif Miyan's teastall, and run to him, okay? They'll follow me." Avi turned his Street Cat towards the teastall. Sharif Miyan would protect him.

As Avi disappeared into the evening crowd, Dev had the sudden impulse to follow him. A vivid image flashed through his mind: Avi was on the ground, howling, as Bappa's fists struck blow after blow to his head. "Dev! Dev! Help me!" Dev shook his head. The image didn't go. Had he taken a wrong decision? Would the boys go after Avi, instead of him? He had to lure the older boys away. He turned right, towards the cemetery, where large open spaces awaited him.

Bappa's cycle reached the junction.

Dev looked back.

Bappa had turned right, towards him. The two remaining boys followed Bappa—they were not shouting anymore. Dev laughed and pedalled hard.

Beyond the cemetery was the little stream with the bridge on it. And beyond that was Shastri Nagar, where he lived.

Dev was exhausted. He would last another ten minutes before his stamina gave out. Bappa was the running champion of the school—he would keep coming. Dev had to lose him in the next few minutes. He entered the cemetery with his legs completely numb. Suddenly, there was silence around him. The hot wind on his sweaty body was soothing, but enervating. He could hear himself panting. In the silence of the cemetery, Dev could hear Bappa panting too.

He skirted the graves. Bappa had immense stamina, but manoeuvring around the old graves was beyond him. Dev quickly gained distance. He heard Bappa's frustrated howl and laughed. He reached the end of the cemetery and realised he had left Bappa behind. He didn't need to look back.

And that was when the stone hit him.

On the back of his head. Blood spurted out. He looked to see Bappa picking up another stone. He kept going. The second stone just missed him as he passed the huge iron gates of the cemetery.

He put a hand to his head, but the bleeding had stopped. The sight of blood on his white school shirt made him feel giddy and weak. His knees buckled, his vision blurred. Pushing the bike across the little bridge, he looked back one last time. There was no one in sight. Ahead, he could see Shastri Nagar and the green walls of his house.

Dev pushed open the door, expecting darkness in the tiny three-room house. But he was surprised to find his mother standing in the middle of the main room.

Her hands flew to her mouth when she saw him. "My God! You've been in another fight, haven't you?"

"No. I fell off the cycle," he said without looking at her.

"Liar."

Dev's mother was just thirty-six years old, but looked twice that. She picked up the rusty lock. Dev wanted to laugh. He wondered what a burglar would steal if he entered the house. Would he want the old frayed bed sheets, or the groaning metal bed? Would he consider stealing the soot-coated stove from the kitchen? Perhaps he would try the three-legged wooden cupboard, to see if there was anything in it. Or, maybe, the two plastic chairs with cracks running from top to bottom.

"This is the last time I'm taking you to the doctor after a fight," she said and walked out.

Dev followed her.

Avi sat on Sharif Miyan's little blue plastic stool, chewing his nails. The older boys had not chased him, but he anxiously scanned the Sarafa Bazaar Street imagining those big bicycles riding him down. He had seen those boys beat up other kids many times. Savage bastards, he thought. His stomach churned as he remembered the sight of them chasing Dev.

He gazed at the sky and wondered if God had seen his cowardice and had noticed how he'd left his friend alone to face the bullies. How heroic Dev was when he stayed behind to protect him! He could have pedalled away like the wind. How shameful his own meekness was in comparison, when he had rushed to the safety of Sharif Miyan's teastall. But he knew they would never be able to catch Dev, and that his friend would be unharmed. His friend, freed from the burden of saving a coward like him, would be so fast on his bicycle! He imagined Dev letting out a cry of triumph as he left those bastards far behind.

Avi turned to watch the teastall owner. Sharif Miyan's gestures were those of an expert. A huge aluminium kettle simmered on the stove. Sharif Miyan would lift it with his right hand and pour the boiling tea into the glass at a sixty degree angle. The brick red liquid defied gravity to land safely in the glass—not a drop wasted and always filled to the brim. Avi had tried that at home once, and the tea had burned his feet badly.

Sharif Miyan's teastall didn't just provide tea. For the harried traders of Sarafa Bazaar, it was a place to find a momentary respite from their endless negotiations. Sharif Miyan knew how every shop owner liked his tea—some loved it with cardamom, some with ginger, some wanted it as sweet as sugar, some as bitter as medicine, some wanted it milky white and some wanted it brick red. For the people visiting the bazaar, it was the last stop before they went back to their homes. Sharif Miyan had a few chairs, but these were rarely used. People stood about, sipping their tea and sharing their stories with him. He was the eternal guardian of their secrets—floundering businesses, conniving relatives, recalcitrant children, fatal diseases. Sharif Miyan was a boundless well of sympathy in which people dumped their miseries hoping to get a soothing word in return and he never disappointed them.

Then there were the politicians of every religion, caste and ideology who never missed an opportunity to visit the stall. For forty years, all the politicians had been trying to convince him to join them. Sharif Miyan had given every one of them a long, patient hearing, smiling indulgently, nodding at their pleas and had sent them away with a gentle but firm 'no'. Many people of the town said Sharif Miyan had eked out some acts of goodness from all those politicians—the new instruments in the squalour-ridden general hospital and the sporadic joint celebrations of Hindu and Muslim festivals were among the things believed to have happened because of Sharif Miyan's influence.

The teastall had a little sitting room where there were a few plastic tables and chairs. There was a small kitchen where Sharif Miyan made tea. He forbade everyone from entering the little kitchen. "This is the most sacred place in this teastall, where I add warmth to the tea," he had once told Avi. He spent two hours every morning meticulously cleaning every little crevice in the teastall. "You cannot keep your workplace dirty," he would smile and say. But what Avi liked best about the teastall were the biscuits and toffees that were freely available to him and his friends.

He was reaching for another biscuit when someone whispered in his ear, "They beat you up because you are a eunuch." Avi recoiled. Abbas laughed, baring his paan-stained teeth as though it was the greatest joke. Sharif Miyan was busy serving tea to his customers, so Avi was completely at Abbas's mercy till the crowd dispersed.

"What are you looking at, eunuch?" Abbas whispered and sprayed blood red, *gutka*-laden saliva near his feet. A few drops fell on Avi's shoes. He felt queasy. Abbas quickly wiped the floor with his chappals, his face creasing with deep worry-lines. Sharif Miyan never tolerated spitting in the teastall.

"Nothing," Avi murmured, eyes glued to his shoe.

"I cannot understand why my senile uncle likes you little assholes so much," Abbas said through clenched teeth. Avi nodded, equally perplexed. He knew there was no escape from Abbas's vitriol. Avi wondered how Sharif Miyan could have a nephew like him. How was it possible that a troll like Abbas was born in the house of a saint?

The older boys talked about Abbas as if he were a hero. He was kicked out of school after failing nine times in the seventh grade, but not before he taught many boys the art of smoking. Avi had heard about his famous collection—hundreds of photographs of nude women. Avi had also heard that Abbas's long dead father used to beat him with a leather belt. The image of a cowering Abbas trying to dodge the whipping belt flashed in front of his eyes. He could not stop himself from smiling.

"What are you grinning about, you freak?"

"Nothing."

"Those older boys call you a rat, don't they? I've heard them. You are a freaky rat. You and that friend of yours, Dev Gokhale," Abbas said and laughed again. Avi prayed Bappa and Jagan would not be looking for him if he left Sharif Miyan's teastall. A few minutes more, and he would end up saying something to Abbas that he would regret later.

Sharif Miyan finished serving the last customer and turned to speak to Avi. "Will you have more biscuits, *beta* Avi?" He pronounced 'biscuit' as 'bis-kut', which Avi always found very funny.

"No, I've already stuffed myself with a packet."

Abbas slithered away to the neighbouring paan shop.

"Have those boys left now?" Sharif Miyan asked.

"I cannot see them," Avi replied, nervously scanning the street.

"Don't worry, *beta.* I will teach them a lesson if they come this way."

"Thank you, Sharif Miyan."

"Oye, Abbas! Look after the stall. I will drop Avi home."

Abbas was sitting on the bench in front of the paan shop. He stifled a yawn as he nodded. Abbas watched Avi, hatred replacing the sleepiness in his eyes.

"Come on, *beta* Avi. Let's go home."

Avi thought Sharif Miyan resembled a lion with his flowing beard and thick, hennaed hair. He walked in Sharif Miyan's shadow, which was big enough to cover five boys his size. He was the biggest man Avi knew.

"How long have you been making tea Sharif Miyan?"

"Oh, it's been decades, *beta,*" he said with a little smile.

"And how do you make it so wonderful? Everyone in the school says you have a secret land where you grow a special tea. Is that true?"

Sharif Miyan laughed with his head thrown back. His laughter was full of warmth.

"No *beta,* I don't," he said and ruffled Avi's hair. "I wish I did though. Own some land, that is. My family owned it once when I was a young man. It's all gone now." Sharif Miyan's eyes had a faraway look in them, as if he could still see the land.

"Where did it go?"

"We lost it during the Partition. My family owned many farms in Punjab—the one in Pakistan."

"But land does not go anywhere, does it?"

"You are right. Land does not. It's the people who go away. I know where my land is in Punjab. I can see it. I can walk on it. But it is not mine. Isn't that terrible? I can never forget the day when those landgrabbers held my family at gunpoint and told me to leave. I didn't think I would have to leave the country."

Avi nodded to show he understood. They reached Civil Lines, where Avi's house was.

"Avi!"

Avi turned back and saw Jayant on the IND-Suzuki motorcycle he had bought just a few days back.

"What happened?" Jayant stopped next to him and looked at Sharif Miyan with narrowed eyes and undisguised hostility.

"Nothing. My bicycle broke down on the way. Sharif Miyan was dropping me home," Avi said, sincerely hoping that Sharif

Miyan would not say anything about the older boys who had chased him.

"Why do you need someone to drop you home? You are a big boy, aren't you? Now go home, your father must be worried," Jayant said.

Jayant was Avi's eldest cousin. A morsel of *gutka* was forever wedged in his cheek, and he had the revolting habit of flicking his tongue on his lips which made them shiny red. He patted talcum powder on his face, creating patches that gave him a clownish appearance. He smelled of a nauseating mixture of unwashed sweat and sugary *gutka.* Already a prominent member of Bhausaheb Bhoite's 'youth' brigade, he fancied himself as a big leader of the town.

"Okay *beta.* I think you can go from here. I will head back now," Sharif Miyan said and ruffled his hair. Avi hated people treating him like a little kid but loved Sharif Miyan ruffling his hair. Sharif Miyan turned back and walked away.

"Why were you walking with that man?" Jayant asked.

Avi didn't answer him as he dragged his bicycle.

"Hey, answer me!" Jayant demanded.

"I am not a little boy. You just said that. I will do whatever I want."

"You are becoming very arrogant, you little rat," Jayant said. He knew Avi hated being called a rat.

"You have a lot of powder on your face, Jayant."

"Okay, smarty. You just watch your mouth." Jayant drove away.

Avi sighed deeply as he approached his house. Sometimes he wondered whether he really knew how many rooms there were in it. But he was sure he didn't know the exact number of people who lived there. Shah Sadan, as his house was called, was a palace his grandfather had built decades ago. He opened the huge wrought-iron gate and parked his Street Cat in the garage behind two Maruti 800s, three Fiats and many bikes. The house reverberated with the bawling of his cousins. There were at least ten children, aged between six months and eight years, and someone was always crying. All his memories of the house echoed with ubiquitous wailing.

"Why are you so late today?" his mother asked him as he sank onto the velvety sofa to remove his shoes. She was wearing a bright red sari and had a huge bindi that covered almost her entire forehead. He wondered how his mother always knew when he came home. She was invariably the first person he spoke to after entering the house.

"My cycle broke down," Avi said.

"Your father is angry," she whispered and glanced behind her. "Run to your room."

But it was too late. His father saw him and raised his hand to show that he wanted Avi to stay where he was. Avi stopped in his tracks and stood with his head bent.

"What's the story now?" his father asked.

He was a short bald man with a huge pot belly. Whenever his father gave him a tongue-lashing, Avi kept his head down and could only see the lower half of his father's figure.

"My cycle broke down." He was tiring of the lie.

"Nonsense! You have been loitering with that Gokhale boy. How many times must I tell you—he and his family are lunatics!"

Avi said nothing. He knew that all the people in the house had heard his father's voice and would be rushing out to view the daily entertainment. And the very next moment, he spotted the familiar faces of his uncles, aunts and cousins all looking at him gleefully. As if he was the performing animal everyone waited for in the evenings.

"Answer me!" his father yelled.

Avi said nothing. He wondered what he was supposed to say.

"When are you going to the shop?"

"Baba, I don't want to," Avi said and looked at his mother who was standing in the corner with a pained expression on her face. She was the other performing animal in the house—the eldest daughter-in-law of Shah Sadan, who had sired only one son after sixteen years of marriage, and that too, a sickly one.

"Shut up!" his father shouted, rather angrily. "How dare you answer back?"

"Baba. I'm sorry. But I don't want to become a shop-owner. I want to be a scientist."

He had never dared to talk to his father like that. It was a new twist in the entertainment and he thought he heard suppressed laughter from someone in the crowd.

His mother sat down on a chair, the strength suddenly sucked out of her. She would be crying a lot in the next few days and he felt a terrible sense of guilt.

"Sejal, what the hell have you taught this boy?" his father asked his mother. His words felt like acid, scorching Avi's heart.

"He will go to the shop from tomorrow, won't you Avi?" his mother said, her brow knitted in worry.

"He had better! Scientist my foot! Does he have any sense? You must've fed him these stupid ideas."

Avi's mother loved his science books. She secretly gave him money to buy them, though she never said that she wanted him to become a scientist. He thought she was simply too afraid to say it.

His father walked up to him and savagely yanked his head up holding a clutch of his hair. Avi let out an involuntary yelp.

"You'd better start work at the shop from tomorrow," he said in a low voice, let go of his head and with a jerk, turned and stormed out.

Avi heard his relatives muttering as they moved away. "Serves him right." "Sejal has totally spoilt the boy." "Stupid rat."

"Run to your room at once," his mother said; her voice was shaking.

He trudged away to his room, which he shared with two cousins. They farted all day and snored all night. Avi had never gotten used to it. He sat on his bed and wondered what was more upsetting for his father—his wish to become a scientist, or his very existence?

As he stared at the floor, two familiar feet appeared in his line of vision. His mother sat down on the bed beside him.

"I hate everybody," he said, trying not to cry.

"Shh…" She had a hundred rupee note in her hand and a smile on her face. Her eyes were red, though—she had wept before coming up to him. "This is for your book," she said.

He took the note and hid it in his school bag.

"I know you will do something in the world of science, Avi. Just don't tell anyone about it, okay?"

"Okay."

"When you finish your schooling, I will ask uncle Ranjit to take you with him to Canada."

He nodded. His mother's brother, Ranjit, owned a computer hardware business in Canada.

His mother laid her head against his. "Now this is our little secret, okay?"

They both laughed.

Chasing Dev and Avi, Jagan could not balance himself on his bicycle, and all the other boys rushed past him. He dropped the bicycle and clutched his heart. The palpitations were like a pounding hammer, causing him to breathe shallowly. He tried to shout an apology to the disappearing form of his brother Bappa, but the scream died in his constricted, throbbing chest. Yet another day when he had let down his elder brother. He'd asked him for help to beat up that bastard Dev, and now he could not pedal alongside even for a kilometre. Dev was responsible for this humiliation and Bappa would catch him and thrash him, but he would miss it—something he had dreamt of the whole day. He slumped on the ground as the dizziness engulfed him.

Two men, who were chewing tobacco standing near a paan stall, laughed at him.

"Shut up!" he shouted at them.

"What did you just say, boy?" one of them said.

"Shut your mouth, you bastard," Jagan snarled, his heart was still hammering.

The man walked up to him and instantly raised his hand to slap him.

"Bhausaheb Bhoite is my father," Jagan said, looking into the eyes of the man.

There was the expected reaction. The men leapt back. Jagan smiled, his heart quieting, gladdened by the fear his father's name evoked. He laughed as the men scurried away. He dragged his bicycle back to his ancient sprawling house that was proudly called Bhoite Wada—the Bhoite manor—and waited for Bappa on the terrace from where the entire town was visible. Leaning on the parapet, he surveyed the town, just like his father, a Member of Parliament and the most powerful man in town, did every evening while sipping his whisky. The Bhoite family had ruled the town for hundreds of years. There was a big hall full of portraits of all the rulers in the house—his proud lineage. Jagan had spent hours in that hall aping the poses in those ancestral portraits, imagining his own next to his father's and brother's. Bappa would look so regal and imposing and people would laugh to see Jagan's emaciated form next to it. Perhaps his father would never allow his portrait to be painted or put up.

Bappa and his friends returned just before sunset. Bappa was cursing his friends loudly, blaming them for being weak and cowardly. Clearly, they had not caught Dev. Jagan felt a deep, aching hollowness in his stomach. Bappa's anger knew no bounds when he didn't have his way. There were many bruises on Jagan's body from when Bappa had mercilessly beaten him for the smallest of transgressions. Bappa gave his friends a dismissive wave. They were not worthy of his words any more. His lips were twisted in a silent rage that would be vented on someone.

Jagan ran up to the huge water tank on the terrace and lifted the lid. The water tank had two compartments and one of them was always empty. He jumped into the empty compartment and closed the overhead lid. The damp smell in the little space was comforting. He had discovered it a couple of years ago, when he had accidentally broken Bappa's badminton racquet. He had been so desperately scared that he saw the cold, dark place in the water tank as a sure refuge from the terrible prospect of getting beaten. Since that discovery, he always hid himself there. It was his little place, his secret place where nobody could reach him, not even his powerful brother. The tiny holes in the cover provided enough life for his weak lungs.

After a long time—long enough for Bappa's anger to subside—Jagan hauled himself out of the tank, walked up to the room he shared with Bappa and glanced inside. Bappa was furiously pumping his biceps with a dumbbell, his face contorted with the effort. Body-building was the latest of his brother's passions and, in just three months, he had developed rock-hard muscles.

"Come inside, you timid idiot!" Bappa said through his grunts.

"I am sorry, dada," Jagan mumbled and plunked on the bed, head downcast.

"What else can I expect from a weak moron like you?"

Jagan could not utter a word. Just a few years ago, Bappa's irate voice would make him pee in his pants.

Bappa kept pumping his muscles for a long time. Jagan didn't dare to look up, afraid that Bappa would hurl the heavy dumbbell at his face if he said another word.

"Don't worry. That bastard cannot escape forever," Bappa said after a long time, wiping the sweat off his face and body.

"Can I do it as well, dada?" Jagan asked, gently touching the dumbbell.

"You are weak, Jagan. So is your heart. Don't even try," Bappa cautioned and walked out of the room.

Jagan lifted the warm, sweaty dumbbell his brother had used, wondering if it could work its magic on his body too. His hand wobbled with the weight. With excruciating effort, he pulled the dumbbell to his shoulder and felt a knot-like pain in his biceps. His hands were weak. Had Bappa punched that fat boy, he wouldn't have been able to breathe. And Bappa would not have retreated as he did when Dev threatened to tell the Principal. What could the white-robed idiot, Father Cyriat, do to him? Would he even dare touch the younger son of Bhausaheb Bhoite? But he had dithered and retreated. He had let down the Bhoite name, let down his brother, let down his father. It was not just his hand—he was weak from head to toe.

"You will see, dada. One day I will be as strong as you and I will make you very proud," he whispered and gingerly put the dumbbell back in its place.

He touched the little yellow metal cup Bappa had won a few weeks back in school. The entire school stopped to watch when Bappa ran, his hands pumping like two pistons, every muscle in his legs showing, his mouth blowing off steam, his eyes unblinking and focussed on the finish line. Bappa left behind plumes of dust on the tracks. And Jagan coughed on the side-lines. He would never win a cup like that. His father had said so.

Whatever Bhausaheb said was always true. Bappa concurred. His mother didn't say anything, but perhaps she too agreed. But his dada would win many cups, even bigger ones. That was enough. His dada would always be there for him. He would cherish all the cups won by Bappa, and he would be happy.

That bastard Dev Gokhale won every cup for class seven. Gokhale, too, must have a lot of cups. Perhaps, even more than his brother.

He shuddered with anger and coughed for a long time.

Bappa had thought of smashing the heavy dumbbell on his wimpy brother's head. The sight of the scrawny moron writhing on the ground would be wonderful. How could he and Jagan be brothers? The feeble had no business to be born in a house of rulers. Why did his father not realise the burden of carrying a son like Jagan and send him away some place?

He walked up to the huge living room of the house where his father was sitting on a high chair. All his father's cronies were fussing around him like gnats trying to get his attention. His father looked so powerful.

"Here comes my heir!" Bhausaheb Bhoite said loudly when he saw Bappa. Bappa's chest puffed up with pride. "Come, sit with us and understand the life of a politician, son."

Bappa walked up to him and stood behind the high chair. All the cronies were smiling at him, telling him that, one day, he too would sit in the high chair and they would serve him.

His father and the cronies talked about votes, about the opposition parties and their schemes. The cronies repeatedly said they were so happy Bhausaheb Bhoite was leading them. They were sure his father would overcome the opposition and triumph in the upcoming elections, just like the last time. Then they talked about money. It was amazing how much money his father had. He would own all that money one day. He would buy ten cars, all of them Marutis—the best car in the country. He wondered if his father was thinking of bequeathing some of those crores to his little weasel of a brother. He smiled. Even if his father bequeathed any money to Jagan, Bappa would still control it. He just had to kick Jagan's ass to make him pee in his pants.

"Bappa, ask your mother to get dinner ready," his father said and Bappa snapped out of his reverie.

"Yes, Bhausaheb."

Bappa went and told his mother that Bhausaheb wanted dinner to be served. Sometimes Bappa wondered if his mother was mute. She rarely spoke and, whenever she did, it was in monosyllables and grunts. Bappa knew about the several women his father had. Some of them, he flaunted openly. He had heard his father call those women his 'property'. His father generally twirled his bushy moustache whenever he said that. Bappa knew it was a thing to be extremely proud of. He couldn't wait to grow up and replace his father as the ruler. He hated the stupid school, the teachers and the kids. And he hated Dev Gokhale the most—Dev's father had called Bhausaheb a liar and a thief in front of hundreds of people.

Bappa hated every single human being who had the audacity to listen to those terrible words. How could they not have beaten up the shameless bastard when he accused Bhausaheb, their king, of being corrupt and tyrannical? Bhausaheb was so angry that day, he had shouted at Bappa. He had never done that before. Jagan was the one supposed to be shouted at, not him. And then his father had asked him about his report card. When he said he had failed in class nine, Bhausaheb had called him an incompetent fool, unfit to rule. How could his father be angry with him, the heir to the great Bhoite empire? It was all Dev's father's fault. Bappa wrote 'Anand Gokhale'—the name of Dev's father—on a paper, spat on it, crumpled it and stepped on it. Then he burnt it, vowing to make Dev pay for Bhausaheb's anguish.

Dev was the champion of class seven. That lunatic's son winning as many cups as him was an unbearable thought. He had a sudden urge to go to his house, drag the bastard out in the middle of the night and beat him up with his hockey stick. He took a few steps towards the door but stopped himself. "Always plan your move"—wasn't that what his father always said? Dev had escaped today, but he would not be able to every day.

He fantasised about Anita as he tried to sleep that night. She was so different suddenly. He wondered what it would be like to have sex with her. He quickly looked around, afraid that his father would hear his thoughts. One thing his father didn't entirely approve of was his loitering in the town. He told Bappa, from time to time, to behave himself. But he always did so with a smile hidden behind his thick moustache. Perhaps he was secretly proud of his heir's activities. However, his father would not forgive any harm done to a girl as it could damage his reputation. What if he did it in some remote place, where nobody was around, no witness.

A deep shiver ran through his body. He had an immense erection. He laughed at the word. What was it his friends called his thing? A tent pole. He laughed again. He wondered how Anita would react on seeing his purple-headed tent pole. Would she be fascinated and readily open up for it?

Or would he have to use a lot of force?

He went to the bathroom, removed his lungi, closed his eyes and imagined using a lot of force on Anita.

"Abbas! Abbas!" Sharif Miyan shouted and shook him, waking him up. "You cannot sleep in the afternoon, *beta*."

Abbas's stupor—after he had smoked two joints bought with money stolen from his uncle's cash counter—was unavoidable. He rubbed his eyes, but they remained unfocussed and bleary. His uncle reeked of sour milk and had a look of profound disappointment on his face, as if Abbas had committed some heinous crime by taking a nap in the hot afternoon. Why did the bastard always sound so disgruntled with him?

"Wasn't feeling well," Abbas mumbled.

Sharif Miyan nodded and sighed deeply. Abbas got up and dusted the bottles filled with chocolates and biscuits.

"I cleaned the stall in the morning. You're soiling it by flapping that dusty cloth all over."

The cloth was not dusty, the teastall was. Sharif claimed to clean it every morning, but it was promptly soiled by the first customer who walked in. With the town always seeped in filth and dirt, what was the point of cleaning the shanty-like teastall? And what was the point of making the monkey-piss tea? What was the need to ask everyone who came to the stall about his well-being? What difference did it make if someone's mother or father was dying? Or if their son never wrote? Or if they had diabetes, typhoid or fucking cancer? What was the need to know all this?

Sharif Miyan lifted the tea kettle slowly and placed it on the burner. "No customers seem to have come while I was away."

Abbas had a sudden urge to smoke another joint. Would Haidar, the flower shop owner who sold weed, lend him one? The sweet smell of marijuana smoke was heavenly. He feared that the only thing he would smell all his life was the burnt milky tea. The sugary vapours emanating from the boiling tea reached deep inside his brain and wedged there. He felt like vomiting after hours of stirring the tea pot. That *haraami* Uncle Sharif had somehow developed a sixth sense . The bastard always shouted whenever Abbas stopped stirring in order to breathe some air that was not infused with tea vapours.

Sharif Miyan shook the kettle of tea simmering on the bright blue flame. "I asked you something."

"No, not many."

"Have you noticed people don't come to the stall when you are alone here?"

"Uh... Yes."

"It is because you have no affection for the town and its people. One day you will realise the importance of spreading warmth."

His father, the madman, used to beat him mercilessly for no reason. It hurt for days. But he preferred that over listening to Sharif Miyan's agonising sermons. The stick-wielding father was dead and he was no longer beaten, but Sharif Miyan would be around for a long time to inflict his words upon him. This remarkably agile bear of a man was not going to die like the madman, although he was five years older. His father's heart was fragile and had stopped one day while he was chasing Abbas. Frothing with fury at Abbas's smoking, and ignoring Sharif Miyan's advice of patience, he had chased him all over the mohalla. He had collapsed at a turn in the road and never woke up. Abbas returned after two hours only to find out his father would not chase him anymore.

Sharif Miyan kneeled down on the prayer mat. Abbas joined him, pretending to contemplate what Sharif Miyan had said, intently imagining Sharif Miyan's head split wide open with the devastating blow of a hammer. Sharif Miyan had fed him after his father died three years ago. His sister told him their father was alive for a few moments after Sharif Miyan reached him and had whispered his dying wish—"Take care of Abbas"—in Sharif Miyan's ear. All trumped up claims. The bad-tempered fiend had never liked him. He still had the marks on his body, permanent reminders of his long-dead father's violence. So what if he started smoking when he was fifteen? So what if he took some money from his brothers' and uncles' pockets? So what if he had fucked the neighbourhood girl, Shama, when she was eighteen and he was sixteen? So what if she became pregnant and had to undergo an abortion? So what? The bitch deserved it for not taking care. Everyone thought he was the black sheep of the family. He smiled bitterly at the word 'family'. You cannot call sixteen people living in two dingy rooms a family. You end up farting in each other's faces.

Abbas was desperate to do something. And he had insinuated as much to his uncle, only to suffer a harrowing, one-hour, gravelly-voiced lecture on the importance of limiting one's desires to the means available. All he wanted to do was to leave this suffocating town full of hurtful memories and go to the Foreign. Sadiqbhai, the best man he knew, had promised him a job there. Sadiqbhai's own son was there, earning money by the bucketful and bedding beautiful women. He was an agent who had sent many young boys to foreign lands from where they never returned, free from the claustrophobia of the town. He just needed two lakh rupees to pursue his freedom, which Sharif Miyan refused despite his incessant pleading.

Sharif Miyan had the gall to doubt the veracity of Sadiqbhai's character, calling him a treacherous snake and Abbas a gullible young man. Abbas tried to explain that Sadiqbhai had sent his own son to the Foreign, but Sharif Miyan said that his son ran a scam to fool young men from his mohalla. There was no job in the Foreign—at least not the kind Abbas was expecting. It was something far more sinister.

Sharif Miyan was rolling his prayer mat when Sadiqbhai walked into the teastall.

Sharif Miyan ground his teeth. "What do you want?"

"A few words of wisdom from you and a cup of tea," Sadiqbhai said. He was a short man of less than five feet, who always seemed to be in a hurry. Abbas liked the sweet words and the occasional pack of cigarettes he had for him.

"I don't have either for you. Leave!"

Sharif Miyan's voice was stunning. Abbas had rarely seen his uncle lose his temper. He was very agitated, and his anger made him look pitiable.

Abbas liked the effect Sadiqbhai had on the old bastard. His façade of sainthood was ripped apart by the stronger man.

"Uh huh. I think I can live without either for a while. Abbas, I need to talk to you."

Sharif Miyan shaking with rage—a sight to behold!—commanded, "Abbas, put the milk kettle on the burner."

If Sadiqbhai could transform his uncle, there was no limit to his powers. Sadiqbhai looked at Abbas with scrunched-up eyebrows and a lopsided grin, confident of the choice he was going to make.

"Abbas! Listen to me," Sharif Miyan's voice sounded desperate, perhaps aware that he was in the vicinity of a far superior man.

Abbas shook his head and walked out with Sadiqbhai.

"Your uncle is a misguided fool."

"Uh huh."

"Why does he hobnob with them? Does he not know what they have done to us?"

"Uh huh."

"Why are you quiet? Are you scared of your uncle?"

"No!"

"Sometimes I feel like killing that bastard."

"Sadiqbhai…"

"What do you think of him, Abbas?"

"I…Uh…"

"I know you also think like that, don't you? And not just sometimes. Always, right?"

"No…"

"You're lying! Don't you hate living on the crumbs he throws at you?"

"Uh huh."

"If I were in your place, I would have taught the bastard a lesson."

"He is my uncle."

"Are you blind? He hates you. Does he miss a single opportunity to humiliate you? Everyone knows you want to go to the Foreign. But he won't let you."

"He will. I will convince him."

"Convince? Are you a *hijda?* Why do you have to convince him when the money is yours? The house was owned by your father too. You have a claim on it."

"I know. But where will my family live if I were to sell the house?"

"They will live in a palace! When you return from the Foreign with bagfuls of money, you can kick your uncle out and live in a palace with your mother."

"Uh..."

"If he is not giving it to you, you need to seize it. I would gladly kill him if I were you."

"Huh?"

"Think over it. Beautiful women and lots of money, or an elderly, dying uncle. You choose. The way I see it, you would be doing the old bastard a favour by putting him out of his misery."

"I need to go now."

"You promise to think over it?"

"Okay... Yes."

"Good. God bless you. You are like my son."

The alarm clock rang punctually at six, but Jeet didn't feel like opening his eyes, tired after fighting off tears long into the night. He had lain awake till an unknown hour with only the distant, agitated barking of a dog for company, replaying the day's events over and over again. He was never very comfortable with girls. Three years ago, when his father had shifted to Poona, the boy's school was too far from his home. So, for the first time in his short life, he had been admitted into a co-ed school. The girls in the new school seemed like a different species—exotic and untouchable—with whom he lacked the courage to speak. Since then, every subsequent school had presented a new set of these unknown, dauntingly unapproachable creatures, and by the time the remote possibility of interaction came his way, his father had already been issued an order to pack and leave for a new place. Till that day, he was certain they were unaware of his existence because he had always avoided initiating any contact with them. Everything had changed in one day. The girls knew he existed now, and in the worst possible way—as a cry-baby.

"Jeet, get up! It's ten past six!" his father's voice boomed.

His father stood near his bed, dressed in an ironed blue tracksuit. He wanted to tell his father he had a horrible first day at school and he was too tired for exercise, but could not. The look of disgust on his father's face at the ten-minute delay was enough to get him off the bed.

"You've lost ten minutes already. Now get ready in the next ten."

"Yes, Daddy," Jeet murmured without looking up.

Jeet hated his own track suit. The several-sizes-small elastic of the pants dug into his belly, leaving red marks. His father had bought it for him, ignorant of what was most conspicuous about him—his stubbornly clinging fat.

He came to the drawing room of the government house they had moved into two days ago. His father, the new Collector of the town, waited impatiently for him at the door, already warming up by inhaling deeply with his nose and exhaling with his mouth. His mother sipped her black-tea-with-honey on the sofa. She wore a bright yellow gown hugging her body like a second skin.

"Measure your weight before you start your run," she said, pointing towards the master bedroom where the weighing machine waited to announce the day's verdict.

Jeet entered the master bedroom and saw the photograph of his parents adorning a wall. Everyone who saw the photograph, taken on their wedding day, said they looked like film stars. And everyone said they still looked like film stars. He stood on the weighing machine and focussed on the needle, which flickered before settling between sixty-one and sixty-two. His weight had not reduced in the last six months. The needle doggedly stuck to sixty-one-and-a-half kilograms. He willed it to move leftwards, but it didn't budge a millimetre.

"How much is it?" his father asked from the living room.

Jeet didn't answer, hoping his father would get the idea from his silence. But he was wrong. His father was determined to make him utter the number, perhaps for the millionth time.

"Well, what is it?" his father asked—a lot louder this time.

"It's sixty-one-and-a-half."

There was silence in the drawing room. Then his father sighed, "Okay, let's go."

Jeet took a deep breath and walked out for yet another morning of jogging and exercising. His parents differed on almost all the aspects of their shared existence, but were unanimous in the belief that the only way to whittle down their son's fat was a relentless regime of exercise, yoga and jogging. They had zealously pursued it. His father had even called it a project. But the weighing machine's verdict had not changed over the past two years.

Little clumps of filth lay in Dev's house, providing obstacles for the racing mice. The ancient paint on the walls peeled away to spawn dirty blue papads. Flies whizzed over the unwashed utensils in the kitchen. The sugar in the round aluminium container coagulated to form little balls, and amber-coloured cockroaches stuck to them, flapping their wings, drunk on the sweetness. The long defunct plug-points were homes for bees. His mother had stopped finding anything wrong with it all. She didn't know how to clean it, or where to start.

Dev touched the old, threadbare curtain hanging limply over a coil bolted into the wooden frame of the door. It had not always been frayed. When they bought it, it was fresh and crisp, as was the design of flowers on it. In the cloth shop on the Sarafa Bazaar Street, his mother had touched the curtain as if it were some exotic animal. His mother could haggle over a sprig of coriander for hours. He'd braced himself in anticipation of the guffaws at the mention of the curtain's price, but she hadn't uttered a word. His father had bought the curtain immediately. It was the last time his parents would smile at each other. A few weeks later, his father abandoned them. The flowers on the curtain now resembled a child's painting with water splashed on it.

The neighbours and relatives always looked at him with pity. Tch tch. That's what everyone said when they thought he was not looking. They sounded like the house lizards he swatted many times a day. Tch tch. He told Avi he imagined two giant lizards talking to each other in their language and they had laughed. He could not say this to his mother, though. For the first few days after his father had disappeared, she had carried on as normally as possible, like a strange wind-up doll, treating the abandonment as an aberration that would soon be righted. She cooked for three people, made the chapattis and vegetables just the way his father liked them, set aside a glass of buttermilk for him and waited for him to return. But he never did.

After a week, she suddenly discarded the illusion of normalcy, stopped caring about the house, and sat on the bed staring at the photographs of her marriage for hours. These photographs, tucked into four paper corners on the black pages of the album, depicted her at a time when she was happy, bejewelled and *nauwari*-clad. He saw his father standing or sitting with his back ramrod straight. His eyes, partly hidden behind thick glasses, were distant, perhaps searching for a way out. A small frown of detachment was permanently plastered on his face. His lips were drawn in a grim line, barely suppressing his impatience with the ritual. The photographs were black and white, devoid of the colour his mother tried to find in them. The only colour was the yellowing of the bad paper, slowly eating away those photographs like acid.

Then, one day, she called him into the bedroom and told him his father had left them, as if breaking the news to him for the first time. He nodded. She stared at him, pained at the inadequacy of his reactions, waiting for the emotions to pour out. But he had stared back at her, unaffected. His life had been a numbing, repetitive sequence before his father abandoned them. He would return from school to find at least five people sitting in the front room of the house with their heads together, whispering. Some words would escape—"revolution", *"inqualab"*, "upliftment" "injustice". He would bring trays filled with tea in glass tumblers, steel tumblers, intact cups, cups with broken handles and cups with zigzagging cracks leaking tea. This would be in response to cries of "Anuradha, tea!" There would be a tightrope walk, balancing the tray, followed by relief—he would later tell Avi, proudly, that he had never dropped it. Then the men would walk out, leaving behind a house smelling of sweat, paan and cigarette smoke. He would sleep next to his mother every night, drowsily aware that she was wide awake all the time.

He had nodded in relief, happy he wouldn't be carrying the heavy tray again, at ungodly hours.

The neighbours called him the son of a revolutionary. They usually laughed after that. He understood the revolutionary part very well. That's what his father was. But he could never understand the laughter. Once, he asked them what was so amusing. They had laughed even harder, as though he was some idiot who was yet to get the joke—the way he and Avi laughed when Anita couldn't understand what they said to each other. There were two words he understood, though. It was a name—Bhausaheb Bhoite. Avi said that perhaps his father worked for Bhausaheb Bhoite. Dev's chest puffed up with pride. His father worked for the biggest man in town! He had asked his father one day if he worked for Bhausaheb Bhoite. His father had laughed. He had not understood that laughter either.

"What are you thinking?" his mother said.

"Nothing."

She always seemed to smell of Amrutanjan balm. She rubbed her forehead every half an hour with the gooey, snot-like balm, so vigorously that it was always red, like a permanent blister.

"Can you get me a postcard?" she asked, and handed him a twenty-five paisa coin.

He said yes and walked out of the house to the grocery shop. She wrote a letter to his father every two days. She recounted the terrible times they were going through in the little yellow postcard, which she never posted. How could she, when there was no known address? Her old almirah was overflowing with these postcards. He once asked her why she wrote them.

"Someday, I will come to know where your father is and then I will send all of them to him," she snapped.

The grocery shop owner saw him and handed him the postcard without saying a word.

Dev wondered how Bappa and his friends would handle yesterday's defeat as he stood in assembly before the morning prayers. Would they be waiting for him and Avi today? Would he be able to defeat them again? And how long would this struggle continue?

"How's the new boy?" Anita asked. She was standing next to him, in the girl's row for his class.

"He's all right."

"Does it hurt?" she said, looking at the white bandage on his head.

"No. It's very pleasant, feels wonderful! Of course, it hurts! You amaze me with your stupid questions."

"Someone's very testy today. Have you lost a bit of brain too?"

"Yes, quite a lot. But it's still bigger than yours."

"Oh please," she said and rolled her eyes.

Avi, who was standing in front of Dev, then let out a suppressed laugh.

"And why are you laughing, you owl?" she asked him.

"You look like a frog with those big eyes," Dev said.

"Just tell him I'm not talking to him," she said to Avi.

"You can tell him yourself. I'm not your Private Secretary. And anyway, men can't be Private Secretaries."

"If I tell him, I would be talking to him, you idiot. And who says men can't be Private Secretaries?" she said.

The PT teacher, D'Silva, who was getting everyone to stand in a line, heard it and walked up to them.

"What's going on here?" D'Silva was fastidious about maintaining silence before prayers.

"These three were talking, sir!" Manoj, the creep, said. Dev could never understand how Manoj managed to hear everything they said. He had spoken of it to Anita, but she had laughed and called Manoj a harmless little toad.

"You shut up!" D'Silva scolded Manoj, who cowered.

Dev laughed.

"Out! All three of you, now go and stand in the donkey's row," D'Silva said.

The donkey's row was the row for kids who had broken discipline during prayers. After the prayers were over, they would get a stern lecture from the principal, Father Cyriat. He would also cane the palms of a few kids.

"You guys are rotten. I get into so much trouble because of you," Anita grumbled as they trudged to the donkey's row.

"And I thought you were not going to talk to me," Dev said and slapped his forehead. They all laughed.

"So, tell me, have all you little morons done your homework?" Bokade asked.

Everyone except Dev nodded.

Bokade wasn't carrying his wooden scale. The classroom always reverberated with the sound of Bokade tapping his thigh with it. The silence that day was deeply unsettling. Bokade slowly walked down the aisle next to the row in which Dev sat. As he crossed bench after bench, the petrified kids let out inaudible sighs of relief. Doing homework didn't prevent beatings from Bokade. All the boys had bruises from the severe beatings they had got over the last year, as did the girls—Bokade knew no distinction when it came to punishing children. He walked up to Dev's bench and stood there for a few moments. Dev didn't blink as their eyes met. He was the only one who could do it in the entire school.

"Have you done your homework?"

Dev slowly shook his head.

"Stand up!" Bokade bellowed.

Dev stood up on shaky legs. His body was pulsing in anticipation of the day's beating. But Bokade didn't stick to his routine that day. He smiled at Dev for a long moment. In that moment, Dev knew something terrible was going to happen, something far more frightening than a mere beating. Bokade's smile hid a brutal anger that paralysed Dev. Perhaps Bokade had found a way to break his will.

Bokade pulled out what looked like a thin, steel cylinder from his trouser pocket.

"Do you know what this is, Gokhale?"

It had a dull shine to it. A shiver ran down Dev's spine.

Bokade removed his glasses and put them in his shirt pocket. His eyes shone brighter than the steel in his hand.

"This is a TV antenna, Gokhale. It broke yesterday. I thought it could be put to good use," he said and slowly pulled the little knob at its end.

It made a low hissing sound as it telescoped out to four times its original length. Dev stared at it with fascination, the faint realisation sinking into him that Bokade was going to beat him up with a steel antenna.

"Walk up to the front of the class!" Bokade shouted. "I want to make an example of you today."

Dev walked out, numbness already spreading across his body and mind.

"Look, all of you. This is what will happen if you disobey me," Bokade said with a smile as he followed Dev.

Dev reached the front of the class and turned to face it. The kids gawked at him with their mouths open.

Bokade walked up to him, tapping the antenna on his left hand. He suddenly whipped it in the air. It made a sound, as if the air had cried out in pain. Dev closed his eyes and waited for the lashing. It would be a new agony for his body. He didn't know how it would react. He bit the inside of his lip so hard he tasted blood.

A moment later, Bokade raised his hand again once again. Dev flinched.

"Bokade!"

The deathly silence in the classroom was pierced by Father Cyriat's deep baritone.

Dev then slowly opened his eyes and saw the white-robed figure of Father Cyriat standing at the entrance to the classroom.

"What are you doing?"

Bokade stared at him with his hand still in the air.

Dev feared he would hit him with the antenna in front of Father Cyriat, but Bokade slowly lowered his hand.

"Disciplining these children," he snarled. There was a frightening frustration in his voice. Years later, when Dev recalled it, he thought Bokade wanted to hit him with the antenna at least once, just to see how he reacted, to experience the sensation of one end hitting Dev's flesh as it was transmitted to the other end, which he held.

"With that thing in your hand?" Father Cyriat asked him somewhat incredulously.

Bokade said nothing and stared hard at Father Cyriat. Dev knew he was grinding his teeth behind the thick beard.

"That means all the complaints are true. What these children's parents have told me is true."

Bokade looked at the class slowly. Every kid in the class saw something beastly in his eyes that day; it was as though his eyes were recording each face in his memory, for future punishment.

"Please come with me," Father Cyriat said and turned to leave. "Now!" he commanded when Bokade didn't move.

Bokade walked up to the entrance of the classroom and looked back at the kids once more. The kids recoiled at the sight. Then he followed Father Cyriat.

When Father Joseph Cyriat had proposed setting up a school in Amrapur to Bishop Braganza of the neighbouring city, Bishop Braganza had laughed. "You certainly have the ability to amuse us from time to time," the Bishop had said. When he saw the determined, slightly offended face of Father Cyriat, he had stopped laughing abruptly. Father Cyriat's ambitions were plain. The son of a British woman and an Indian Syrian Christian from Kerala, he had come to India on a mission to study Hindu scriptures. Within a few months, he had learnt all the Vedas and Upanishads and was considered an expert on the Bhagawat Gita.

Nobody in the seminary knew why a man nearing sixty needed to know so much about a religion, but his grasp of it made them marvel. When asked, he had smiled and said he just wanted to know what the fuss was all about.

The real reason for Father Braganza's laughter was the history of Amrapur. It was a quaint town, nestled amidst barren mountains. The Hindus and Muslims living there were perpetually warring with each other, reacting violently at the slightest provocation. It had started a long time ago, this squabble, and had escalated into a terrible war. Some people say it started centuries ago, but many believe it started when the country gave one final, fierce shrug to rid itself of British rule. The shrug quickly became a relentless shuddering, and countless people were uprooted and flung into the air. Many didn't survive. Perhaps the mountains of Amrapur absorbed the deracinating wave. People weren't cruelly plucked from the town. They remained there, festering, becoming irate and harbouring murderous desires. And while the country was desperately trying to heal its near-mortal wounds and move on, Amrapur's dormant volcano erupted. Momentary and overlooked, but devastating. Leaders emerged on both sides and, driven by greed, they fed off the town's ignored bloodshed. They created ravines out of cracks, fostered hatred and grew richer. The Bhoite family, the erstwhile rulers of the ancient town, adopted the legacy of their British rulers—divide and conquer.

Father Braganza knew there was no place for a third religion in that town.

Father Cyriat took it as a challenge.

Armed with a ready smile, boundless patience and an ear for everyone, Father Cyriat built relationships with both communities. He convinced the leaders that convent education was the greatest gift from God—their own God. They, the leaders, could go right ahead and claim credit for the great act of imparting education to their kids. It would make them look like saints for saving the children's future and helping in nation-building. The leaders liked Father Cyriat and his calm, soothing words. They granted him a little spot on a hillock, under the perennially hot sky of Amrapur.

Father Cyriat had taken great care while building the school. Every brick and every teacher was personally inspected and approved by him. The school was to be his legacy, his little imprint on the history of this boundless, at once fledgling and grizzled, hot and cold, turbulent and tranquil nation.

Within four years, Father Cyriat had managed to achieve his dream.

And inadvertently, unbeknownst to his proud soul, birthed a terrible nightmare.

He had personally selected Bokade sir, hadn't he? How could he be wrong? Surely the man deserved some chances. It wasn't the first time Bokade had walked into his office. There were many incidents in the past. Some teachers said he smoked in the school. They also told him that Bokade was perpetually drunk, was always angry and misbehaved with women teachers. But Father Cyriat firmly believed in redemption. Long before Bokade walked into his little office, Father Cyriat had decided to give him yet another warning. It was a decision which he would come to regret bitterly two days later.

Bokade sat on the chair, his back straight, staring hard at Father Cyriat.

"You cannot continue like this, Bokade sir," the old bastard said, steepling his arthritic fingers. He laid a special emphasis on 'sir' as though it were some kind of abuse. There was an expectant smirk on Cyriat's face. Perhaps the bastard expected him to fall at his feet, begging for mercy, "Forgive me Father, for I have sinned."

Bokade said nothing.

Patting his beard as though it were some exotic animal, the senile bastard said, "I have been receiving many complaints over the past few weeks."

"Who has complained?" Bokade asked. Bokade knew Cyriat was a strict disciplinarian and had his own cane. The kids were scared of the conceited bastard. The old man had no moral right to question him.

"Who has complained?" Bokade repeated, in a rather low growl.

"That is not relevant. You know I believe in punishment. These little children are like putty in our hands. Sometimes, we need to use force to shape them. But what you are doing is not right, Bokade sir."

"Who has complained?" Bokade repeated, ignoring the sermonising idiot.

"I said, it does not matter!" Cyriat said so loudly that the walls of his little office shook. After a few moments, the good Father calmed down and wiped the perspiration off his reddened forehead with a clean white handkerchief. He neatly folded the handkerchief and shoved it into a pocket. "You have to promise me that you will not beat up the kids anymore," he said, trying hard to be calm.

Bokade stood up with such force that the chair toppled behind him. He walked away without even looking at Cyriat. He imagined the expression on the old bastard's face—incredulity, followed by sheepishness or anger, followed by helplessness. He lit up a cigarette standing just outside the teacher's room, and felt the smoke singe his lungs and heart. A few teachers gaped at him. He smiled while exhaling the smoke slowly. Then, crushing the cigarette in the middle of the entrance, he walked out of the school. Faint sounds of laughter emanated from the school's bowels, mocking him. He took out the steel antenna and expanded it. It was hot to touch, angry for not having had its fill. He pressed the little knob, subduing the monster, promising to quench its thirst very soon. It wouldn't take him too long to find out who had complained. All that was needed was to ask the peon. Scared and gulping air, the peon had told him who it was. Bokade smiled and handed him a five-rupee note.

Naveen Desai had a hole in his heart when he was born. He had popped out of his mother's not-so-bloated stomach in seven months. The doctors had given up hope of his survival. His parents, both devout followers of the goddess Durga, sat before the idol, trying relentlessly to invoke her blessings for their only child. After two days and nights of praying, the little baby won the battle against death. It wasn't a clear victory though—Naveen grew up, and the little hole in his heart grew too, swallowing up copious amounts of medicine, prayers, sleepless nights and money. Naveen's parents never complained. They thought of him as a gift from the goddess, their own little Krishna who had tamed death.

The death waited for twelve years.

Naveen sat on the side-lines while his classmates played volleyball. His hands were weak, like those of a seven-year-old, and he could never play games with kids his age. There was something sickly about him that warded off bullies, like Jagan and his gang. He looked fragile, like a wax mannequin.

Bokade walked up to the volleyball game. He pointed at Naveen and flicked a finger to catch his attention. The volleyball game stopped. The white ball bounced a few times and lay still. Shaking uncontrollably, Naveen gaped at Bokade with his mouth open, paralysed by the recognition in his eyes. Until that moment, he had managed to stay away from the terrifying gaze of the class teacher, somehow enveloped by his little hole, hiding in it, invisible. But the monster had seen him and wanted him to come closer. When he didn't move, Bokade walked up to him, slowly. Naveen wanted to scream, somehow aware of Bokade's wrath.

Bokade grabbed a handful of his hair and yanked him up. Naveen screamed.

"What did you tell your parents?"

Nothing coherent came out of Naveen's mouth. His weak, seven-year-old's hands clutched the sweaty, slippery arms of the class teacher, as he hung in the air.

Bokade slapped him hard.

The hole had made his entire body weak. The brutal slap dislodged his teeth. He felt them on his tongue. He began to sob.

Bokade curled his fingers to form a fist. His fist was bigger than the hole in Naveen's heart. It was bigger than his heart. It was bigger than Naveen.

He pulled his hand as far back as he could. The fist was very big. It blocked the raging sun, it hurtled down. On his hole. On his heart.

The hole didn't stay inside his heart. It consumed his heart. It also consumed him. Then there was just darkness—comforting and liberating.

Bokade dropped the twisting little vermin when he coughed up a spray of blood. He wiped his hand on his trousers. The weak insect could not endure a single punch, and he had the audacity to complain to his parents. "Now why don't you go and complain?" he said and pushed the cockroach lying on the ground with his foot. The boy didn't move. He pushed harder. The boy lay still.

Bokade stepped back and looked at the kids on the volleyball court. They were frozen, like statues. Just behind them, Dev Gokhale, Avinash Shah and the new fat kid stood with their mouths agape.

Dev was the first to move. He bolted through the school grounds towards the administrative block, where Father Cyriat had his office. Bokade watched him run. He was followed by Shah and the fat boy. It set off a chain reaction. The children came to life and they ran.

Bokade looked at the body of the little vermin on the ground and smiled. This was a unique design. His greatest yet. He wondered if he would get to do it again. He laughed long and hard.

Father Cyriat, a trained doctor, rushed to the spot after Dev Gokhale told him what had happened on the volleyball court. He watched the round-shouldered Bokade walking away from the court with his raucous laughter. Father Cyriat called out to him, ordered him to stop, even let out a profanity for the first time in many years. But the man just walked away. As though he had not heard him at all.

Father Cyriat tried valiantly, but Naveen had gone far away. Massive heart failure, from the looks of it. He lifted the boy's weightless body and said a silent prayer for his soul. Two large tears escaped his eyes and disappeared in the boy's blood-soaked shirt.

He turned back, while all the teachers of his school, every one of them personally interviewed by him, stood absolutely dumbstruck.

"Call the ambulance. Call the police," he said, and carried Naveen's body to the little dispensary that was in his administrative block.

The ambulance arrived and took the body away, leaving the blood on the volleyball court and on Father Cyriat's habit behind.

Policemen—clad in sweaty khakis, their bellies bulging over large metallic buckles—landed on the hallowed grounds of Father Cyriat's school. They walked up to the administrative block in their noisy brown leather shoes, the sound of which reverberated through the silent, mourning walls. They questioned the teachers. Nobody had seen anything. They questioned Father Cyriat. He sat blankly at his desk, looking at something visible only to him, answering their questions in monosyllables.

Police Inspector Raut, irritated by the lack of information on a seemingly open and shut case, was almost on the verge of arresting Father Cyriat, when Dev walked up to him and tapped his back.

"I saw it. Everything," Dev said. His words were soaked in tears. Naveen Desai was not his friend, but he was a sweet boy, in awe of Dev.

Dev told Inspector Raut what he saw—the volleyball game, Bokade's walk, his slap, his punch, the blood and the death. Raut patiently heard him out, noted down certain things, patted his back when his voice choked and told him to go home.

Raut grabbed Bokade within the hour. Bokade was amused when told he was being arrested for killing a student, Naveen Desai, age twelve. He said the vermin died, he didn't kill him.

There was a difference. If he had wanted to kill him, it would have been different. Inspector Raut, unable to control his anger any more, slapped him and loaded him into the open jeep.

"Who told you these lies?" he asked the Inspector.

"Keep your filthy mouth shut."

"Was it Dev Gokhale and his friends?"

Raut said nothing and looked ahead. He had dealt with criminals who had committed crimes far more heinous than Bokade. But Bokade's smile sent a faint shiver up his spine, as though his soul felt the primitive fear of being around a predator with no motive other than the pleasure of the kill.

"Dev Gokhale."

Those were the last words Raut heard Bokade speak for a long time.

A few days later, Dev and Avi showed Jeet their secret place—the riverside—hoping its magic would lift their new friend out of the fearful gloom he had plunged into since joining school. Jeet sat in the classroom the whole day with downcast eyes and never ventured out during break.

"This is beautiful! When did you find this place?" Jeet said as he sat on the green grass, soaking in the magic of the riverside, a smile breaking through the perpetual look of dread on his face.

"Avi found it actually. Last year."

"Hey look! We can make a fort here," Jeet said.

"A fort?"

"Yes, a fort. Almost every river in India has a fort next to it. Our riverside should have a fort too! What do you say?"

"That's a good idea," Dev said.

"I'll draw it tonight. Let's start from tomorrow!"

"Okay," Avi said glumly.

"What happened? Why do you sound as if someone just died?" Dev asked.

"Whatever we do, Jagan and his brother just want to destroy it."

"Don't worry. They don't know about the riverside. They won't be able to touch our fort."

"But how are we going to make the fort? Will we need cement?"

"Oh, no! The soil here is wonderful. We can just use the soil. I have built so many forts. There is a fort in every city I have lived in," Jeet said with a lot of pride.

"Every city? How many cities have you actually lived in?" Dev asked.

Jeet had hardly spoken in the classroom. A fortnight had passed, but the only thing they knew about Jeet was that a big Fiat car with 'Government of India' written in red letters on its hatch came every evening, after school, to pick him up. Many kids, and some teachers, watched him get into the car with a familiar deference to those three imperial words.

"I have attended school in six cities in the last five years."

"Why? Do they kick you out every six months, fatty?" Avi said and they all laughed.

"My father is the Collector of Amrapur now," Jeet said.

The only reason he had never been bullied in any of his previous schools was because of his father's position. It protected him, like a magic spell, from the common punishments, even causing the teachers to plunge into unstinted fussing over him. They eagerly admired his handwriting, complimented him for solving simple maths problems and effusively praised his diction. This privileged treatment alienated him from his classmates, who never harmed him but never befriended him either.

"My God! We have the son of the Collector amongst us!" Avi said. "Why don't you get the police to beat up Jagan and his brother?"

"Can he do that?"

"Oh, yes! He is the Collector. He can do anything."

"I'll ask him tonight!"

"Avi! Don't be ridiculous. You think Jeet's father is going to waste his time on our little fights?" Dev said. "This is a communally sensitive town. I think your father would have a lot of work. But why did you attend so many schools?"

"Daddy says honest officers always get transferred. So we were in a new city every year or so. I have overheard so many arguments between my mother and father over these transfers," he said, and suddenly realised he had said something he should not have. But Dev and Avi ignored it. Jeet had never been this friendly with anyone—and that too, in just two days. He vowed to make the finest fort, one that would stand forever on the riverside. He hoped his father would not get transferred any time soon.

"All right, then. We're all set," Dev said.

"But what about Jagan and his brother?"

"We can all rush to the riverside immediately after school. They don't know about this place. Do you want it in writing?"

"Okay," Avi said frowning deeply. His Adam's apple jumped a couple of times.

"One day, you watch, that rabbit is going to jump out of your throat, Avi."

They all laughed.

That evening, Jeet sat at his study table with a big white sheet in front of him. He needed peace to concentrate, but the drunken laughter coming from the living room was too shrill. His father had invited several people for a party. Jeet got up from the chair and walked to the living room. At least fifteen people were there, in various stages of drunkenness. The women wore beautiful saris and held tall glasses full of red liquid—his father's wine. The men wore suits and had amber and cola coloured liquids in their glasses. It was his father's favourite scotch and rum. He was surprised to see that the little town of Amrapur could conjure up people dressed in such expensive suits and gaudy jewellery.

Before they had shifted to Amrapur, his parents had a huge quarrel, hurling hitherto unheard abuses at one other. She called him an ignorant coward; he called her a shallow nag. They quickly went through the bitch-bastard routine, and then the exotic insults were bandied. She called him an uptight asshole; he called her a money-obsessed cunt. It spiralled into a recital of abuses, painful for Jeet to hear. They stopped after an hour. Perhaps they had run out of foul names. The reason was that his father had refused to comply with accepted practices at work—namely, ignoring or participating in the all-pervasive corruption, and indulging the criminals masquerading as politicians. As a consequence, he had been transferred for the sixth time in five years. His mother's reaction had escalated with every transfer: she had maintained a reproachful silence during the first couple; she was grumpy and spiteful during the next few; and adamant and furious during the last two. However, shifting from Bombay to

Amrapur was absolutely unbearable to her. His parents stopped talking to each other, loaded their belongings into a truck, and uprooted their lives once more.

Jeet observed the people in the living room and thought his parents would not miss Bombay too much. They still lived in a government house, the parties sounded the same, the brands of alcohol they drank had not changed, and the compliments they received echoed those they had received earlier. The familiar scene superimposed itself over memories of their fights, and whatever remained felt farcical.

"I tell you Mehra sahib, this town is hell on earth," said an old bald man with a white moustache; he was dressed in a white suit. He held Jeet's father's hand by the elbow, weighing it in his palm.

"I know Agrawal sahib," his father said, nodding. "There is a lot of communal tension here. It is always vulnerable."

"Yes. You know, in the communal riots in 1978, a hundred and twenty people died? Although the media reported just fifteen deaths."

"Uh uh."

"I think, over the past twenty years, there have been so many problems that I have forgotten what it is they fight about... Hey! Is that your son?" Agrawal looked at Jeet and spoke with practised enthusiasm.

Jeet had heard the same sentence several times before. The surprised and excited tone was always amusing, as if the people who said it were amazed that a Collector could father a human child.

"Jeet, say hello to Agrawal sahib," his father said.

"Hello uncle," Jeet said dutifully. This was another thing he had done often. Sometimes he wondered if he held the record for the the largest number of uncles in the world.

"Oh, isn't he cute?" What he meant was, "Isn't he fat?"

"Thanks uncle. Daddy, I have to finish my homework. Can I go to a friend's place?"

"Who is your friend?" his father asked, his eyes filled with doubt. This was the first time Jeet had made a friend so quickly.

"His name is Avinash Shah. He stays close by. He told me his house is called Shah Sadan."

"Are your referring to the Shahs of Shah Garments?" Agrawal asked.

"Don't know."

"Well, they are the biggest trading family in this town. They have, I think, eight garments shops in all," Agrawal said, nodding.

"Make good friends, okay Jeet?" his father said, satisfied with a relative stranger's approval of Avi's family-pedigree, but not trusting his son to make the right friends.

Jeet began to lose interest in the conversation. "Yes Daddy. Now can I go?"

"Okay," his father said as he went back to talking with Agrawal.

His mother was deep in conversation with a lady wearing garish makeup. She had bent her head and was listening to her with great attention—more than she ever paid Jeet.

He slipped out of the house.

Amrapur's indolence was in stark contrast to the frenzied chaos of Bombay. People walked slowly, in no hurry to reach their destinations. Their journeys didn't warrant changing modes of transport, from train to bus to rickshaw, as in Bombay. Their expressions were calm—both, because the sun had gone down, and because the landscape was unchanging and familiar. The streets were littered with uncollected garbage and animal shit, through which the people walked, unaware or uncaring. The houses were of a wide variety of styles, in wildly contrasting colours, and were not uniformly maintained. Some were big, with porches sprouting dense overgrowths of flowering plants and fruit trees. Some were small, with entrances next to the road. Some were painted in garish colours, like maroon and green. Some were an austere white. Many were old, proudly displaying the year they were built—Joshi Wada, 1961, or Raut, 1965—and a few were new. Avi had told him his was a palatial house that he could not miss even if he wanted to. It was a two-storeyed building made of marble and was drenched in bright light, as though the family celebrated Diwali every day of the year. 'Shah Sadan' was written in large golden letters on the two pillars that sandwiched the huge iron gate.

What if his father had been a businessman instead of a government servant? They would have stayed in the same city for years together. He would not have had to get used to a new room in a government house every few months. When they arrived in a new town and went to their new home, he could still smell the repulsive disinfectant. He could not sleep for several nights, because the new house was alien to him. His parents had closed the door to their bedroom from the inside, leaving him alone to grapple with the strangeness of the house. He had walked up to their bedroom in the middle of the night, bleary-eyed, despondent and on the verge of banging the door, and had walked back to his bedroom because he could imagine his parents' disappointed faces and hear their long drawn sermon on the importance of independence. It took him several weeks to adjust to the new house. He felt as if there were invisible beings staying there that had been disturbed by his arrival, and they made every attempt to prevent him from getting accustomed to the place. Even the mosquitoes in every new house bit differently.

He opened the huge iron gates of Shah Sadan. There was a big lawn in front of the house littered with toys and bicycles. He walked up to the entrance of the house and was surprised to see it ajar. The first thing his father had taught him—perhaps even before he began to walk—was to close the door of the house. A lot of noises emanated from deep within. Suddenly, two kids, a boy and a girl, came rushing out. The boy held two lollipops in his hand and a catlike grin on his face. The girl was crying loudly and chasing the boy.

He walked inside. The living room had a large sofa upholstered in blood-red velvet, a patterned carpet, wall units populated with strange artifacts, vases and wedding pictures of couples, and a huge picture of a pride of lions. Two grandfatherly men sat on the sofa, watching TV with the sound on very loud.

A woman came out holding two silver glasses. She placed them in front of the two old men and shouted, "Milk," in their ears. Much to his surprise, she completely ignored him and went back inside.

He stood at the entrance, unsure of how to find Avi in this house bustling like a zoo.

"Hey, fatty! What are you doing here?" Avi said, standing at the top of the marble staircase.

"Trying to find you, you owl."

"Come up then."

"You are so lucky, Avi," Jeet said, as they sat on the bed in Avi's room.

"Why?"

"Well, you have such a big house as well as such a big family!"

"Does it make me lucky?"

"Then what does? You have stayed in the same place all your life. I wish I could have done so. I envy you for that."

Avi laughed.

"Did I just say something funny?" Jeet asked with his eyes narrowed.

"I hate this town, Jeet," Avi said. "And I hate this house even more."

"What?"

"Yes. And I can't wait to get out of here."

"Now you're joking, right?"

"No, I'm not. Forget it. Can we draw that sketch now?"

Jeet was stunned by what Avi said. He was used to having a lot of unknown people around, all of them either government officials or socialites, who drank too much and, often, puked too much.

He wondered what it would be like to have a big family like Avi's, where everyone stayed under the same roof for many decades.

But he didn't ask Avi.

Instead, he said, "Where does Dev stay?"

"Shastri Nagar. It's on the other side of town."

Jeet wondered what it must be like to have a friend throughout your life. It would be fantastic if his father stayed at his posting in Amrapur forever.

He could spend the rest of his school days sitting next to Dev and Avi, and stealing glances at Anita.

That evening, the two boys drew the sketch of the fort. And, as Jeet had promised Dev and Avi, it was the most beautiful fort he would ever build.

Anita walked back to her house that evening with Jeet on her mind. His fat made him look like an overgrown baby, an adorable overgrown baby. A goofy smile never left his pudgy lips. He must be shy, she thought, because he glanced at her furtively. Humiliated on his first day by Jagan, he'd wept because he was ashamed, not because he was in pain. It would be such a relief if Jagan failed the year—at least she would not have to witness his brutality every day. Bappa was sure to fail and would be in her class the next year. The prospect of sharing the same space with Bappa and Jagan gave her the shivers.

She made her way home via Mehrab Street, which was dotted with dingy bars that played loud music. Sweaty, pot-bellied men sat for hours at the grimy tables and drank vast quantities of alcohol. They misbehaved with women, which led to noisy clashes that sometimes escalated into fistfights. She hated walking through this street, but could not avoid it.

"Hey, look! It's my *janeman!*" Bappa shouted.

She had been lost in thought, unaware of Bappa and his gang loitering around Shambhoo's paan stall. She stopped. Until that moment, Bappa had never said anything to her. There were the lewd whistles and grotesque catcalls, but never words. Bappa lit a cigarette and walked up to her. She glared at him, her eyes unblinking, hoping her face didn't betray her fear.

"I see you are aroused to see me," Bappa said and blew smoke into her eyes. It was acrid, like the stench of something rotten.

"Get out of my way," she said through clenched teeth.

People on the street stopped to watch the unfolding drama. A few men lingered around Shambhoo's paan stall with lascivious grins plastered on their faces. Bappa's friends cheered hysterically as if Bappa was doing something heroic.

"You've developed a sting since you started wearing a bra," Bappa said. There was a crazy desperation in his eyes. He was trying to accomplish something much more than humiliation.

In his warped mind, perhaps he had equated hurting her with hurting Dev. If that was true, then Dev's strength was her strength too.

"Your father will be very proud to hear the new things you have learned, Bappa," she said with so much viciousness that Bappa actually took a step back. She took a step forward. "Maybe I should walk up to your house right now and tell him about it?"

He laughed loudly, hiding his nervousness. He was a repulsive sight. His teeth were decaying and horribly twisted, as if they had been pulled out one by one and fitted clumsily back. He was tall and wore clothes that were several sizes smaller. His ropey muscles bulged out of the tight sleeves of his T-shirts. His hair was cut close to his scalp and reeked of a sickeningly smelly hair oil.

"Oh, you wouldn't dare," he said, gasping, trying hard to appear nonchalant.

"I can and will do that."

He stopped laughing abruptly and took a couple of steps forward until his face was an inch away from hers. The smell of his hair oil was nauseating.

"One day, I am going to fuck you," he said, turned around and walked back to his friends.

She fought hard against an overwhelming desire to weep. Some men laughed, as though it was a fitting climax to the drama—an arrogant shrew tamed, shown her place by one of them. Bappa's friends slapped his back and laughed raucously as he blew rings of smoke.

"What's going on here?" a voice boomed.

There was only one voice that could make a busy street go quiet. Sharif Miyan stood opposite Shambhoo's paan stall, looking at the boys snickering near the paan stall, with quiet fury in his eyes. They were silenced instantly. Men who had gleefully observed Bappa's behaviour walked away, avoiding Sharif Miyan's glare.

"Anita, go home," Sharif Miyan said to her gently, his tone at odds with his anger. The warmth in his voice gave her the strength to walk on, although her legs still wobbled and she feared she would collapse in the street.

Sharif Miyan walked up to the boys.

"Bappa, I have seen you pester that girl often," he said.

His tone was civil, giving Bappa an opportunity to apologise. Bappa was a kid too, albeit a misguided and confused one, blindly following his father's hideous example.

Bappa snorted and started laughing. "Didn't you enjoy it old man? Don't you miss your youth?"

Sharif Miyan's hand moved so quickly and forcefully that it left Bappa sprawling on the ground. Tears welled up in his eyes and he could not help but let out a pained sob.

"You have a foul mouth, Bappa," Sharif Miyan said.

Bappa sobbed again. His left cheek was numb. His friends were looking at him, stunned, recording his humiliation forever in their memories. He was the leader, wasn't he? The heir to the Bhoite Empire? How could this town be allowed to witness his humiliation?

Sharif Miyan gestured with his finger to Bappa's friends, asking them to come closer. They moved back a few steps, then turned and ran.

"Don't run away, you morons!" Bappa screamed. It was unbelievable—the very people he was going to rule one day ran away like a bunch of cockroaches.

Sharif Miyan walked up to him and pulled him up holding his right ear.

"You're such a wimp, Bappa. What will your friends think of you if they see you crying again?"

"Leave me alone you bastard! You are dead! My father will kill you!"

"Your father will certainly kill you if I tell him what you did today."

His father revered Sharif Miyan. Bappa had never understood what made his father bend before this old man who reeked of tea and burnt milk.

"Now, will you pester her again?" he asked and yanked his ear savagely.

Many bystanders were staring at him. A few had the gall to laugh. He was helpless, made impotent by a ferocious assault from a man not worthy of cleaning his toilet.

"I cannot hear you at all. I am holding your ear, not your tongue."

"No," Bappa said and tried to jerk his ear out of Sharif Miyan's grip.

"Good," Sharif Miyan said and released his ear. Bappa ran away, wiping his tears on his sleeve with the laughter of onlookers echoing in his ears.

Anita's house was in the older, claustrophobically congested part of town. Most people lived in tenements that were as old as the town itself and were haphazardly constructed. In the labyrinth of narrow lanes, people did their chores in the open: old men and women performed the early morning puja to the rising sun; teenagers stole suggestive glances; men wearing dirty vests riddled with holes lolled around; women slouched in groups on the doorsteps, animatedly chatting about family politics, while the little kids played a noisy game of cricket. The aroma of singed chapattis and spicy curries floated out of the houses and merged with the stench of open sewers.

She barely managed to reach her home, her knees wobbling with fear and her eyes stinging with unshed tears, but she willed herself to continue. When she was home, she could collapse and cry her heart out.

Her mother's voice singing "ta-thai-tat-thai" rang loud and clear as she opened the creaky wooden gate. It was accompanied by the jingling sound made by *ghungroos*. She entered the veranda where her mother sat on a small stool in front of a dozen girls practising Kathak. Her mother saw her and raised her left eyebrow—she was late, which was not acceptable if she wanted to perfect her dancing. She nodded at her contritely, wondering if her mother could sense something was wrong.

She ran to the bathroom and splashed water on her face many times, even though she feared she would start weeping the next moment. She closed her eyes and resolved never to permit Bappa to make her cry. Her mother's "ta-thai-tat-thai" was laden with concern. She wiped her face with the towel and rushed to the small room that she shared with her mother in their tiny house. She quickly changed into a salwar kameez without looking at herself in the mirror—the sight of her bra would definitely make her cry.

She ran to the veranda and joined the girls, mid-step. Soon, she forgot Bappa and his terrible words, the tight elastic of her bra and the smell of his hair oil. She concentrated on her mother's voice and her own attempts to match it with her footwork. After two hours of relentless dancing, she lay on the bed, sweating freely. The limply rotating table fan was inadequate in this heat.

The sound of the front door banging was followed by a loud burp, even as the reek of alcohol spread through the house. The monster was in the house. He lived in the front room, which was forbidden territory for her.

"Malti! You motherfucking bitch!" His speech was slurred, but she understood what he had said. The monster could never speak like a human—the words dribbled out of his mouth along with alcohol-laden drool. He was a short, short-sighted, gnome-like man who was capable of extreme cruelty.

She closed her eyes. The whirring of the table fan could not drown his voice. Her mother walked into the front room, holding a steel plate full of food. A few moments later, she heard loud munching and slurping sounds.

"This is absolute shit, that's what it is. You call this food, you bitch?"

The plate clanged as it collided with the wall. She wondered how much of her mother's cooking had been thrown at that wall over the years. And then she heard him slapping, punching and shoving her mother, all the while uttering the vilest abuses. Her mother remained silent. She could never determine what hurt her mother more, the words or the blows.

She whimpered soundlessly, too afraid to add her tears and cries to the daily ritual. She had stopped crying a very long time ago.

Her father would tire after a few minutes. He would sprawl on the bed in the front room and start snoring, as if the violence were a precursor to this stupor between bouts of drinking. He often vomited in his sleep, with the green bile seeping through his mouth.

Her mother would wipe the vomit from his face and the tears from her own, before she walked into their bedroom. She would then kiss Anita while weeping silently and pretend to sleep.

The old rusty metal bed groaned as Dev's mother twisted and turned on it, clutching her head and moaning. A week ago, she had told the doctor that her migraines felt as if a small animal was biting at her brain. That animal was relentless, and it chewed very slowly.

The ancient metal cupboard had a large fading mirror on its door. She had pasted his father's photograph on the top of the mirror two days after he had abandoned them. His father was smiling in that photograph—it was perhaps the only photograph in which he did so. Dev was lost in thought as he rode his bicycle. So he didn't see Bappa or the wooden staff with which Bappa wrecked his cycle wheel. He fell off the bicycle and hit the ground hard. He was getting up when Bappa hit him square on the jaw with his right hand. Bappa's cronies smashed his bicycle, turning it into scrap metal.

"That's for the other day, Gokhale," Bappa said and landed another blow on his left eye. The world was blank for a moment. It returned vehemently with Bappa's next blow. Bappa grabbed his collar. He was at least six inches taller than Dev. He lifted Dev off the ground. In that moment, Bappa's desire to show the world that he could lift his opponents like Amitabh Bachchan did in the movies, made Dev taller than him. Suddenly, Dev felt the strength returning to his body. He rammed his right leg into Bappa's crotch. Bappa's eyes bulged. He dropped to his knees, clutching his balls and wailed. Dev raised his right hand and smashed it against Bappa's nose. "My nose!" Bappa cried clutching his balls with one hand and his nose with the other. It was a sight that made Dev smile—he felt he would never stop smiling now. The five older boys and Jagan were stunned to see Bappa thrash around on the ground.

"What the hell are you guys staring at? Beat the bastard!" Bappa shouted through his pain.

In a flash, the six of them sprung upon Dev. They beat him up with their hands, kicked him with their boots and whipped him with their belts. It lasted for a minute before passers-by intervened and dragged the boys away. Dev lay on the ground and could see the blood dripping from a cut just above his eyes. They had rained blows on his body but he was still elated because he had incapacitated Bappa. He wanted to run to Avi, Jeet and Anita and tell them that he had floored the bastard.

"Kid? Kid? Are you alright? Can you hear me?" a man said, bending down to him. He could barely hear the voice, which seemed to come from a distance. He sat up abruptly and thought he would collapse once again.

The men rebuked Bappa's gang, but they were defiant and ran away. Bappa got up unsteadily, still clutching his groin. Dev laughed as he watched Bappa lumber away groaning.

"Let's take him to the hospital," one man said.

"These kids are hopeless. One day they're going to kill each other," another said.

He wanted to tell them that he was all right, there were just some bruises. His mother would not be able to bear the sight of her son in the hospital. The men lifted him up. He was vaguely aware that they put him in a rickshaw for Amrapur General Hospital. He was wading through a sea of iridescent white milk but he knew it was only a soothing illusion. He was tired and didn't want to leave the sea. There was light on the horizon, which grew in intensity, as if its source had its back to him and was slowly turning to face him. Soon the light covered the entire sea. Then he heard voices, familiar and heartening.

"Dev? Dev? Can you hear me?"

He slowly opened his eyes. The world was bright and chaotic.

Avi stood next to him. His eyes looked twice their size through his glasses, and he had large drops of sweat on his nose. Next to him, Jeet fidgeted, chewing his nails furiously.

"Are you going to eat your fingers today?" Dev asked with a faint smile.

"Thank God!" Avi said and removed his glasses. There were tears in his eyes. He wiped all the sweat and tears off his face with his sleeve.

"You were unconscious for a long time," Avi said and glanced at the entrance to the general ward. Dev's mother stood there, intently nodding as she listened to the nurse.

"You mother was crying all this while," Jeet said in a whisper. "I'll call her. I think she'll be relieved to see that you're awake."

There was a lot of noise in the huge general ward of the hospital. It stank of antiseptic and urine. On the bed next to his, an old man coughed relentlessly. He was in wretched pain, the kind that increases every minute, but no one sat next to him.

He had been in the same ward two years ago when his mother had pneumonia—a month after his father had abandoned them. The doctors were on strike then. And his mother had coughed just like the old man next to him. He stood despondently next to her bed, watching her twist about. He took help from a neighbour to send his uncle a telegram. His uncle lived in the neighbouring town, just a hundred kilometres away. Nobody came. After two days, the strike ended and the few doctors resumed duty. His mother lay there coughing away for some more days before the doctors could attend to her. A young doctor brusquely told him that there were very few doctors in this "shithole of a government hospital". The neighbours fed him and his mother too, their reluctance conspicuous after a week. Perhaps they were compelled by pity for a ten-year-old boy and a woman who was near death. They all concluded, though, that humiliating a ten-year-old boy was not such a great transgression. He gave them silence in return for food and derision. "Where is your revolutionary father now?" "Your father should be flogged in public!" "This is what he has reduced you to—begging!" When he heard these words, he looked at the ground and raised his hands to take the food. After a week, Sharif Miyan had turned up at the hospital. He carried a big tiffin-box with food in it. Sharif Miyan sat with him on the benches outside the general ward, gently patting his back as he cried in his lap. He told him that nothing would happen to his mother, that she would be all right within two weeks. He never asked the neighbours for food again, and they were happy to neglect him. Sharif Miyan brought the tiffin every day and paid for the medicines. After three weeks, his uncle sent a small money-order, but no letter. His mother got discharged. She thanked the neighbours profusely for taking care of her son. He stayed silent. The roles that he and his mother had played a year back were reversed. Avi and Jeet slid out of the general ward when his mother returned.

"Who hit you?" she asked.

Averting his eyes, he said, "Jagan and Bappa."

"Why did they hit you? Answer me!"

"Because they hate me, *Aai!* I stand up to them in school and they hate me for it."

She sat next to him and held his hand. "I don't want to lose you, Dev." Two large tears trickled down her cheeks.

Then, for the first time, she said something he thought she had always wanted to.

"Your father left us. Was that my fault? You think it was my fault, don't you?"

He looked away from her.

"Dev, look at me please."

He turned his eyes towards her.

"Promise me that you will never get into any scuffle with anyone from now on."

"I don't blame you for it, *Aai.* I was the reason he left, didn't he?"

"No! Don't you ever think like that," she said. "Your father left us because he believed in his cause. He is a good man." She insisted on using the present tense when speaking of his father.

He could never do that. "Promise me that you will not fight with anyone. Promise me that you will finish your education and become a big man."

Dev nodded. That was the line she kept repeating—study hard and become a big man.

His mother had three brothers, all of whom had refused to give them shelter after his father disappeared. She wrote letters to all of them, telling them about his father's disappearance, obliquely suggesting that she and her ten-year-old son, their nephew, might starve to death.

None of them responded.

She wrote more letters but never visited them, perhaps ashamed that her husband had abandoned her.

After two months, her eldest brother visited their house. He had purchased return tickets for three people for a journey the next day by the state transport bus. She refused because it would be a burden on him. She told him to send money instead, and keep a record of that money. She would return it soon after she got a job.

"Job? What job?" his uncle had asked.

"As a teacher in a primary school."

"Haven't you had your fill of adventure when you married that man? I told you he'd run away one day, didn't I?"

"Yes you did. Will you send me some money?"

"And didn't I tell you that he was a fool? A man who was good for nothing? He was…"

"*Aba,* you can leave now."

"What?"

"If you expect me to put up with you insulting my husband as the price for helping me, you are wrong."

There was a long silence in which her brother regarded her with a pained hopelessness, watching her drown in her own illusions. He nodded after a long time, said he would send money every month, patted Dev's head and left.

Her migraines started that night. She searched for a job for three months and got one that paid a pittance. His uncle never stopped sending money. She could never pay him back. Her migraine never left her, but her dignity did.

"How are you *beta?*" asked Sharif Miyan, who stood behind his mother.

"Mother worries far too much, Sharif Miyan," Dev said and smiled.

His mother touched Sharif Miyan's feet. He patted her head. Dev's father had told him that Sharif Miyan was their guardian angel.

"I am going home to bring you some food, Dev," she said and walked away.

Sharif Miyan sat on the bed.

"Why are you always fighting, son?"

Dev said nothing.

The sallow cheeks of the twelve-year-old boy were a sad sight. Sharif Miyan remembered the chubby boy he had seen when Anand and Anuradha had come visiting. He was so full of life. And they were such a lovely family.

"Your father is a great man, Dev," Sharif Miyan said.

"So everyone says," Dev said, and instantly regretted the sarcasm in his voice.

Sharif Miyan took a deep breath and nodded as though he understood the pain behind Dev's sarcasm. "I am sure you will learn about him one day. And you will be proud of him. I am sure you will make him proud too, son."

Dev said nothing. Sharif Miyan was perhaps the only man in town who had that impression of his father.

"Do you want to hear a story?"

"I am too old for stories now," Dev said.

Dev remembered every single story that he had heard from Sharif Miyan. He liked to tell stories to all the kids at night, after he returned from his teastall. These were stories about princes and kingdoms and heroes and warriors. And all the kids were in awe of Sharif Miyan.

"Once, there was a young man who loved his family. They were a good family—he had a wife and a son. The man knew the son was special. He vowed to always be there for him. Then, one day, while he was working in a factory, a man's hand was caught in the jaws of a crusher. People tried to save him, but the iron monster gobbled up his hand. The owner of the factory was furious, not because his man lost an arm, but because production was stalled for two hours. He came to the shop floor and shouted at the workers. Someone said to him that a man almost died. The owner kicked him. The family man saw everything. He knew that safety norms were not being followed in the factory. The old machine should have been replaced a long time ago. He went to the injured man's house after a few days and saw that the hospital had discharged him, as the man had no money to pay for his treatment. He had a three-year-old son and a wife. The little boy didn't understand anything and kept on crying. Our family man took out all his savings and readmitted the injured man to the hospital. His co-workers thought he was a great man. They asked him to talk to the owner to give some money to treat the injured man. He went to the owner's place to make the request. The owner and his men locked him inside a room and beat him for two hours, then threw him out on the street."

Sharif Miyan took a deep breath, as though reliving a heart-wrenching memory. Dev stared at him wide-eyed.

"The man somehow reached home. But he was not the same man. He knew there were many injured men in the past whose families had been abandoned. There were many three-year-olds who were orphaned. He took a new vow—that he would not allow another little kid become an orphan, or allow another worker to lose his hand, or allow another family to be destroyed because of the greed of a few people. It didn't mean that he forgot his vow to his son. But it meant that he had too many people to take care of now. Since then, the man saved many families. He saved many kids from becoming orphans. He stood up against the greed of some dastardly people."

Sharif Miyan held Dev's hand. Dev's tears soaked the dirty bed sheet.

"Your father is a great man, Dev. And he loves you," he said and patted his head.

"What is a Naxalite, Sharif Miyan?"

"Everyone calls your father that, don't they?" Sharif Miyan said. There was a wry smile on his face.

"Yes."

"It doesn't matter, son. He is your father. And you will make him very proud one day."

A few days later, Dev went back to school. He had a deep scar on his face, just above the left eye—God had gifted him another eye.

"Hey Mr Three Eyes! Can you see me with your two eyes closed?" Avi said as he and Jeet saw Dev entering the school. Dev had walked to school. He missed his cycle.

"My third eye is Shiva's third eye! It will burn you down if I open it," Dev said theatrically. They all laughed.

Jagan and Bappa were nowhere to be seen when the three of them joined their row for morning prayers. Anita, as usual, stood next to Dev in the girls' row.

"Jagan and his family have left town for the next ten days on a pilgrimage," she said and laughed.

He laughed too. "This is the best news I've heard in days," he said. She had an irresistible urge to caress the scars on his face with her hands. Would she hurt him by doing so, or would she assuage his pain? What would his face feel like if she touched it? And his body? Her cheeks were hot. She could not speak to Dev and was grateful when the PT teacher, D'Silva, whistled, which was the cue to start the prayers.

After school got over for the day, Dev, Avi and Jeet ran down the hillock to the riverside. Jeet spread out the sketch of the fort to show Dev.

"This is beautiful, Jeet. You're an artist!" Dev said.

The smile was back on Jeet's face after a long time.

"Avi and I made it the other night."

"That's hard to believe. I thought our owl was only good at maths."

"I taught fatty how to draw," Avi said folding his hands and raising his eyebrows.

"In your dreams," Jeet snorted.

"Well then, let's start!" Dev said and the three boys started to work at building the fort.

Jeet taught them everything—how to build the foundation, the boundary wall, the gateway to the fort, and the pathway that curved up to the fort.

Over the next two days, the fort gradually began to resemble Jeet's sketch. They were so excited that they went to the riverside during lunch break on the third day.

"Where do you boys disappear during lunchtime?" Anita asked when she saw their soiled hands as they returned to the classroom.

Jeet could not look at her. He sensed the intensity of the aura that surrounded her. It made her intimidating, unreachable, even though she stood just a few feet away. It amazed him that she was the first girl with whom he was friendly. Why was she not short and chubby—a more approachable person?

Avi was so casual around her, either indifferent or oblivious to that aura. Perhaps it was the result of being in her vicinity for a very long time.

With Dev, it was inexplicably but conspicuously the opposite—she was in awe of him. There was an ancient bond between them, beneath their bickering, which concealed her devotion to him. It manifested itself many times during the day, in her furtive glances in his direction, followed by her smile. She would twist an unruly strand of her hair and look at Dev through it. When she laughed at a joke that her neighbour whispered in her ear, when she answered a question correctly in class, she would look at him. At times her glances lingered upon him, but sometimes they were clandestine.

"Are you learning pottery?" she asked, pointing at their hands.

"Yes. We intend to break those pots on your head," Dev said.

"That's very funny. I pity those pots."

"We know you have a thick skull, so we are making them hard," Dev said.

He and Avi laughed. She rolled her eyes, twisted her lips and walked away.

"Why do you talk to her like that?" Jeet asked Dev.

"Like what?"

"As if you're always trying to humiliate her."

"And you think she is always praising me?"

"They've always behaved like that, ever since we met in KG," Avi said. "I don't know why, but that's the way they talk to each other."

Jeet woke up at some unknown hour of the night. His bed was wet with sweat though the overhead fan rotated at its highest speed.

It was a full moon night and the moonlight filtered through the mosquito net. He got up from the bed and walked up to the window. He could see the quiet, empty streets of the town. He heard the faint barking of a dog somewhere far away.

A strange dream had woken him up. He was with Anita. They were holding hands on the banks of a silver sea. It was cold in the dream and Anita was very close to him. Her body was covered with sand from the beach. He could not remember what she wore—maybe she did not wear anything, or was wrapped in the grainy coarse sand. The sand shone and he could not look at her for more than a few seconds. All he could see were her dimpled smile and her blue eyes. They were quiet, but it was not because they had nothing to say to each other. It felt like the quiet that comes after long hours of talking, after they had said and heard all that they wanted to say and hear. All that remained was the afterglow of the time spent together.

He was not sweating on that beach. He could vaguely remember Anita saying that she loved his smell and his smile. He looked down at his body hoping to see his flabby belly spread like an octopus on the sand, but it was flat. He touched it and it was hard as wood. She touched his stomach too. And he thought he would just melt and be lapped up by the waves of the silver sea. She smiled her impossibly beautiful smile. She said that she loved his body.

That was when they both heard Dev's voice. It didn't come from any specific direction. He could not hear or understand the words. Anita stood up in a flash and responded. Again, he did not hear what was said. He wondered if the wind was so strong that it carried their words far away from his ears. Perhaps he was not meant to hear those words. Her face was animated, but not with anger. She was so ecstatic on hearing Dev's voice that nothing else mattered, including Jeet's presence. She walked towards the sea laughing, as though Dev had told her some private joke. Then she walked on the silver sea.

Strangely, Jeet was not at all angry to hear Dev's voice. It was as if he had known all along in the dream that this would happen—that she would not sit with him for long, that she didn't belong next to him. He peered at the sea and could not see her. She continued walking, on the sea, farther and farther away from him, till she became a tiny speck.

He woke up in the wet bed. He had carried back some of the sea water from the dream.

Everyone called him Manoj the creep, and he was proud of it. His mother had asked him once why he grinned when people called him that. She said it was not right that the other kids made fun of him. He was surprised that she thought it was humiliating and told her so. His mother had looked at him for a long time. He heard her talking to his father the next morning.

"All of Manoj's friends used to call him a creep," she said in a whisper.

"So? Even my friends called me that," his father said. His father resembled a clown. Tufts of hair, like candyfloss, were scattered on his balding pate. His bulbous nose and squinting eyes completed the appearance of a clown. Everyone told Manoj that he had taken after his father.

"You worry far too much," his father said as he did his morning puja.

"The way they humiliate him is horrible. But he doesn't seem to mind. It gives me the jitters."

His father started humming the mantras. Manoj wondered what his father hummed and to whom. The assortment of idols in the corner of the house was a mystery.

"Are you listening?"

"He will be all right."

"I sometimes wonder what happened to that little puppy," his mother said.

"What?"

"The puppy that Manoj was so fascinated with has a broken leg. Vishal says it fell from the roof. Not once or twice, but several times. The puppy barks crazily whenever it sees Manoj."

Vishal, his elder brother, was a nosy bastard.

"You're losing your mind. Now let me go ahead and complete my puja."

"That's all you do! Puja for twenty-four hours a day! You're a good-for-nothing."

She continued nagging. God must have been fed up with the continuous nagging of his father's mantras, and had punished him by making his wife nag him. Manoj laughed at that joke, which he never shared with anyone else.

He liked secrets. Such as the dirty thing that Vishal did with his penis in the bathroom. He had heard Vishal grunting one day as he stood outside the bathroom waiting his turn. His elder brother was such a fool—he didn't know that there was a hole in the overhead window of the bathroom. One day, when his brother had gone to bathe, Manoj quietly got a ladder, climbed it and peeped through the hole. Vishal was shaking his penis. And his penis had exploded. He didn't share this with anyone either.

Nor did he tell anyone about the little hearts that his sister drew in her notebooks, with the name of a classmate in them. She guarded her notebooks, but he had torn a page from one and had neatly folded it inside one of his own school books.

There were the countless little conversations his parents had about things he was not supposed to know, such as why his father's sister was not able to have children, or why his grandmother was always unhappy with his mother.

There were many ways of discovering a secret. Some secrets were obvious, waiting to be uncovered. Some needed more effort. Would a puppy die if it fell from a height? He had looked into the puppy's eyes before he threw it from the terrace. There was a curiosity in the little dog's eyes, its pink tongue protruding expectantly from between its little teeth. He flung it high in the air. He smiled when it flayed its limbs in all directions. You cannot swim in the air, didn't the stupid dog know that? His smile had broadened when the puppy fell on the ground with a soft thump. He had expected more noise, though the movements that the puppy made after falling more than made up for it. It tried to get up but collapsed with a tiny cry. Perhaps the pain was too much for it to cry any louder. Manoj wanted to clap when he saw that the puppy's leg was broken. It managed to get up after many attempts, dragged its twisted feet for a few steps and collapsed again, this time wailing loudly. His elder brother came out on hearing the barking. Manoj quickly hid behind the terrace wall, hoping that his brother had not seen him. He silently ran down the stairs to the back of the house, ecstatic. Manoj knew everything. And he never told anyone that he knew it. When he told Anita that he loved her, she laughed aloud. He loved that laughter.

"What did you just say?"

"I love you, Anita," he said again, tickled all over by her laughter.

She kept on laughing. She had stopped in the middle of the road while heading to the school. She bent over, clutching her stomach as though she was going to vomit. There were tears in her eyes.

"Manoj Jadhav, you are the creepiest person I know," she said trying to control her giggling. But she could not.

He could stand there in the middle of the road and hear her laugh like that forever. If he could make her laugh, that meant she liked him. He wanted to tell his mother that being creepy was not such a bad thing after all. How could it be, when it made Anita laugh?

And then she had walked away from him with her hand on her mouth. He was certain that she loved him.

Two days later, Avi told Anita what they were doing on the riverside. They were talking about the impending semester exams when Avi casually said that they should complete the fort before the exams started. Dev slapped his head.

"What fort?" Anita asked.

"Uh...Did I say fort? I meant 'course'. Our course for the semester," Avi said, biting his tongue.

"Oh, come on! 'Course' does not sound like 'fort,'" Anita said, flicking a troublesome strand of hair from her left eye. Jeet wondered if anyone else noticed her little mannerisms, each of which made his heart beat faster. "What fort are you talking about?" she asked, narrowing her eyes.

"Uh...Umm," Avi looked at Dev.

"It's a little fort that we're making," Dev said, nodding.

"Where?"

"At the riverside."

"Riverside?"

"Hey! Enough of your questions, okay? You're a nosy, nagging witch!"

"I won't let you guys go before you tell me," she said, her lips set in a determined line. Jeet had never seen anyone who looked so ethereal even when frowning.

"Okay!" Dev said. "Come with us during lunchtime."

He stomped off towards the bench muttering, looking angrily at Avi, who followed him with his head bent.

During lunchtime, the three boys, followed by Anita, ran down the hillock. Jeet was struggling to keep up and he felt miserable when he saw that Anita was a faster runner than him.

"Hey! Run faster, fatty!" Avi turned back to yell at Jeet.

Jeet wanted to wring his little neck for calling him "fatty"—a word that Avi used often, but it never felt offensive except in Anita's presence. Sweating profusely, he breathed in short, pained bursts.

"Shut up, four-eyes!" Anita yelled back at Avi.

She stopped and waited for Jeet to catch up. He could not look at her. There were dark, wet patches of sweat all over his shirt. He wondered what Anita would think.

"I'll run with you," she said. There was neither condescension nor pity in her voice—there was a faint interest. Perhaps she had thought about being with him, just the two of them. The riverside was not very far, but he was grateful for whatever he got. If his fat was the reason she was to run with him, he was glad to be fat.

He smiled at her. She smiled back, and they ran side by side. He was fascinated by her hair and her legs, as well her frown of concentration.

"Look ahead. You'll fall otherwise," she said and laughed. There was no hint of exhaustion in her voice.

"Sorry," he said, embarrassed that she had actually caught him staring.

He thought someone had poured petrol on his lungs and ignited them, but he continued to run. He didn't want her to regret staying behind with him. They reached the riverside and saw that Avi and Dev had already started work on the fort.

"This is simply beautiful, boys!" Anita said.

"It is Jeet's design," Dev said.

"It's amazing," she said, looking at Jeet with admiration. Jeet thought he was going to collapse with dizziness, and it had nothing to do with his running.

"Well, don't just keep standing there! Get going," Avi said, smiling.

"How can I help?"

"Why don't you just sit and admire the men at work?" Dev said.

"Oh, I can do better than you," she said and looked at Jeet with her eyebrows raised, waiting for an affirmation from him.

"I think you can work on the staircase of the royal entrance," Jeet said. "It's the most beautiful part of the fort."

And the four of them began to work.

Manoj felt the incredible elation of knowing a secret.

He had followed Anita that day, as he had for the last six months. When Anita had joined school that year, he had sensed a profound change in her. Before that, she was a sombre girl who sat quietly in the classroom, unremarkable and almost unnoticed. She didn't have any friends apart from Dev Gokhale and Avinash Shah. But that year, she appeared to have transformed, and that intrigued him. Her face had a perpetual freshness that he found mysterious. She smiled a lot, as though she knew a secret. He had followed her—with his eyes in the class, and with his legs out of it—and had fallen in love with her. She had, unknowingly, already revealed a secret that day. He saw the four of them lost in building that little fort. Now he would become friendly with Jagan and Bappa. They would not ignore him anymore. Not with what he had to show them. That was the power of secrets. His smile broadened at the thought. He walked back to the school.

Jeet sat on his haunches, trying to shape a pillar, when he saw her against the splashed saffron of the setting sun, like a painting he once saw at the *Jahangir Art Gallery.* She stood with her hands on her hips, with little patches of mud smeared over her school uniform. Her face was glistening with a thin sheen of sweat. There was a tiny smear of mud on her cheek. A large strand of hair fell over it. He drank in all the details, till he could almost visualise it on paper. He wondered if his painting would be as beautiful.

"What are you looking at, fatty?" Avi asked with a knowing smile.

Jeet sheepishly returned to fussing over the pillar. He stole a glance at her and saw her frowning in concentration, with her head tilted at an angle. She looked back at him with an indulgent acceptance, perhaps aware that he was infatuated with her. She then looked at Avi, tilting her head in the opposite direction.

"What?" she asked him.

"Our man here was doing some sightseeing," he said pointing a finger at Jeet.

"Don't you have any other work, you owl? That boundary wall needs your attention," Jeet said.

"Jeet, what does the entrance of the fort look like?" Dev asked.

Jeet stood up and peered at the entrance from many angles. "This is the best entrance I have seen ever, Dev," he said. "And look at Mr Owl's boundary wall."

They ribbed Avi for a long time after that, while Avi ridiculed everything made by them. They sat on the rocks at the edge of the stream. Their minds relaxed, watching the sun set, while the running water massaged their tired feet.

"So this is the place you boys disappear to every lunch break," she said, looking at Dev. There was hurt in her eyes. Somehow, Dev had betrayed her by not letting her in on something special in his life. Jeet wondered what else they had already shared. Dev nodded after a long pause. Her sadness was intense but fleeting, and disappeared after the infuriatingly inadequate response from Dev. Jeet looked away, giving them space, allowing them to share that intimate moment.

"How do you protect it from rain?" Anita asked Jeet the next day. This had struck her the day before, as she practised her dancing. She had missed a step and could not match it for the rest of the evening. Jeet was making the watchtower. He froze at her question. The six forts he had built in the six cities where he previously lived had all been washed away, gone forever. By the time he had friends to help him make the fort, his father would have been transferred. By the time he finished building the fort, the truck transporting their belongings would have been loaded.

The fort was abandoned, the friends were abandoned, as was the government house. Unlike the government house, there was nobody to take care of the fort and the lost friendships. He had known this would happen, but had refused to think of it. When Anita raised the issue, he realised that his forts had already been destroyed. How foolish he was to build those forts, knowing but not acknowledging their eventual destruction. Why did he build those forts when they would be destroyed? They stared at him intently, awaiting some brilliant idea from their architect, but he had none.

"I don't know," he said and then flopped down on the ground.

The three of them looked at each other. He knew what they were thinking. Stupid fat kid. Just like his body, his brain is fat too.

"This is the first time I have built a fort so soon after moving to a new city. It took me months to make friends in every other city," he said.

"What an intelligent question. We build a shed to cover the fort, you stupid girl," Dev said to Anita.

"A shed," she said, readily, agreeing for the first time, perhaps, with Dev's assessment of her—that it was stupid of her to sadden Jeet.

"Yes. We cover it with tarpaulin. Don't we Jeet?"

"Huh?" Jeet said. Dev was looking at him with his eyebrows raised. "Yes. That's a good idea."

They all knew it was not a good idea. The flimsy tarpaulin was inadequate defence against the inevitable destructive onslaught of nature. But it was something upon which to pin their hopes.

"So why have we stopped working? Let's get going! Avi, you're the slowest, you know that?" Dev said and got back to the rear entrance of the fort.

"You get to do easy things like the door!" Avi said. "Fatty, this is not fair. This wall is very hard to make."

Anita was contrite all evening, refusing to leave at her time of *riyaz,* atoning for the turmoil she had caused.

"What do you think?" Jeet asked them that evening.

"I think it's just one more day away from completion," Dev said. Avi and Anita concurred, satisfied and excited.

It would be the best fort that he had made. He had been inspired by Rajgarh, Shivaji's fort. They promised each other that they would finish it the next day. And from that day, the great fort of Rajgadh would proudly oversee the riverside, a sentinel of their secret place.

Many years later, Jeet wondered if they should have completed the work that day itself. They were tired, but they should have carried on. Maybe they would all have been scolded by their families.

If they had completed it that day, perhaps the memory of it would have been complete too.

Two hours before the blast...

The members of the Shah family were doing their weekly shopping in Sarafa Bazaar. The aunts haggled raucously at the fake jewellery shop for hours and bought cheap gaudy jewellery, their faces drenched in sweat from the exertion and exhilaration of bargaining. The uncles indulged their wives, admiring their reflections in mirrors with forced smiles and approving snorts. The clamorous children threw tantrums and made their parents buy hideous toys—a rubber alligator with red eyes, a banjo-playing monkey with a creepy grin, plastic guns—that they never played with afterwards. After finishing their shopping, the family members gorged on chaat. Every week, Avi was amazed by the deep-rooted gluttony of his family. They ate the pungent chaat as if it were their last meal.

It was a tradition in the Shah family. His uncles and father never tired of describing what they did in Sarafa Bazaar—the family had no other stories to tell. The last few Sunday excursions had become unbearable to him. But there would be no respite. As long as he lived at Shah Sadan, he would have to endure these trips. His mother forced him to go with them, in the vain hope that his father would somehow, eventually, accept him. She stayed home, cooking and guarding the house, while Avi dragged his feet behind the Shah flock.

One hour before the blast...

Dev smelled something delicious cooking in the kitchen. His mother was dipping handfuls of chopped onions into batter, before plunking them in boiling oil.

"I am making *bhaje* for you!" she said excitedly.

There was a faint fetid smell in the kitchen from the many unwashed utensils, but it was suppressed by the aroma of the deep-fried *bhaje*. She had a childlike thrill on her face, as though she had suddenly discovered that she could cook.

"That's nice, mother," he said, trying to match the enthusiasm in her voice.

"Why don't you run and get some *shrikhand?* I'll also make puris for you today!"

"Maybe you can make the puris next time?"

"You're worried about the money, aren't you?"

"No."

"Don't. Just take the money from my purse and get the *shrikhand*."

"But *Aai*, we..."

"Shh...Do as I say. Go now!" she said and stirred the *bhaje* that were turning a crisp brown in the boiling oil.

She had filled the pan to the brim. It could have lasted them the entire month. The *shrikhand* was not cheap and would cost them a few meals. He stood in the kitchen entrance, wanting her migraine to return and hating himself for that. She waited for a few moments and ran past him to the bedroom, snatched the worn purse and fished out a few notes.

"I want you to act like a twelve-year-old sometimes." She held his hand and put the money on his palm, before rushing back to the kitchen.

He walked out of the house and wondered what she really meant.

Forty five minutes before the blast…

Jeet combed his hair. He was going to Sarafa Bazaar for the opening of a new shop. His father was the chief guest, and he was never late for any function. His mother stared at her image in the vanity-table mirror for hours before getting up. That habit was the remnant of the countless high society parties they had attended in Bombay.

"Have you taken the gift, Mrs Mehra?" his father asked his mother. They never called each other by their names. It was always Mr Mehra and Mrs Mehra. He wondered when they would start calling him Master Mehra.

"Yes, Mr Mehra," she said and adjusted an errant strand of hair.

They stood in front of the mirror and admired themselves for a few seconds. The opening ceremony would take place in fifteen minutes. His father estimated that it would take fourteen minutes to reach the shop.

Thirty minutes before the blast…

Her mother was adamant that Anita would not wear the old *ghungroos* that had, long ago, become unmelodious.

"Come outside," she whispered in Anita's ear.

There was the smell of alcohol in the entire house. It was strongest in the little living room, where her father sprawled on the floor with his clothes soaked in cheap liquor and bile. Her mother washed his clothes every day for hours. She banged the little washing bat on the clothes to remove the smell of alcohol. The sounds of the washing bat and the *ghungroos* pervaded their life.

"Take these thirty-nine rupees and tell the shop owner Gangadhar that I will pay the rest later."

"*Aai,* I really don't need new *ghungroos,*" Anita said.

"The old ones have said their last words. Dancing without *ghungroos* is like singing with no *sur* or *taal.* Now don't argue and go buy yourself a new pair."

The thirty-nine rupees, made up of old musty notes and a few coins, were not enough. But Gangadhar, the old lecher, would give her mother anything for free. She quietly walked out of the house to buy new *ghungroos* and to breathe in air that did not reek of alcohol.

Five minutes before the blast…

The narrow street that led to the old masjid was, as usual, filled with people who ate grilled chicken with naan, who drank *thandai,* who shopped for saffron flowers, who admired *chadars* and who haggled over the prices of trinkets.

Inside the masjid, Sharif Miyan knelt on his prayer mat to pray for his nephew. He knew Abbas hated him. He prayed for peace for the troubled boy. He prayed for the soul of his departed brother. He had a faint regret that he had failed his dead brother, who had entrusted him with Abbas's well-being. He knew the boy was going astray, that he was listening to dangerous people in the mohalla. He hoped God would show him the right direction.

When the bomb exploded, Sharif Miyan was bending down on his prayer mat for the third time. The ground shook. For the next few moments, there was a stunned silence, broken only by the fearful chatter of birds fleeing skywards, afraid of man and his anger.

The three flower shops were obliterated. The petals of the once-dewy flowers and their sellers' flesh burnt together. The people reacted and, unlike the birds, they did not react in unison. They ran towards the narrow streets near the masjid, trampling over the old and limping beggars. They pushed and shoved and cursed and cried. The birds circled in the air, pitying the humans who had lost their humanity.

Sharif Miyan ran to the burnt shops. He peered into the blaze, searching for a sign of life. There was none. The bright orange flames had devoured all the colours—the saffron of the flowers, the purple of the *chadars*, the rainbow colours of the *mithai* and the red of blood.

"Ya Allah!" He banged his fist against his head.

The three flower shop owners were young men who had grown up on his stories. Their faces flashed in front of his eyes. He screamed and ran with tears streaming down his face and with a prayer on his lips for the dead and the living.

The town of Amrapur and its fragile peace would shatter into a thousand pieces. The soul of the town was to be lynched in Sarafa Bazaar where, haplessly, his little teastall stood.

Abbas had been smoking his third joint of ganja in Haidar's flower shop. He took a long drag and didn't exhale for a long time. Soon he was flying with the clouds in the sky. It was so wonderful there, where none of his stupid family was around to berate him. This is what heaven must feel like, he thought. The deafening blast was a dull thud in his ears.

"Hey Abbas! Just get out of here very quickly! It's a bomb!" Haidar shouted.

Abbas could not understand what he said. His limbs refused to obey his commands. Haidar ran out of the shop cursing him loudly.

The street that led to the old masjid was filled with the cries of frightened and stampeding people. It was the noise he used to make when his father beat him with a leather belt, amplified a million times. The memory of the beatings roused him. He stood up so suddenly that he had a painful cramp in the small of his back. He walked out of the flower shop with laboured steps.

The shops near the masjid were burning. He smiled. A realisation illuminated his foggy brain like a bolt of lightning: Sarafa Bazaar would burn. And, with it, his *haraami* uncle too.

Avi drifted away from the Shah horde. The uncles and aunts would not bother about his whereabouts. His father didn't acknowledge his presence in the house, so he would not fret either. He would wander around the crowded Bazaar Street for a few hours and join the family when they went back home. If he went home before everybody else, his mother would be disappointed.

The driver of the government car honked relentlessly. People scurried away as though it were a raging bull. Jeet lowered the window of the car.

"Don't do that," his mother said.

The car was an air-conditioned bubble gliding through the hot, dusty Bazaar Street. The walls of the car insulated Mr and Mrs Mehra from the concoction of smells and smoke pervading the street. They got down from the car in front of a shop. It was buried under a thick canopy of garlands. The owner of the shop smashed a coconut at the entrance. Everyone clapped. His parents would smile condescendingly at all the people. The people would say nice things to them and then they would comment on him. It was a depressing pattern that he had endured all too often. He looked away.

He saw Anita walking into a shop. She had a pair of *ghungroos* in her hand. There was a wistful smile on her face. Would he ever see her dance?

"Jeet, say hello to Gurudas uncle," his father told him. He could not tear his eyes away from Anita.

"Jeet! Jeet!" his father said a little loudly.

"Huh? Uh, sorry. Hello Gurudas uncle."

He saw that his father was angry. It was there in the way his lips twisted while he smiled, in the exasperated sigh, in the little push that he gave Jeet. His anger never manifested itself in a more violent form, but those little expressions were enough to frighten Jeet.

"And now, say hello to Phartade uncle. He is the Superintendent of Police."

Phartade was huge, and wore a policeman's uniform. He was flanked by three constables. "Don't be naughty, or else uncle will lock you up!" he said and laughed. The constables and his father laughed dutifully.

Jeet stole a little glance in the direction of the other shop. Anita was talking to a middle-aged, paunchy, bald man. It seemed they were haggling over something—perhaps the price of the *ghungroos*.

When Dev walked out of the sweets shop, all he had expected was a guilt-ridden journey back home. What if he had not liked *shrikhand* so much? Perhaps he would have resisted his mother's efforts and that money could have been saved. He walked with his head down.

It started as a low rumble. A few moments later, the cries were audible. Down the Sarafa Bazaar Street a wave of people carrying swords, iron rods, hockey sticks and cycle chains roared like one terrible beast. The people on Bazaar Street froze like wax statues.

And then the carnage began.

"Bastards!" a man carrying a big, shiny sword shouted.

"Kill them! Kill them all!" another carrying an iron rod bellowed.

The mob flanked the street at both ends, like a two-headed python. The men carrying swords attacked two people, a woman and an old man. In seconds, they were on the ground, dead even before they hit it.

The people ran. A shopkeeper tried to close his shop and his hand was severed. It dangled from the shop's door handle, spurting blood. The mob burnt him, along with his shop.

For the first few moments, Dev stood hypnotised by the violence. He screamed, shaking off the stupefaction, when he saw the severed hand dangling from the shutter. The by-lanes of Bazaar Street were clogged with screaming and stampeding people. He ran towards Sharif Miyan's teastall—the only place where he felt safe.

The man next to Avi was stabbed in the stomach with a sword. Blood erupted from his stomach in a geyser. A few drops fell on Avi. A man wielding a bicycle chain ran towards him. Avi stared at him, transfixed with the realisation that he would be dying on Bazaar Street. Instead, the man attacked another person who stood in front of him. Avi ran.

Anita ran out of the shop just before Gangadhar locked himself inside. Instinct told her that staying inside the shop was going to be very dangerous. The terrible sight of people being cut made her vomit violently. A man whose face was spattered with blood saw her. He licked his lips and ran towards her. She ran. She looked back once to see the man attacking people who came in his way with a sword. She was sobbing and hoped that Sharif Miyan would be able to save her.

Jeet could see Anita running towards the other end of the street.

"Jeet! Get into the shop!" his father shouted.

"Anita!" Jeet called behind her.

Two men attacked their car. The police constables raised their guns and shot them.

"Jeet!" his mother screamed.

She and his father were pulled towards the shop they had just inaugurated by two constables. The third constable rushed towards him. Jeet turned and ran. The three constables with their guns would protect his parents, but Anita was alone on the street. There was no way he was going to leave her alone.

Sharif Miyan stood right in front of his teastall with his hands spread.

"Stop, for God's sake!" he shouted.

"Sharif Miyan!" Dev cried.

"Dev! Get in the kitchen! Quick!"

Dev ran and hid inside the little kitchen, the sacred space in the teastall.

Avi and Anita reached the stall at the same time.

"What are you kids doing? Get inside!"

Jeet screamed her name. She turned back.

"Run Jeet!" she shouted.

Jeet reached the teastall. Sharif Miyan pushed him inside as well. They all tried to hide in the little kitchen but there wasn't enough space.

"You stay here. I'll hide behind the counter!" Dev said and stepped out of the storeroom

"No! Wait!"

"Anita, listen to me," Dev said and held her by her shoulders. "Nothing will happen to me."

He stepped out of the storeroom and shut the door before they could protest any more. He hid under the teastall counter, knowing he could be dead in the next few minutes. Giant flames, fanned by hatred, lit the old bazaar. Smoke from the bazaar's burning shops filled the air. Dev shuddered at the thought that the rioters on the street would burn down Sharif Miyan's teastall, and they would all burn to death. He bit his lip to stop himself from crying.

Sharif Miyan's blood-curdling cry stunned him. There was a horrified shock in that cry. Dev peeked above the little counter. Abbas had buried his sword deep in Sharif Miyan's heart. Abbas laughed, his teeth bared in a snarl, at Sharif Miyan's writhing form. He pulled the sword out with so much force that the blood spurted out of Sharif Miyan's chest. Smothering his instinctive yelp, Dev ducked back under the counter.

Dev wept violently. Shivering uncontrollably, he closed his ears with his hands but the anguished screams broke through that feeble resistance. Sharif Miyan's dying cries were drowned in the sea of cries that the Sarafa Bazaar Street had become.

Abbas laughed. Sharif Miyan's body lay still on the ground. Abbas kicked Sharif Miyan's ribs with such force that the old bones cracked. Abbas didn't stop at one kick. He kicked Sharif Miyan's body as though it were a dusty carpet. "Now what will you do, you bastard! Bastard! Bastard!" Abbas screamed. He spat upon Sharif Miyan's face. His frothy spit spread over the bloodied face. "Say salaam to my father!" For a moment, Abbas stood still, his sword lowered, blood dripping to the ground—as though comprehending the enormity of what he had done. Then he spat on Sharif Miyan's face one last time.

He slowly turned towards the teastall counter. Perhaps he sensed someone was under it. Dev ducked back under the counter and put his fist in his mouth. Should he just run? Abandon his friends? He shook his head. He would die before Abbas could harm them. Biting hard on his fist, he waited, certain that his life was over.

He was so shaken that he urinated in his pants, even as he shoved his hands into his mouth to prevent a torrent of sobs. Closing his eyes, he waited for Abbas's sword. Moments ticked by. He would die without saying goodbye to his mother.

Abbas wrapped a scarf over his face, raised his sword and ran.

Dev sat beneath the teastall counter, surrounded by the endless cries of rioters and their victims, and the raging inferno that spread through the street, devouring everything in its wake. The fire spread, fanned by intense hatred. Everything burnt—shops, vehicles, people. All were transformed into dark grey ash. The hockey sticks and iron rods covered the street with broken bones, torn flesh and spilled blood.

The little teastall, in which Sharif Miyan had served tea and warmth to the people of Amrapur for forty years, didn't burn down, as if it repelled the hatred of the people like a shrine. The ground was fast turning crimson with his blood.

Sharif Miyan died, and with him died the soul of the little town, its humanity and its harmony. His body lay in front of the stall, guarding the four of them. After an interminable time, Dev dared to look at the street. There was an eerie silence, punctured occasionally by the strident noise of frightened birds.

He opened the storeroom door. Anita and Avi were crying nonstop. Jeet was shaking like a leaf in a tornado.

"Oh my God…Sharif Miyan!" Anita said, sobbing.

"Should we go out there and help him?" Avi asked.

"He…He is dead!" Dev said, and they cried for the man who had protected them with his own life.

"Jeet! Jeetu!" The panicked cries of Jeet's father broke through the rumble of the Ambassador car.

"Father!" Jeet said and stood up.

They walked out of the teastall and stood a few feet away from Sharif Miyan's body. Anita walked up to the body and squatted next to it. She gently touched the blood-soaked face. She held his hand and kissed it.

"Jeetu! Get in the car!" His father held him by his shoulder and pushed him towards the car.

"They are my friends!"

"Shut up!"

"Father, please!"

His father slapped him hard. He dragged Jeet to the car and flung him into the back seat, where a constable held him. Jeet banged the car window and screamed, begging his father to stop and help his friends, but the car didn't stop.

Amrapur was engulfed in funereal silence the next day. The streets were empty. The stillness was pierced sporadically by loudly wailing people mourning the dead. Special police forces were scattered all over town. The khaki-clad, helmeted policemen stood guard with stony faces and shiny guns.

The people spoke in hushed tones in the confines of their homes. It was all a big conspiracy, they said. Barely minutes separated the blast and the riot. It was a staged carnage, they believed. No one dared to name the puppeteer behind the massacre. Everyone knew that nothing happened in the town without the blessings of the king of the town, Bhausaheb Bhoite. The news slowly filtered in that Bhausaheb and his family had cut short the religious yatra and returned to the town. People waited with bated breath.

A curfew was imposed that barred more than two people from meeting on the streets of Amrapur. The policemen had their fingers on the triggers, ready to shoot down anybody breaking the curfew. However, twelve-year-old children were spared.

The four friends met at the riverside. They held each other's hands.

"We just hid like cowards," Avi said, wiping his tears.

"Yes, we did," Dev said and broke down. He buried his face in his hands, ashamed of those fleeting but intense moments when he had thought of abandoning them. The echo of Sharif Miyan's dying cries didn't fade away. Avi embraced him first, then Jeet and Anita.

They sat facing the stream. Nobody uttered a word for a long time.

"The police will help us, won't they, Dev?" Anita asked, uprooting a few leaves of grass.

"We can't let that bastard live," Dev said and got up. "We will go to the police now."

He raised his palm.

"Together?"

Anita put her palm on his. Avi and Jeet followed.

"Together," Anita whispered.

They began walking back.

"Well, well, well...We have an orgy here, don't we?"

They stopped in their tracks at the sight of Bappa laughing hysterically.

"What are you doing here?" Anita said. Her voice wavered like a badly tuned musical instrument.

"Looking at you having fun with three boys," Bappa said and spat on the ground. "Now who is going to save you? That senile bastard is dead. I heard they cut him into a hundred pieces." He started laughing again.

"Bappa, we don't want any trouble, okay?" Dev said.

Intense anger clouded Dev's vision, but he did not do anything as he had promised Sharif Miyan that he would not fight anymore.

Would Bappa let him keep that promise? Bappa ignored him and looked at the fort that had escaped the fury of the town.

"What do we have here?"

"Bappa...Bappa! Look at me. We have had a lot of trouble already. Let's all go back to our homes, okay?" Dev said trying to pacify Bappa.

"Trouble? You think you have seen trouble? You're mistaken, you're going to see it now," Bappa said.

He let out a loud cry and ran towards the fort so suddenly that all four of them were stunned into stillness. He jumped high in the air and landed with a sickening thud on its roof.

The fort didn't break but burst in an explosion of mud. Jeet let out a wail of such intense anguish that it shook them out of their fearful trance but it was too late. The fort lay in ruins. It was not supposed to look like that so soon. Maybe five hundred years later. But not five days later.

Dev bellowed and slammed his shoulder into Bappa's chest. Bappa did not expect that. He cried out in pain. There was a crack of something breaking, but it was not his bones. It was the wooden skeleton that supported the fort.

Bappa punched Dev squarely on his face. Dev's head whiplashed and a thin spray of blood erupted from his mouth.

"Bastard!" Jeet roared, and threw a clumsy powerless punch at Bappa. It landed on Bappa's shoulder like a woollen ball. Bappa smiled, showing all his deformed teeth, amused by the audacity of the fat boy. He slammed his right fist on Jeet's nose, breaking it. Bappa let out a short burst of laughter. The sight of Dev and Jeet writhing on the ground made him feel like ejaculating. Those few seconds, when he stopped to congratulate himself, led to his death a few minutes later. The stone hit him on his right eye. He shrieked. He lost his vision immediately. He touched it. Blood was pouring out of his eye. Avi's stone had smashed Bappa's eye to pulp.

"I am blind!" Bappa shouted through his pain. It came out like an awful wail.

In that instant, Avi knew that Bappa would kill him. He ran.

"Bastard! Bastard! Bastard!" Bappa's cries made his heart sink in the pit of his stomach.

After a few moments, Avi let out a frightened, defeated cry. He had run straight towards the stream. The ground under his feet became soft as he approached the stream. He looked back and saw Bappa just a few feet behind him. He was like a ghoul, with his face covered in blood and the specks of flesh that were once his eye.

Bappa flew at him. He grabbed him by the waist and they landed close to the water. He landed furious punches on Avi's face and head and neck. Each punch devoured Avi's consciousness till he felt he was going to pass out. A deep realisation that he was leaving this world engulfed his consciousness. He gave up trying to protect himself.

"You're drowning now! Do you hear me? I am going to bury you deep in this water!" Bappa said and dragged Avi into the stream. He held his head in a vice-like grip and dragged him till the water was up to his waist. He punched Avi's face once, and then dunked his head in the water.

Dev stood up and bolted towards them. His jaw hurt with every step he took, but he ignored it and ran as fast as he could. He reached Bappa, who was making strange animal sounds as he held Avi's head under water. Dev hit him on the back of his head with rapid punches.

Bappa's grip on Avi's head loosened. Avi shook violently under water, rejuvenated by a little hope. His mouth and nose were filled with water, choking him. He pried Bappa's loosening hands with desperate force and rose to the surface, retching violently. When his vision cleared, he saw Bappa and Dev exchanging a blur of punches. The water around them was frothing. Avi felt like crying. Once again, his friend had saved him. He clenched his teeth and attacked Bappa.

Anita ran towards the stream with cold dread in her heart. She had seen boys fighting many times. But what she was witnessing was something far more violent. Dev and Bappa were locked in a deadly embrace and were flailing their arms at each other. Bappa was three years older than Dev, and at least six inches taller. His blows were far more devastating than Dev's. She thought Dev was tiring. There was panic in his eyes. That was when Avi, who till then had been thrashing about like a dying fish, suddenly attacked Bappa from the back. She ran into the stream.

Jeet thought he was going to drown in the blood from his nose. His mouth filled with blood that felt hot and tasted salty. He spat it out. His vision was hazy, but he could see Bappa trying to drown Avi, Dev attacking Bappa, and Anita running into the stream. He stood up on his wobbly feet and ran towards them. He fell a couple of times and thought it would take him a lifetime to reach them.

"Leave him alone you animal!" Anita shouted and tried to slap Bappa.

Bappa was raining impossibly fast punches on Dev. He knew Dev was struggling to stand in the stream. Avi's weak, flapping blows had no effect on him. Suddenly Anita grabbed Bappa's head and pulled it back. Bappa threw a punch at her that landed on her mouth. Anita felt as if her teeth had been shaken out of their sockets.

Dev jumped up and managed to grab Bappa's neck in the crook of his right arm. He pushed his head under water.

"You bastard! How does it feel?" he screamed.

But Bappa was too strong for him and clawed on his hand to wriggle out of the grip. That was when Avi grabbed his head and held tight.

"I am coming! Don't let him go!" Jeet shouted as he reached them. He too gripped his head.

For the first time, Bappa felt pure horror. He could have wiggled out of Dev's grip, but all three of them were holding his head under water. He flailed desperately to no avail.

All the years of abuse. Calling me all those terrible names. Making my mother cry after she dressed my wounds. Dev stiffened his grip.

A lifetime of fear. The humiliation. Years and years of hiding. All the cousins laughing and calling me timid. Coward. Eunuch. Avi pushed Bappa's head.

My most beautiful fort. Fat boy. Hurting my friends. Jeet held his flabby hand to smother Bappa's face under water.

Had Dev, Avi and Jeet released their grips fifteen seconds earlier, Bappa would have lived to torment them forever. But those fifteen seconds passed and took Bappa's life away with them.

Dev thought he heard Anita calling his name.

"Stop! Stop, Dev!" she shouted.

Bappa's legs floated to the surface of the water. Dev released his grip first, then Avi and Jeet released their hold on Bappa. There was absolute silence. The froth on the water slowly disappeared. They all stared transfixed at the floating body. The flow was strong enough to gently push it into the middle of the stream. They were completely paralysed and could do nothing as Bappa's dead body was carried away by the current.

"My God," Avi said. It was a whisper, but they all heard the sheer terror in it.

"What have we done?" Jeet said and put his fist in his mouth.

They could still see Bappa floating. Avi lunged into the stream, but Dev caught his hand and pulled him back.

"He is dead," Dev said.

"What do we do now?" Avi looked at Dev.

"Let's go to the police and tell them," Jeet said, sobbing.

"We will be hanged now, won't we?" Avi said, still looking at Dev.

A tiny voice in Dev's head told him that there was something very wrong with Anita. "Anita?" he whispered.

She didn't move. She stared fixedly at Bappa's form floating away from them.

Dev touched her shoulder. She jumped. She looked at Dev's drenched face and turned back. Suddenly she ran.

"No! Wait!" Dev said and ran behind her.

"We killed him! We killed him! We killed him!"

Dev reached her and held her tight. Her cries were steeped in an anguish so deep that Dev thought the riverside was shaking.

"Shh…Shh," he gently patted her back. "We will never talk about it. Ever. We just have to promise this to each other. Right now."

"What? We are going to the police right now, Dev!" Jeet said.

"No! You want to die? They will lock you up forever. He was the son of Bhausaheb Bhoite. You think Bhausaheb will spare your families?"

"But what about Sharif Miyan?"

Dev was silent for a few long moments.

"We can't do that now." Dev thought an eternity had passed after they had decided to go to the police for Sharif Miyan's murder.

"Dev…You…you are a bastard!" Jeet said grabbing his collar.

"Shut up! I'm doing this for you and your families."

"Coward!" Jeet tried to slap him.

"My family has suffered a lot because of Bhausaheb. I won't let that happen to you." Dev's voice was suddenly very calm as he held Jeet's hands. "It was a terrible mistake. We never wanted to kill him," he said.

"Didn't we? Didn't you?" Anita asked.

"Don't you dare accuse me of a crime! He would have killed Avi."

Avi made soft mewling sounds, touching his throat. The memory of Avi drowning broke their resolve.

"Listen to me, all of you. We can never talk about this. Ever. We have to promise today."

Dev raised his hand with his palm towards the sky.

"Promise me. Now!"

They placed their palms on his, and promised.

Bappa's body was discovered three hours later by the police. The stream had carried it to the old bridge that connected the town to the highway. The police took the dead body to the morgue, where the doctor recognised Bappa.

A hiatus of twenty-four hours was all that the town got. It went up in flames after Bappa's dead body was discovered.

The Bhoite family, after a violent outpouring of grief, summoned its followers and armed them with weapons. Bhausaheb Bhoite, grief-stricken, raging and on the verge of losing his sanity knew who had killed his eldest son. He knew it wasn't one man, it was an entire community. One half, the worst half of the town he had forever despised.

Bhausaheb led the mob with a gun. The town burned again.

Many years later, Dev thought the four of them had died that day too. After that day, the only thing that lived in him was a terrible guilt.

The distance between the Shah Sadan and the railway station felt like an eternity to Avi. Ranjit mama, his mother's brother, had finally agreed to take him away. His mother had spent an entire night convincing Avi that he had to go away. He had asked her repeatedly why she was doing it to him. She had stoically refused to answer him. When he had wailed long and hard, she had said it was because she wanted him to live.

Avi's father didn't see him in the morning. He had told Avi's mother that he had nothing to do with a son who was so stupid as to abandon his family and get caught in the riot. Nobody survives by abandoning the family.

For days after he had returned from the riverside, Avi hadn't spoken a word to anyone but his mother. He had abandoned his books, paid no attention to the relentless heckling from the family and lied to his mother for the first time that he was fine. When she had asked him again, he had cried and told her he hated his books and didn't want to do anything with them. He didn't step out of the house and told her he didn't want to meet his friends, especially Dev.

She knew something fundamental had altered in her son. And she had to do something, or he would be forever lost.

The train was three hours late. The railway platform, drenched in rain, was deserted. Two little children frolicked in the puddles, their parents ignoring them. The railway track was covered in faeces. A brood of pigs gorged on it ecstatically.

Avi dug his nails into his mother's hand.

"Don't be scared. We will meet very soon," his mother said, evading his eyes.

His uncle, Ranjit, restlessly walked the length of the platform, muttering curses at the delayed train. Avi didn't want the train to come.

"Ma…Why don't you come with me?"

She stared at the empty railway track as if she had not heard the question. She had answered it patiently the first twenty times he asked. Then she became irritable and snapped at him.

"You study very hard, okay? We will meet very soon," she said after a while. She repeated, "We will meet very soon," like a mantra. He didn't believe her.

The black engine appeared on the distant horizon, spouting plumes of black smoke. His uncle walked up to them and lifted the bags, ready to pounce on the train the moment it arrived.

"Pick up your bag," she said to him, her voice filled with tears. He lifted his bag. He was angry and despondent at her curtness.

The train came to a reluctant, screeching halt. They boarded the train in a hurry as it stopped only for three minutes.

"Eat what your aunt tells you to and also write to me every week."

He nodded. His uncle patted his back.

"Don't worry," Ranjit mama said to no one in particular. He was a taciturn man, perhaps already worried about the responsibility of bringing up a nephew.

The train began to move, slowly dragging his mother over the platform as her grip suddenly tightened on his hand. He started crying silently. "We will meet very soon!" she said one last time, before the speeding train prised her fingers from his hand. She stopped at the edge of the platform and waved at him. He strained through the cage-like windows to see her. The train followed the turn in the track and she disappeared. He didn't see her for three years.

Dev stood behind a tree, just beyond the railway platform. He waved his hand at the tear-drenched Avi. He thought Avi saw him but didn't wave back.

"Goodbye, Avi," Dev whispered.

"Anita…Anita," her mother whispered in her ear. She woke up with a dizzying suddenness.

"*Aai?* What happened?"

The house was pitch dark.

"Shh...Be quiet!" her mother said, putting her palm on Anita's mouth. "We are leaving right now."

Anita nodded. There was a calm finality in her mother's voice, as if she had practised saying it for a long time. They quickly grabbed a bag and dumped a few clothes into it. Her father continued to snore. Anita looked at his sprawled form once and had an overpowering desire to kick it. She swallowed hard and followed her mother out of the house. It was raining. They hurried through the darkness and the rain, not caring about getting drenched. A noisy, red bus arrived at the bus stop after they had been waiting a few minutes.

"Poona. Two tickets," her mother said to the sleepy bus conductor, who disdainfully punched two stamp-sized tickets. The tickets quickly became sodden in her mother's wet palm. Her mother stared ahead, refusing to look out of the window as the bus hurtled out of the dormant town.

Anita put her head on her mother's shoulder and cried. "I'm sorry for abandoning you, Dev," she whispered as the sun peeked over the distant mountains.

This time, Jeet's parents didn't fight when they were packing. Mr Mehra had decided to send his wife and son away from the 'hell on the earth'. *This is for you,* his father had told Jeet. *This town is just too terrible.* Mrs Mehra had agreed. Mr Mehra would be joining them as soon as he could get the situation under control. He had already engineered his transfer and would leave the town after the situation stabilised and he could hand over charge to his successor.

"What are you going to do?" Jeet asked Dev, as they looked at the men loading the Mehras' belongings into the truck.

Dev said nothing. His cheeks were sallow. There was a haunted, distant look in his eyes that made him look far older than twelve.

"Will we ever meet again?" Jeet asked.

"I don't know. It's better if we don't." Dev got up and walked away. He never looked back.

Two hours later, the Mehra family departed from Amrapur.

She hanged herself from the ceiling fan.

Dev sat down with his back to the wall. She looked like a hideous doll: her hands limp, her feet twisted, her tongue caught between her teeth. She wore her purple-coloured marriage sari—a grotesque caricature of the beautiful woman in the photograph.

He sat there with her for a long time.

The neighbours sensed something was wrong. They walked into the house, saw him sitting, vacuously staring at the dead body. They shook him, trying to get his attention, but his eyes were fixed on her. They lifted him and took him out of the house. They asked him his uncle's address. He told them in a strangely detached tone. They tried to feed him. They tried to talk to him. He didn't respond. He never cried.

The uncles and aunts arrived the next day and quickly finished the funeral. They whispered about him in the night, worrying about his future, which could affect their already stretched incomes. He could hear words like "orphanage", "burden" and "fate" long into the night.

At the break of dawn, a commotion broke out in the house.

His father was home.

His father walked up to him and patted his head tentatively. He was hardly recognisable. The terrible life of a fugitive had ravaged him. He had always been thin, but he looked like a skeleton now. His face was covered with a flowing black beard. His hands were coarse. But there was an amazing light in his eyes.

"Come with me Dev," he said and held Dev's hand.

Dev walked out of the house with him.

The four friends would not meet each other for the next twenty years.

2009

A painful groan made Maggie stir in her sleep. She gently patted Jeet's chest, which pacified him for some time, but he began to groan and mumble again. Sometimes, he cried in his sleep. She wiped away his tears. Sometimes she kissed them off his wet face. His traumatic sleep was a mystery. There was a dreamland that he traversed each night only to be tortured. She found it frustrating not to be able to comprehend his pain. She never asked him about it, because she feared his answer would take him far away from her.

Dawn was breaking in Jeet's studio apartment when he said, "He is drowning!"

She froze, searching through their shared memories of six years to recall another instance when he had uttered intelligible words in his sleep, but couldn't. His mumbling had always been incomprehensible. She listened intently. Several moments passed but Jeet didn't say anything else. Had she heard him clearly? Who was drowning? There was no incident that had involved drowning in the time they had been together. Jeet became very still, as though he had expressed all his agony in those three words. She could not sleep for a long time.

"How does it look?" Maggie asked him as she turned the easel in his direction. He stood near the window, peering through the steam that rose from his untouched cup of coffee.

"Good," he said.

"You're not even looking at it," she said, sighing deeply.

Sighs were always the first indicators of people losing their patience with him. She had been sighing a lot in the past few months, and they were becoming deeper and longer. Jeet said nothing and kept staring out of the apartment window. The grey uneven wall of the neighbouring building blanked out his view of the world.

"What is it? What are you thinking?" she asked, her voice tinged with a desperation that had been very pronounced in the last few days.

"Nothing," he said, not looking at her and hoping she would not say any more.

"Is it the sex?"

"What?"

"Have you realised that making love has been an empty and angry activity for us, of late?"

He smiled. The question seemed frivolous. She shook herself, as if to stop shivering. Her eyes were red—the only sign that she had been crying. She was anything but frivolous.

"You are being melodramatic now," he said. The urge to laugh it off was overwhelming.

"No Jeet. I am not. I love you," she said.

The pain in her eyes was too burdensome. He went back to looking out of the window. After a few moments, there was the sound of the apartment door slamming. There was a finality to it. Perhaps, she would never open the door again. He should have told her he loved her too. The last time he had declared his love for her was almost a month ago, on her birthday, after they had made love. She had wept for a long time after, and he had stopped saying it. He banged his fist against the window pane. The pane shuddered for a few moments and the imprint of his fist formed on the cold glass. If only he could hit out at his past like that.

Maggie had come closest to knowing what had happened twenty years ago. But a promise was a promise—that's what

Dev had said. If even one of them broke the promise, they would lose everything. The memory became clearer each time he grew close to someone. It was as if he was forced to relive the darkness at the centre of his life.

The nightmare brought the entire incident back with a grotesque clarity. He did not know how Maggie would react if he told her the truth. Would she love him or would she abandon him? Would she find nothing wrong about loving a murderer?

He took off his clothes and started his routine of two hundred push-ups. His muscles bulged—he had already exercised in the morning. He doubled the speed and felt his muscles ache, but he didn't relent. "No fat," he said to himself through gritted teeth.

His phone rang but he didn't pick it up, letting the answering machine respond.

"Son, how are you? It's our wedding anniversary today. I thought I'd remind you this year as well. Your mother expects you to call. Please call between five and six in the evening, India time. We should be back from my book launch by five and the anniversary party starts at six. I would prefer it if you call at five thirty."

The phone disconnected. He had not spoken to them for months.

After the Mehra family left Amrapur, Mr and Mrs Mehra were deeply concerned about their only son. For three months, he was continuously and violently ill. Mr Mehra summoned the best doctors in Delhi, where he had managed to get his family settled while he figured out how to get out of Amrapur. The doctors were perplexed. The fever was not accompanied by any other symptoms. It was as though something burned inside the twelve-year-old boy's body. They had no equipment to detect the smouldering guilt and shame inside him.

However, Mr and Mrs Mehra were secretly happy. They didn't express it openly, especially not before Jeet, but he could sense a perverse elation in them: His fat had been an intolerable intruder, a fourth person in the Mehra family, but this undetectable illness was melting it away. It was as though Jeet had needed to undergo this ordeal to finally be called a Mehra.

The fat was replaced by silence. He had never been a garrulous boy, so the Mehras didn't really notice. They attributed it to the inexplicable illness—it was a small price to pay. His lack of words was never an embarrassment in front of their guests. In fact, it was good. He was praised as a good-looking, obedient son, who never raised his voice.

The Mehras had been, reluctantly, avoiding social events during his illness, but when he recovered, they returned to their social life with a vengeance. The silence in the new government house seeped through his emaciated body quickly and surreptitiously.

At school, he was ignored by kids, either because they sensed his need for silence or because he no longer looked like an easy target. He had no friends or enemies, but he painted beautiful watercolours and oil paintings. A teacher in his school told the Mehras that their son was a prodigy, that they should do everything to enable him to explore his talents. Mr Mehra was ecstatic when he heard this. He didn't think it was odd that a stranger should remark upon his son's talent. He provided Jeet with art coaching after school, along with equipment and a studio and, finally, encouraged him to sit for the entrance examination to Bombay's J.J. School of Arts. Jeet not only sat for the exam, he topped it. He packed his bags, and with the blessings of Mr and Mrs Mehra, boarded a flight to Bombay. His silence was unnoticed. He carried it in his clothes, in his brushes, in his memories, in his smile.

He sailed through his years at the J.J. School of Arts. He was a quiet boy, slowly metamorphosing into a quiet man. He painted and he exercised till he collapsed from exhaustion. He was polite to his classmates and deferential to his teachers. All of them absolutely loved his smile. His silence thrived beneath his veneer of easy approachability and friendliness.

He rented a little flat in a Bombay suburb, instead of staying at the hostel. It was, thus, easy for him to disappear in the city's organised chaos. He wanted the noisy city to assault his numbness, to subdue his memories. He travelled by local trains, from Churchgate to Virar, completing many journeys every day. He soaked in the movement of the trains as well as the startlingly inane chatter of the travellers. The pointlessness of the journeys soothed his mind. He carried his aloofness everywhere.

Dev Gokhale, Avinash Shah and Anita Kulkarni faded from his memories. He could no longer recall his childhood clearly, but the emotions it had aroused became stronger. His paintings were spectacular, which prompted his professors to use all their influence to get him a scholarship to the University of the Arts in London. The Mehras were thrilled—Mr Mehra even said that it was a good return on his investment. They threw a big party. Even the Home Minister of India attended it, as Mr Mehra was the incumbent Finance Secretary to the Government. When he boarded the flight, they wished him well, without ever saying that they would miss him. Mrs Mehra wore kohl, a sure sign that she was not going to cry.

The University students roomed together in tiny London flats, but Jeet found a top-floor room with an ageing couple. He stayed alone.

A year later the Mehras came to London to meet him, when he did not respond to their letters. His parents' letters were unopened, lying neatly stacked on a shelf in his cupboard. They didn't stay with him, choosing to call him instead to an expensive hotel suite. Mrs Mehra wore her immaculate eye-liner, painted lips and sleeveless blouse. Mr Mehra had a pouch with assorted bottles of lotions and a suitcase full of new suits. The suite reeked of Godrej shampoo, Old Spice aftershave, Godrej hair dye and Park Avenue scent, and brought back memories of loneliness. They still looked like film stars, albeit ageing ones.

They confronted him immediately. "What have we done wrong, son?" his father asked him. The question was rhetorical, even a little insulting. How could they pretend to be so ignorant? He became more silent when he was with them. Words lost their meaning and all that remained was a vague sense of loss. Mr and Mrs Mehra stayed for some time. He ignored them and remained in his little room.

"What is wrong with you?" his mother asked him one day. She wore no mascara—she was prepared to weep. But he said nothing and stared at the blank canvas on the easel. They would never understand their grown-up son's silence, just as they had never understood why he was so fat when he was a twelve-year-old boy. They left after two weeks.

He met Maggie on the first day of his second year in the university. She had a beautiful dimpled smile and blue eyes. Two days later, they moved in together. Six years flew by.

"All your paintings are too dark, Jeet," Malcolm Fontaine said to him when he saw the canvas. The elderly owner of the once-prestigious and famous gallery was already imagining a price-tag of six thousand pounds on it. "Why don't you explore something on the brighter side?"

"This is what I've got Malcolm. Do you want it or not?" Jeet asked with a shrug.

"Of course, of course! I was just, you know, suggesting," Fontaine said with a sheepish smile. He could not afford to let Jeet go—the art gallery was back in business because of him. The forty per cent proceeds from the sale of his paintings were the gallery's only assured source of income. And he knew that the young man was bloody good. He feared that one day he would lose him to the big sharks in the business but, surprisingly, Jeet had renewed his contract two months ago. He asked him once if he had been approached by someone else. "You gave me my first exhibition, Malcolm. I'll stick with you," he said. Fontaine later wondered if he had really heard Jeet correctly, or if he had just imagined it.

Jeet said goodbye to him and walked out of the gallery. He stood outside and breathed in the smoke-filled London air. Could this sprawling city with its crowded streets finally slay the demons of his past? So many millions walked these streets. Could he not merge with that mass? He could just run into the sea of flesh and bones and, perhaps, emerge a new person on the other side, cleansed of all his memories. Could a city be burdened with that responsibility?

Sameer often sensed a deep melancholy in Anita, despite her beautiful smile and tinkling laughter. He had never seen her brooding or looking sad—her melancholy manifested itself in her dance. Often, in the middle of a joyous step, she would look grief-stricken. He could not understand why she suffered because she had never discussed it with him, but he loved her for not succumbing to it. He dithered over the question for three months. It was as if it was burning in his mouth, scalding his tongue, even though he knew what her answer would be.

"Will you marry me?" Sameer asked, as she sat down after a rehearsal.

Her first reaction was irritation. It was the fifteenth day of the rehearsal and the troupe was still nowhere close to perfection. She wiped the dewy perspiration off her brow with a finger. An errant drop escaped and slid down her nose. She stared at him as though he spoke an unknown language.

"No," she said with a small shake of her head that hid great resolve. It was rehearsed. Perhaps, she had anticipated the question and honed her reply. She didn't look at him but gazed fixedly at the ground, almost contrite.

"I'm not going to ask you why, or whether there is something wrong with me," he said. "I simply accept your decision."

"Thanks," she said, surprised.

He was surprised too, but relieved.

She walked away without looking at him again.

She desperately wanted to tell him why. She had almost blurted it out when he didn't ask her. It was an overwhelming urge to cut loose from the shackles of the past, say yes to him and walk into the dazzling future, leaving behind a heart pining for a long-dead love. It was not to be, because her heart was no longer a small part of her being. It had spread itself long and deep, even into her mind, and forced her whole being into submission. It reacted violently to any diversion, reminding her of the terrible sin and submerging her conscience in guilt.

He deserved to know the reason why, but he deserved happiness too. He had fallen for her the moment he saw her. And there was nothing wrong with him. In fact, he was so perfect for her. But she knew she would destroy his life. He was the only son of a billionaire, a charming man whose riches did not make him arrogant, the only man who could make her laugh and still be brave enough to finance her dream—he had too much to lose.

Maybe her dancing was to blame. Perhaps it was the only reason why people became attached to her. Maybe she should give it up. But what would she do then? Live like a recluse? Destroy her only dream—of setting up a dance academy for girls like herself—on the still-raging pyre of that sin? Would there be anything left for her in this world then?

"*Aai,* help me here, please," she whispered and wondered if her mother would forgive her one more time.

She had told her mother what happened twenty years ago, not certain that she could hear her. People could hardly be expected to listen two hours before their death. Perhaps the memory of her mother's hand tightening on her fingers after she had told her the truth was just her mind playing tricks. Or perhaps her mother had conjured up a final moment of lucidity in which she heard everything, understood everything, and knew how important her forgiveness was. That tightening of her grip was her final act in her role as a mother. Anita felt thankful that her disease did not permit her to carry the burden of her daughter's grief.

"Ladies! What are you doing? You want to get fired?" she shouted at the girls, who should have been rehearsing. Instead, they were standing around on the stage, giggling.

"Sorry Anita," one of the girls said. They all hastily got back to the sequence they had been rehearsing for the last four days. The remnants of laughter and giddiness on their faces made their attempts at apologising inadequate and a sudden blinding anger erupted in her.

"So am I. For having good-for-nothing people like you," she said and stormed out of the rehearsal hall. She sat in the dressing room, quelling her unbearable urge to smash the mirror. She hated to see her eyes brimming with tears. Haven't they dried up yet?

"May I come in?" Sameer asked after knocking on the door.

She said nothing. He came into the room.

"I know you are angry. Maybe I should not have asked you like that. But you refused every time I asked you for a non-professional meeting," he said apologetically.

"Wasn't that a big hint?" she said and immediately regretted the sarcasm. She was shocked by the coldness in her voice. She had broken his heart and all she had for him were spiteful words.

"Yes it was. But the question was in my mind for months. It had to come out some day, and it did. I hope you don't make anyone else suffer for my mistake," he said.

"Will you please leave me alone for a while?"

"Sure," he said and walked out.

***

She didn't have anyone else to talk to—there were no friends. As though the terrible act she had been a part of twenty years ago had been witnessed by a powerful being who had cursed her forever. She had had imaginary conversations with Dev every night, for the last twenty years. In her mind, he had not aged since they last parted. Perhaps she too had not aged. They were destined to be together, weren't they? She had asked that question so many times, but the only answer she got was silence. Would she ever see him again? And would she be able to accept him as anything except a twelve-year-old?

She wore her *ghungroos,* recalling the promise that she had made her mother—that she would not let the Sharad Kulkarnis of the world destroy any more lives. These were the two opposing forces she was torn between—the promise to her mother, and the one to her three friends, one so pious and the other so heinous.

The cursor on Avi's laptop screen blinked incessantly, reminding him that he had work to do. Vijay, who was sprawled on a chair, yawned.

"You can go home, if you want to," Avi said.

"Huh? I am so sorry, Avinash. It's just that I haven't slept too well..."

"I said you can go home."

Vijay, the Chief Operating Officer of Avi's company, didn't yawn again.

After an hour, Avi's Blackberry vibrated. It was a long-awaited call. He walked to the window of his sixth-floor office. Night had fallen in Bangalore several hours ago.

"Avinash! Time to open the champagne! We've got the deal!" his Vice President, Sales, Mike Krueger, shouted on the phone.

"Did they agree to a two per cent discount?" he said, ignoring the excitement in Mike's voice.

"Uh...No. I took the decision to go ahead with three point five."

Avi said nothing.

"This is one of the most important deals for the company, Avinash," Mike said, his voice quivering.

"I know which deals are important." The coldness in his voice traversed the distance between Bangalore and San Francisco.

"I have signed the deal," Mike said. Avi could imagine him sweating in San Francisco.

"Cancel it," he said and ended the call. He knew that Mike would go back to the client and renegotiate. He would be desperate to please Avi, and would get the deal at a two per cent discount.

"Mike and I had decided on giving a three point five discount," Vijay said.

"I know."

"When will you start trusting us?"

"When you get me the deals I want."

"It's your company. I think I'll leave now."

Avi nodded as Vijay left.

He peered at the cursor and wondered how much he had achieved because of it. And it promised him many more things. He had determined ten years ago that he would turn his company into a billion-dollar enterprise and had written it on a big white board stuck to the ceiling above his bed. He had already made it worth a hundred-and-thirty-two million, and had another eight sixty-eight to go.

"Keep yourself hungry, you monster," he said aloud and smiled.

His personal mobile phone rang. Very few people had that number. Although he did not recognise the number flashing on the screen, he took the call.

"Avi? Hey! How are you?" he heard a voice that he had dreamt of silencing forever.

"Who gave you this number, Jayant?"

"I asked your father for it. I sent you many letters, but didn't get any response so I thought I'd call you up! How are you, little brother? It's been a while…"

"Jayant. Listen to me very carefully. This is the last time I will talk to you. I don't want you to call me on this or any other number, ever. And no letters either. I don't want to hear from you or any of those asshole cousins. Ever. Clear?"

Jayant hiccupped, as if someone had kicked him in the guts. Avi switched off the phone before Jayant could say anything. He leaned back in his chair, closed his eyes and tried to control his anger. After a few moments, he felt like laughing and wanted to call Jayant back—there were many more things he wanted to say. He wondered if his father had been standing by the bastard while he called. Perhaps the patriarch had prodded his stooge to call the rich son. Had the old man no shame?

He opened a private folder on his computer and clicked on his mother's photograph. It was an old, yellowed photograph that he had scanned and stored. She looked so healthy in it. She wore a bright red sari and a huge bindi. She had died ten years ago. His father had stopped talking to her two years before that. Avi knew there was no disease called banishment, but his mother had died of it. His uncle could not reach him when she died. He was in Norway, trying to get his first customer. By the time he returned, her pyre was already smouldering. His father was on his way out of the crematorium when he confronted Avi.

"What took you so long?"

Avi said nothing and stared at the fire that consumed his mother's frail body. He wondered why so much wood was needed to burn a body weighing a mere forty kilograms.

"Answer me!" the old man bellowed in front of the family. Many relatives were smiling behind their façades of grief. Avi remained silent. He felt his mother's presence in the crematorium, wanting to see him one last time. She didn't deserve to see him talking back to his father. He could wait till the fire had had its fill.

The patriarch had kicked the ground and walked away, as had all the other relatives. He stood in front of the fire till it turned to orange embers.

"I have burned everyone with you, Ma," he said softly to her ashes.

“This is our land. Nobody can take it away from us,” Dev said to the farmers’ gathering. The fields, where they squatted in a circle, talking in whispers, were dark.

“Let’s show them that when a farmer wants, he can wield the sickle as a weapon too!” a man said.

“No, Sakharam. Never think like that. One small act of violence from you can cause us great loss. They have guns. There will be carnage if we pick up weapons.”

“You have always told us not to raise weapons, Dev dada, but we are dying here. I would rather kill those bastards than die.”

Agreeing with what the farmer said, Jeevan, his father’s old friend and comrade, looked at Dev with condescension. Dev had refused to follow the violent ways of some of his father’s associates.

“Yes, you would rather kill them, but what will happen then? Do you think killing a few of them will actually stop the atrocities? Do you realise what they could do to your children or your womenfolk? You want them to die with you?”

The farmer stared at him for a long time, then fixed his eyes on the ground.

“We protest with our words and actions. Not with weapons. They have nothing to lose. We have too much to lose, although we are poor…”

The gunshot pierced the stillness of the night. The group of men froze.

“They are here,” Dev got up and said, “Remember, no violence.”

Dev ran through the darkening woods, fearing that the loud crunching sound made by his feet crushing dried leaves would lead the five men and their dogs to him. A branch chafed his shoulder, and he lost his balance and fell down clutching his shoulder. Warm blood spurted out of the wound. He crawled behind a huge fallen tree, stifling a scream. He strained to hear what the men chasing him were saying.

"Bastard!" a man yelled in frustration.

"How did he suddenly disappear?"

"Shut up, you morons! Fire into the area."

The bullets flew past him. Bile rose up in his throat. He held his breath and ran with his head down, hoping that the bullets would somehow miss him. He could outrun any man, but would be caught by the rabid, hungry dogs. He desperately looked around and made a decision. It would determine if he lived or died that day. The men chasing Dev were tiring. They let the dogs loose and followed them as they waded into the jungle, barking constantly and letting their masters know where they were. The dogs gathered under a tree and barked incessantly. The men caught up with the dogs and peered into the tree. Dev's shirt was hanging from the branches. They cursed him and fired some more bullets.

"Stop shooting you idiots! Your sisters don't shit bullets," the man leading them shouted.

After a minute of cajoling from the men, the dogs took up the chase once more. They had lost precious time, during which Dev had gained some distance.

Dev removed his trousers, flung them up into another tree, and ran ahead. His legs were scratched and bloodied. After a minute of running, he did the same with his vest and was down to his underpants. The barks were very near, angry and hungry. He knew the dogs had finally smelled him through their alcohol-induced madness. He had three or four minutes before they caught up with him and tore him apart with their powerful jaws.

There was a small hutment a few hundred metres ahead. He ran towards it, summoning every last ounce of energy.

"Gokhale sir!" a man saw him and said.

"Where is your shitting place?" Dev asked, panting, the words scraping his parched throat like nails.

"Come with me," the man said and they ran.

The dogs chasing him lost the scent when they reached the hutment. They barked for a long time, running around in circles.

The men came and checked each hut. They beat up a few men and groped almost all the women when they could not find Dev. After a couple of hours of abuse, they left.

※※※

"Gokhale sir? You can come out now. They are gone," the man said to him.

Dev peeped out from the bottom of the shit pit where he had been hiding for the last two hours. The men never checked the shit pits in the hamlets. He came out and vomited for the umpteenth time. His body was smeared with shit. He ran to the little stream of water and washed himself for a long time. If the men had not left for another half an hour, he would have died there. He scrubbed his body till it was sore and had turned pink, to remove the overpowering smell.

"Thank you for the help," he said to the man.

"It's nothing, sir. You saved our homes from those monsters. You saved us from killing ourselves," he said and held Dev's hand.

He offered food but Dev refused. The people in those Adivasi hutments could not feed themselves more than once a day. He took a tattered cloth from the man to cover himself and walked away.

※※※

He reached a little town thirty kilometres away. The town was submerged in darkness—there was no electricity for twenty hours a day.

The dull ache of hunger seemed to gnaw at his stomach. The cold wind attacked his almost bare body, making him shiver. There was just one safe house for him in town—Rambhau Patil's.

"You are just like your father, Dev," Rambhau Patil said to him as Dev wolfed down the *khichdi* that Rambhau's wife had hastily cooked for him. He had not eaten for two days. The piping hot *khichdi* had already burnt his mouth badly, but he didn't care and swallowed without chewing. He wondered why his intestines had still not got used to the lack of food. Why did his stomach cry out for food when so many were dying of hunger?

"How is your father?"

"I haven't met him for weeks now," Dev said.

When his father had taken his hand and they had walked away from their tiny house in Amrapur, Dev felt a slight tremor of misgiving. His father had not seen him for many years, yet now he had chosen to take responsibility for him. Wordlessly, they had walked to the Amrapur Bus Station—a fugitive wanted in three states for crimes against the Government, and his twelve-year-old son who was his victim.

His father walked towards a crowded bus. Before he could board the bus, Dev jerked his hand out of his father's.

"Where are you taking me?" he asked.

His father, who had already climbed into the bus, got down.

"We are going far away from this place," he said. "There is a school for tribal children that we have started. You will study there, Dev. You will like it."

Dev turned around to take a look. The town was bustling with its usual frenzy. Nobody would miss him. He nodded and boarded the bus.

All the seats in the bus were taken, and the aisle did not have enough space to accommodate the many people who were standing. Dev was pressed against the coarse fabric of his father's clothes. That's when the tears started flowing. He cried into his father's chest, soaking it.

His father patted his shoulders for a long time. "I am sorry," he whispered.

Dev was unsure if he said that to him or to his mother. He wanted to talk about the countless yellow postcards stuffed in his mother's cupboard, but just could not. He had never read any of them. What his mother wrote on them would always remain unknown. Hers was a life wasted in writing those unread letters.

After a sixteen-hour journey, they reached the little town of Mulgaon, where his father took him to Rambhau and Mandatai Patil's house. Over a cup of tea, his father told Dev that he would be staying with them and studying in the school for tribals. He would visit every week. Rambhau and Mandatai were like his elder brother and sister-in-law, and he would be happy with them. Dev nodded.

The childless Rambhau and Mandatai raised him like a son. For the first few weeks, Dev waited for his father to visit, but he never came.

"Have you seen yourself in the mirror? You look terrible, son," Mandatai said to him, tears filling her eyes. Dev had a long, unruly beard, his eyes were sunken, and there were deep lines on his forehead that made him look twenty years older.

"I don't care, Mandatai," he said. "Your *khichdi* is delicious."

"I don't think you're really eating it. You're just throwing it inside," she said in such a sad voice that Dev stopped eating for a few moments.

"Why are you doing this for us?" Rambhau asked.

Dev gazed at the old sooty lantern that was the only source of light in the house.

"Because what's happening to you is unjust," he said in a whisper. "I cannot tolerate that."

"You're paying a heavy price for it son," Mandatai said, wiping her tears with the tip of her orange sari.

"Why are you both so morose today?"

"Sometimes I wonder what we would have done without you," Rambhau said.

Dev wiped his plate clean. It was an old, dented aluminium plate, perhaps as old as him.

"There should be no sense of obligation between us, Rambhau," he said as he washed his hands. "I am doing it because I want to. I have to leave now. Tomorrow, there is a public meeting in Jampur that I have to address. You know how many farmers have committed suicide there? More than fifteen hundred in the last year," he said and bent down to touch Rambhau and Mandatai's feet.

"One moment, son," Rambhau said and he walked up to an almirah.

"There was a strange letter that arrived a week back. I couldn't make any sense of it. There is no name of the sender and I don't think it came by post. Someone pushed it under the door."

He pulled out an envelope from the almirah, removed a single sheet of paper in it and handed it to Dev.

Tell Dev he has to go back to Amrapur. He thought he will never pay for the twenty-year-old crime, but he is wrong. Tell him I am waiting for him. 20th of next month.

Dev read it again.

"What happened son? You are shivering! Is everything all right?"

Dev looked at the old couple and wondered if it would be the last time he would be seeing the two people who had raised him.

He bent down to touch their feet.

"Dev, why aren't you answering?" Mandatai said.

Dev couldn't speak a word. He stepped out of the house and disappeared into the darkness.

"So tomorrow you visit the Taj, Imo?" Avi asked the Chief Technology Officer of the German conglomerate.

"Oh yes. My wife will kill me if I don't get a photograph with me in front of the Taj," Imo said. Avi chuckled politely. "Avinash, now that we are business partners, I have to tell you something."

There were tiny drops of sweat behind the fluffy hair that covered Avi's forehead. This meeting with the Chief Technology Officer of a multi-billion dollar client was the result of his endless hard work. He would shoot himself if something went wrong at the last minute.

"I know you have the best people working on developing our product. But so do your competitors. Your price, too, is slightly higher than that quoted by your competitors," he said and sighed.

Those tiny drops of sweat would soon become a stream flowing down his nose. He vaguely thought of wiping his brow but realised that he could not move.

"But we...No, I—it's my decision really—I am awarding this contract to your company," Imo said, smiling, as though he knew how anxious Avi was. Avi let out his breath so conspicuously that Imo laughed. "Don't worry. I'm not throwing any last minute surprises," he said. "You are the only reason that I chose your company over your competitors. I hope you won't let me down."

"I don't want to say something clichéd, like 'I will do my best'," Avi said, wiping his brow. "This is the biggest deal of my life and I have to do a great job with it, don't I?"

"Thanks," Imo said and shook hands with Avi.

After the German left, he called his entire senior management team into his cabin and told them the good news. It was the moment for which they all had been waiting. The company would enter a different league with this deal. There were smiles and barely suppressed excitement. They stood fidgeting around, unsure of how to react in front of their boss who rarely showed his emotions.

"That will be it," he said and they started to file out of his cabin, when he stopped them. "Wait a minute. I forgot to tell you that I have booked the *Grande Banquet Hall.* You have a party to attend."

The team hooted with joy and bounced out of the cabin.

"Aren't you joining us, Avinash?" said Vijay, who was the very first employee of his company, and had earlier been his roommate when he was studying at the University of Canada. He was now the second in command.

"No," Avi said without looking up from his laptop.

Vijay walked up to the cabin door and closed it.

"Avi, this is ridiculous," Vijay said. "This is a big day for all of us. You can't be serious about not celebrating!"

"I know," Avi said looking up. "All of us have our own ways of celebrating."

"I know your ways. We're friends, aren't we? So, as a friend, I'm requesting you to come with us."

"Vijay, we are not friends. I don't have any friends. I never did."

Vijay stood still, not believing what he had just heard. After a few minutes, he walked out of the cabin. Avi shivered a little, which then became an uncontrollable shaking. His breath came in short, painful bursts. He pulled out his inhaler from the cabinet and blew the pungent spray into his mouth. It was momentarily soothing, but he seemed to need it more often now. The doctors had told him to slow down, to not burn himself out. They didn't know that he had nothing else in his life. He had decided to run and never look back when he left his mother behind.

Avi reached the office very early the next day. That had been his routine for the last six years. He would arrive when everyone else was still sleeping, and leave it after they had gone to sleep. He checked his Blackberry and started his day by responding to the emails sent by his contacts in the US.

The first email was a request for a meeting to negotiate a contract, which he accepted. The second email was a message of congratulations from the Vice President of Sales for bagging the German deal, which he deleted. The third email was a request for additional finance for a technology festival in Los Angeles, which he rejected.

He opened the fourth email. It seemed like junk mail from someone trying to sell something. The word Amrapur stopped him from deleting the email immediately. He opened the email and realised that his hands were shaking, which made the words on the tiny screen of his PDA blur. The Blackberry just slipped from his hands the moment he read the first two words.

You rat.

It lay on the floor, blinking. He sat down and stared at the instrument, willing it to melt away. It had brought back the word he most hated—rat. He knew none of his cousins would dare to call him that. He lifted the Blackberry and read the words in a daze.

Do you think no one knows? I know what you and your friends did. Remember, twenty years ago? I know you're dying to know who I am, aren't you? Amrapur. That's where I am. I will wait. I know all of you will come. On 20th of next month. I will wait…

He sat on the floor. After an eternity, the first light was switched on outside his cabin. A few minutes later, a few more lights came on. But he knew a darker dawn had broken upon his life, indicating not the end of the night, but the beginning of an eternal darkness.

"This is beautiful, Jeet," Maggie said as soon as she entered his studio.

He stood in front of the canvas, still as a statue. His eyes were fixed on the canvas as though he saw something terrible, yet fascinating in the painting. There were dark patches of sweat on his shirt and his face was wet. The studio was cold. The painting showed a roiling river, with a man drowning in the middle of it. There were two eyes in the sky, malevolent and red. It made her uneasy when she focused on the painting. She closed her eyes and took a deep breath before she opened them again and saw what had unnerved her so much. It was subtle, almost hidden, but she could not tear her eyes away from it once she knew it was there. It was the little brush that the drowning man held in his outstretched hand. She walked up to the canvas and a cold shiver ran up her spine. The face of the drowning man resembled Jeet's, but the drowning Jeet was very fat.

"What does this mean, Jeet?" she asked him.

His expression had not changed. It was as though his soul had been transplanted into the drowning man in the painting and his lifeless body stood before her. He would collapse if she touched him.

"Jeet," she whispered.

He turned towards her but looked right through her, not acknowledging her presence. Then he turned back to the painting. She took a couple of steps away from him. The memories of his dark moments flooded her, but there was a sense of finality in what he was going through that was chilling.

She banged into his computer table as she backtracked from him. The screensaver disappeared, revealing an email:

You fat bastard. You have to come back. I saw it—what you and your friends did twenty years ago in Amrapur. You will have to come. Just like them, on 20th of next month. I am waiting.

The words were incomprehensible. Who was the fat bastard? And what did he do twenty years ago? It could not be addressed to Jeet, who ran five miles a day, did countless push-ups, and ate only fruits and cucumbers.

"I have to go back."

She jumped when she heard his voice. There was an unsettling, fearful timbre to it.

"Where?"

"Amrapur," he said. He had still not moved his eyes from the canvas.

"Okay."

The email was addressed to Jeet. But she was glad that he was talking.

"Okay," she said again. "You do that."

She suddenly realised that she knew nothing about this man whom she loved so hopelessly.

"Don't be scared, Maggie," he said and finally looked at her. The intense sadness in his eyes almost made her sob.

"What is it, Jeet?"

"The sin. Yes, that's what it is, although Dev would not agree with it. But all of us called it a sin that would not go unpunished."

She had stopped breathing. Nothing made sense to her. She almost shouted his name. The Jeet she knew was hiding somewhere deep inside the apparition in front of her.

He fell as though his feet had suddenly refused to carry his weight. He fell backwards on the easel and tore the painting. She rushed to him but it was too late—his head hit the floor and he passed out.

Her mother had told her never to look at the audience when performing. Their approval or disapproval was to be sought after the performance. She had refused to obey that rule the first time she had performed and had suffered. Some eyes had looked at her with rapture, others with denunciation. The audience was a monster that played with its prey's mind. Since then, she had refused to look into its countless eyes. But she could not help forgetting that rule tonight. All the two thousand pairs of eyes were spellbound. She had finally defeated the monster.

The applause went on for a long time after her final curtain. Everyone stood up and clapped. Her eyes brimmed over with tears of happiness. She let them flow after the curtains fell. She staggered offstage, exhausted and elated. Every member of her troupe hugged her and she hugged them back. She knew they were crying too. She had pushed them to the brink of despair in her relentless pursuit of perfection, and they hugged her ferociously, wanting to finally feel her acceptance.

She lovingly touched the pile of appreciative notes that lay in front of her the next day. Her secretary, Mala, had sifted through the numerous letters and kept only the ones that were well-written or the ones that mattered for her to read.

"This was one of the most beautiful performances I've seen in my life. My best wishes for the show." This was from the greatest exponent of Kathak in India.

Then there was a wonderful poem written for her by an eighty-nine year old poet.

"Wonderful!" said the greatest singer in India.

"I didn't feel like leaving. I have never seen something more beautiful..." went a long note from a great cricketer.

"Wonderful performance! Congratulations. But nothing compares to what you and your three friends did twenty years back in Amrapur. Remember, at the riverside? Why don't you come back to Amrapur on 20th of the next month? Your three friends are coming too. And I am waiting for you."

A tiny cry escaped her throat. She read the note one word at a time. The meaning didn't change. The spiteful words shattered the illusion she had been living in for the last twenty years. She got up and ran outside her office. "Who sent this note?" she asked Mala.

"Uh…Umm…" Mala was stunned to see her like that. She had experienced her anger a million times in the past, but what she saw on her face now was something else—it was filled with fear.

"This note, you idiot!" Anita waved it in front of her face.

"I…don't know, Anita," she said.

"What do you mean? You filter the mail here, don't you? Answer me!"

All the people in the academy were shocked to see her so angry. She never shouted except during rehearsals.

"I'm sorry, Anita. I thought it was another congratulatory letter for you," Mala said. The little sob that punctuated her apology shook Anita. She slowly walked back to her office and locked herself inside. It was not Mala's fault. It had to happen one day. Mala was just the medium through which her terrible sin would be exposed after twenty years. She felt like crying again. Just twenty-four hours after weeping for joy, her eyes were on the verge of weeping in shame and sorrow.

She called Mala from her desk phone. "I'm sorry. I have to leave. Please cancel everything."

"What?" Mala said with barely suppressed incredulity. "For how long?"

"I don't know. Just cancel everything for the next week," she said and banged the phone down.

Maggie held Jeet's hand while they waited for his flight to depart. She had packed for him while he'd paced around the apartment in silence. Her fear had escalated—what he had to confront had the power to snatch him away from her. That short email had made him oblivious of her presence, and now he was going away to face something she could not comprehend.

"You don't know much about me, do you?" Jeet asked her, his first words after he'd told her to pack for him.

She knew that he had saved her from certain suicide after the death of her parents, two years ago. He had waded through the sea of her tears to anchor her to the safety of his wonderful, quiet smile. He was the most gifted artist in the art school. He cried and talked in his sleep. Perhaps he spoke more asleep than awake. She knew that there was a wound he consciously tried to push into the background of his life.

"Yes," she nodded.

"I know you deserve to know about it," he said. "But I can't tell you. I cannot recognise reality anymore." She held his hand, which was so cold that it was difficult to believe there was blood running through it. "I have run from it for the last twenty years," he continued, as if talking to himself.

"When will you be back?"

He didn't answer, sensing that she didn't want to hear the truth. His long sinewy hands rubbed her fingers, the way she knew and loved. The intimacy of that touch overwhelmed her.

"What are you getting into, Jeet?"

"I don't know. But I hope to confront it one final time."

She put her head on his shoulder and then wept for a long time.

"Why won't you take me with you?"

"No!" he said with such vehemence that she shuddered. "Promise me you will not come to India till you hear from me. Promise me!"

A few people turned in their direction, then went back to minding their businesses—it was an everyday scene, a young couple going their separate ways.

"Promise me Maggie," he insisted.

"I promise you, you bastard! But you have to promise that you'll come back."

He said he would. She sensed the pathetic lie in it and hugged him tighter.

Standing in a rickety bus hurtling down the barren landscape, Dev read the note once again. The bus moved in jerks. People wore tired and dazed looks. The bus, made of bare, hot metal, was like a furnace. Little children wailed in turns, relaying their anguish.

His father's words echoed in his ears. "Lies always catch up with you, especially the ones you tell yourself." For twenty years, he had lied to himself, punishing his body relentlessly, making it wither, and calling it repentance. But a sinner can neither punish nor forgive himself. Perhaps the time had come to atone for it.

The bus reached Amrapur, rattling and screeching as it halted in the depot that had become more cacophonous and more congested over the last twenty years. The hawkers remained in a time warp, with the same oily samosas and kachoris piled up on their carts. He walked up to the nearest square. One of the roads led to Sarafa Bazaar. It seemed to him, as he walked down the once-familiar road, that he could hear the voices of the dead who still haunted this town.

Now that he had reached Amrapur, what would happen next? Would the man contact him? How? How would he even know that Dev had reached Amrapur? Perhaps the man had followed him all the way in the same bus. Turning back, he scanned the buzzing bus depot, where nothing seemed out of place.

How would all of them look now? Would Avi still have those owlish glasses? Would Jeet still be carrying his fat? And Anita… His heart beat faster when he thought of her. What would she look like? But most of all, he wondered what he stood to lose this time. There was only one place that he could call his own—the riverside.

Dev removed his torn chappals and walked on the grass by the river. It had not grown at all, but was yellow and damp. The trees seemed taller and leafier. The setting sun cast its golden shadow on the stream. He found the stillness disquieting.

He walked to the spot where their beautiful little fort once proudly stood. He sat down there and stared at the stream flowing past. His vision clouded, and he realised he was weeping. He didn't wipe away the tears. He waited for his friends.

Avi saw the chaos on the railway platform. The blue bogies filled with people slowly traversed the length of the platform and halted.

Nothing seemed to have changed in the little town where he had lived till he was twelve years old. The smell—a disgusting mix of boiling tea, frying eggs, shit and cigarettes—hit him. He had not experienced it for the last ten years. Now that he was back, he would carry that smell with him for a long time. He disembarked from the train and walked towards the exit.

"Sahib! Coolie sahib!" And he was surrounded by red robed coolies. He shook his head vigorously, "No." A coolie grabbed the handle of his suitcase. "Don't touch it!" he shouted at the man so loudly that he recoiled. The others dispersed as though he were a freak.

"Where to?" the rickshaw driver asked.

"Shah Sadan," he said and yelped, realising what he'd just said. "No! Wait. Take me to a hotel."

He wondered what else the family had ventured into. Did they still have garment shops all over town? His father used to proudly claim that a Shah Garments shop was as ubiquitous as the post office. His lips curved into a mirthless smile. And finally he saw it—Shah Garments written on a billboard in colourful letters. He felt a sudden rush of bile up his throat, and quickly looked away.

"Which hotel?" the rickshaw driver asked.

"Any," he said, with the voice of a drowning man.

"Are you from this town?"

"No."

"This is a good hotel. The best," the driver said as he stopped. Avi craned his head out to take a look. He nodded, got his suitcase out of the rickshaw and paid the fare.

"Welcome to Hotel Amir, sir," the man at the reception said in halting English.

"Madam?" her driver said.

She woke up as though someone had poured cold water on her.

"Sorry madam," the driver said sheepishly. "We have reached Amrapur."

"Okay," she said and unconsciously looked at herself in the car mirror. The sight was shocking. Her face had aged ten years in a day. There were deep lines that had not been there before.

"Where do we have to go, madam?"

It was a question she was yet to ask herself. Where do you go in a town that you had vowed never to return to? She said nothing. The driver, sensing her disquiet, continued to drive.

She soaked in the sights of the town from the confines of her car. There were giant hoardings of wickedly smiling politicians that obscured the sky. The roads were as bad as she remembered, but there were a lot of changes: a few young girls on the streets were clad in jeans and T-shirts; there were cyber-cafes instead of public telephone booths; large garish shops bordered the roads on either side, replacing the *kirana* shops of her childhood. However, the changes appeared cosmetic. The town itself had not changed.

"Where should we stop, madam?" the driver finally asked again. They had been driving around town for an hour.

"Drop me off at a hotel," she said.

"Hotel?"

"Yes."

"Madam? Can I say something?" the driver asked, squirming in his seat.

"What?"

"It is not very safe for you to stay in a hotel, madam," he said. "This town is a bad place. A lot of things happen here that are not good."

"I know. I grew up here," she said.

"Oh…I am really very sorry, madam. Don't you know anyone here?"

"Don't worry. Just take me to a hotel," she said firmly.

The driver said nothing. After a few minutes he stopped in front of a tall building with a big neon sign—Hotel Amir.

It had to be Dev sitting near the stream. The man had the same ramrod posture and broad shoulders. Only, everything was bigger.

"Dev?" Jeet asked as he approached the stream.

The man stood up and Jeet was shaken. This could not be his boyhood idol. Didn't Avi say that Dev resembled Christopher Reeves?

"Jeet!" Dev exclaimed and they embraced.

"Well, well, well," Dev arched his back. "Don't we have a movie star here?"

"What happened to you, Dev?" Jeet asked in a whisper, as he hugged the skeletal man.

"Ah...Nothing. But look at you! Did you forget to wear your fat today, fatty?" he asked and they both laughed. It was as though they had not been parted for twenty years. He felt as though he had slept through those years and woken up to resume his friendship with his childhood hero.

Avi lost the way. How could it be? He was the one who had discovered the riverside all those years ago, wasn't he? Closing his eyes, he tried to remember. There was a little pathway that broke away from the tarred road on the hillock. It was concealed by bushes with needle-like white thorns. Runaway goats and stray cows grazed on those plants, expertly picking out the tender leaves nestled amidst the barbs. It led to the wild grove of unknown trees, and after seven minutes of running—Avi had timed it once—there was their riverside.

But he could not remember that little path. Did he hate the memories of this town so much that even the best part of his childhood was wiped out? Had he also lost his friends?

"Avi...?"

He turned back and saw a woman with long flowing hair who was tentatively walking towards him. Her eyes stared at him in wonder.

"Anita?"

She laughed, and he breathed a sigh of relief. The memories were not all erased after all—he still remembered her laughter.

Running the last few steps separating them, she hugged him fiercely. A sudden numbness spread across his body. Nobody had hugged him for the last twenty years. Nobody had even wanted to. He stiffened at the unaccustomed intimacy. Sensing his discomfiture, she stepped back.

"How are you?" he said.

Peering at him, embarrassed and hurt, she touched his fingers. "What did you do with your glasses?"

"They're long gone. I don't even recall wearing them," he said jerking his hand back, a little more roughly than he wanted to.

"I cannot imagine you without them," she said biting her lip.

He shrugged nonchalantly, humiliating her memory, not wanting her to arouse his. Turning back, he started walking down the pathway, its old twists and turns suddenly vivid in his mind.

Leaving her behind with rapid strides, Avi reached the riverside. Two men sat near the stream. Sensing the movement, they turned back. Their faces were unrecognisable and stunningly contrasting. He stopped near the edge of the green patch, shocked by the sight of intruders.

"Avi?" the man with the flowing black beard said, his voice gravelly.

Avi nodded and walked up to them. "You must be Dev," he said, extending his hand.

Dev was left speechless by the coldness in those words. He felt an agonising urge to hug his friend, but shook his hand instead. His palm was cold, unfeeling.

"And you are Jeet, right? You have changed a lot," Avi said, as though meeting someone vaguely familiar.

"So have you," Jeet said and looked away, not wanting to say another word to this stranger who happened to share the same name as his friend.

Anita stepped on the little patch of green land. The long-forgotten feeling of being a trespasser returned. She was the last one to know their riverside, a place they had reluctantly shared with her. The remembrance of that betrayal was still painful. Dev used to come here during every lunch recess, while she aimlessly wandered around the school, ignoring her friends, searching for him.

Three strangers looked at her.

The tall, ravaged man broke away and walked up to her. No words were needed—the endlessness of those silent years had made them redundant. Hot tears flowed down her cheeks. His long, bony fingers held her hands. He smiled, his teeth surprisingly white against the unruly beard, his eyes brimming with unshed tears. She gently put her head on his shoulder, the coarse fabric of his kurta grazing her wet cheek. She held him, tenderly at first, and intensely a few moments later. They rocked, drenching each other, finally reunited at the riverside.

After what felt like an eternity, she moved away from him and noticed the awkward, fidgeting man.

"My God! I would never have recognised you," she said, her hand on her mouth.

Jeet hugged her perfunctorily, not wanting to rob her of the memory of Dev's touch. She and Dev were destined to be together, and only something as terrible as their sin could have torn them apart. He had played his part in it, pining for her attention, wanting her so feverishly and cursing their obvious but unrealised love. Perhaps his arrival in their world brought about their separation—something he had wished for, blinded by jealousy.

He was indeed shocked by the resurgence of those guilty thoughts.

"Okay, now that we've had our little reunion, can we get to the point? Why are we back here?" Avi said with his lips twisted unpleasantly.

They looked at him, stunned by the disdain in his voice.

"When did you become such a bitter man, Avi?" Dev asked, his voice quivering.

"Oh, can we do away with all this emotional claptrap? We are back in this shithole of a town because some bastard saw us. I say, we deal with this man and get the hell out of here."

"Yes. You're right. That's what it is all about," Dev said, clenching his teeth.

"I think all he wants is money. And I can give it to him."

"How much money do you have, Avi?" Anita asked him angrily.

"Enough to take care of this man."

"Is it enough to make us forget what we did?"

"You know what? I don't care. It was a mistake and I have paid the price. I am not going to let some bastard ruin everything."

"It wasn't a mistake, Avi. It was a crime and I regret committing it every moment of my life."

Dev walked up to the stream and sat down. The stream was silent and grey, flowing slowly by.

"It is not about money, Avi. He wouldn't have called us back, if it was just money he wanted. Nor would he have waited this long. He would have just named his price, and it would have become an endless cycle of blackmail. He wants more," Dev said softly. His words reverberated in the stillness of the riverside. Nobody spoke for a long time. Anita walked up to Dev and sat next to him. So did Jeet. After a few moments, Avi joined them. They heard the insects chirping away relentlessly.

"So where *did* you get all your money?" Jeet asked.

They were the witnesses to his pathetic childhood, forgotten creatures of the darkness that existed before that train journey from Amrapur to Mumbai. Perhaps they deserved to know how far he had traversed.

"I don't remember how long I cried on that train. I stared out of the window as it left one town after another. Night came, and I didn't sleep for a moment. I couldn't stop wondering why. Why did my family treat my mother like a slave? Why did she endure it all? Why did my father banish me from his life? Why did Sharif Miyan die? Why did we kill Bappa?"

His rapidly heaving chest forced him to stop. The memories were too painful. He fished out an inhaler from his pocket and breathed in a dose.

"The next few days went by in a haze. Canada was cold, very cold," Avi said, his voice suddenly devoid of the cultivated hardness. He sounded vaguely like that boy who had once worn big owlish glasses. "My uncle Ranjit was a very quiet man. I was a burden. With a struggling business and a young family, I was one problem he could have lived without. My aunt didn't speak to me for many years. They put me in a boarding school."

Those days had been endless. The angry whispers between his uncle and aunt had stabbed at him for hours. He used to sleep on an old musty mattress in one corner of the living room. The alien house had felt cold and hostile.

"On the first day of school, some older kids grabbed me in the toilets. They were going to hold my head under the freezing water for five minutes. 'This is the way we welcome new meat,' they said. I looked at their faces one by one, comparing them to Bappa and Jagan. None of them were even close. And I had killed Bappa, right? So when a boy held my head, I did something that kept everyone in the school away from me for years. I bit his finger so hard, it broke. I heard it crack. Blood spurted on my tongue but I didn't let go of his finger. He was screaming. The other boys started hitting me, so I bit harder. A couple of them ran. One kid hit me on my face, breaking my glasses. I let go of the mangled finger and collapsed on the toilet floor laughing, blood dripping from my mouth.

"From that day onwards, I chased my dream. Today I own the fastest-growing company in India. I gave a million dollars to my uncle. He is a good man, the only one who took care of me. Now my aunt wants to talk to me every day, wants to invite me to their new house and wants to cook for me. I don't talk to her."

Twilight came suddenly and then it was night. For twenty years, they had not spoken of Bappa's death. Saying it aloud was a confession of the terrible crime. The words hung in the air. The four friends sat still and silent for a long time. Their riverside, humming with the ghosts of ancient secrets, was a witness to their sin.

"It has to be Jagan," Anita finally whispered.

Jeet shivered. Somewhere deep in his heart, in the place where all his nightmares lived, he still feared his childhood tormentor.

"Why would he wait for twenty years?" There was a fearful note in Avi's voice.

Avi and Anita looked at Dev, unconsciously slipping into their forgotten roles as his avowed followers. For a moment, Jeet saw them as twelve-year-olds, dumping their problems on Dev, waiting for him to tell them what to do. Dev was staring intently into the stream, perhaps watching the forever floating body of Bappa.

Rubbing his gaunt face Dev said, "I want the three of you to leave the town immediately. Hide for a while. I will contact you once this is over."

"Enough! I have had enough of it. You are no superman, Dev," Avi shouted.

"What?"

"Why do you still have to be so fucking brave? Protect everyone? Just let them be! You cannot change what they have to endure. You may just worsen it!"

"You are right, Avi. Maybe I should. Maybe that's what has led to all this," Dev said in a barely audible voice.

"You don't have to be the saviour. The hero."

A tiny voice in Jeet's mind, which wanted to blame someone, agreed with Avi. Why did Dev intervene when Jagan punched him? Perhaps Jagan would have hit him a few more times. Maybe he would have never met Dev and Avi. He would have known about them some weeks later—the lanky, defiant fellow and the owlish class topper. They would have ignored him as they ignored every other kid.

"Why do you think you left everything you built for the last twenty years and came here?" Dev said to them.

They said nothing.

"Don't you think one of us would've acted differently? Maybe would've thought to hell with this man, I won't go? He asked us to come back on the 20th and here we are, all four of us."

They looked at each other but no one spoke.

"We came because we all thought what if even one of us decides to follow what the man told us to. We came back for each other, Avi. Including you. We aren't what we have been for the last twenty years. That was a façade. A lie we told ourselves for such a long time. We are back to being twelve-year-olds who committed that terrible sin. That's the only truth of our lives."

They looked at the silent stream for a long time.

Dev stood up. "Together," he said in a hoarse whisper.

"Together," Jeet and Anita said.

Avi rubbed his face as though trying to wake up from a bad dream. Then nodded his head.

Amrapur's clammy night lay outside the open window. The noises of the town had slowly faded, and she was stepping back to wallow in the sound of Dev's breathing. She had heard and treasured every sound he made—his laughter, his anger, his irritation, his sadness. She lay on the bed, restless and resentful of his deep sleep. They had decided to share two rooms—she with Dev, and Jeet with Avi. When they walked into the hotel room, Dev nodded at her, put the mattress on the floor and slept. They were two strangers sharing a roof, a night, a childhood, a love.

She drew her knees up and hugged them. Dawn was breaking but, as yet, only the birds seemed aware of it.

"You haven't slept, have you?" he asked, suddenly wide awake. Perhaps he was aware of her all the while, his sleep a charade.

"Have you been awake too?"

He sat up on the mattress and said, "I have never slept, Anita."

"What have you done to yourself, Dev?"

"We all reacted in different ways. This is how I responded," he shrugged.

They settled into a long silence. What was there to say? Nothing existed between their separation and reunion. Nothing was worth staying away from him, not even her dream of setting up the institute. Did he remember her the way she remembered him? He was forever a faint spectre in her eyes, never away, never close. Would she have seen him, heard his breathing, shared a night with him, had it not been for that terrible letter?

She said, "I have loved you forever. If we don't survive this...I want you to know that."

"I have loved you since the very first day I saw you in kindergarten," he said, unsurprised.

The room felt warmer as his words hung in the air. He walked up to the bed and kissed her. It was a kiss that had taken twenty-eight years in the making. She hoped it would never end.

The false ceiling in Avi and Jeet's room had worn off. Rotating noisily, the dirty fan sprinkled hot air. Tired and sleepless, Avi stared vacantly into the night. He and Jeet had lain awake for a long time, ignoring each other, before Jeet had succumbed to sleep. He had nothing to say to this man who bore no resemblance to that ever-smiling fat boy who had been a friend, for a while, in a forsaken life.

The PDA in his hand vibrated with the arrival of every email. So many people wanted to talk to him, wanted his attention and wanted to see his words. The boy, once ignored by everyone, was a sought-after man. The Shah clan wanted to talk to him too.

"Kill him…Kill him…Kill him."

Jeet was twisting and turning in his sleep. The two words were clearly audible—the rest was gibberish. Avi was shaken to the core. Jeet was crying, his eyes shut tight, tortured by the relentless dream. Avi silently walked out of the room. Jeet's cries broke through the thin door. Avi soundlessly ran down the corridor. He stopped near the stairs, pulled out the inhaler and doused his exploding panic.

As he walked down the stairs unsteadily, a flicker of guilt rose in him for abandoning Jeet. He brushed it aside. Guilt would make him vulnerable, an easy prey for the man who had called him back. He jumped three steps at a time and reached the dark hotel lobby. It was flooded with red light from a naked bulb. The man at the reception stopped mid-yawn and looked at him as though he was a ghost.

"Is everything all right, sir?"

"Huh?"

"Do you need anything?" the man asked with a knowing flicker of his eyebrow.

"No. No," Avi said, shaking his head.

He walked out of the hotel. The darkness, undisturbed by the dim streetlights, was at once unnerving and soothing. He found himself surrounded by closed shops and old houses.

He saw, or thought he saw, the silhouette of a man covered with a blanket. Avi narrowed his eyes in the vain hope of seeing the man's face, but it was hidden behind the black mask of the night. Avi stood transfixed, unable to breathe. The man—perhaps an apparition—turned around and disappeared into the darkness.

Avi ran on the deserted street.

"Who are you? Wait, you fucking coward!"

The screams bounded off the walls of the lifeless town. Perhaps his eyes were playing their old tricks, showing him things that didn't exist. The tricks that had scared a twelve-year-old boy once. Already, the town was pushing him back into the abyss from which he had emerged.

Jeet woke up with a start. The room was dark and hot. The ceiling fan had fallen prey to the eighteen-hour "load shedding" and had stopped churning the hot air. Wet with his sweat, the bed-sheet had a familiar smell—that of the countless beds he had slept in, in government houses. He rubbed his face vigorously, brushing away the cobwebs of sleep.

"Avi?" he whispered.

There was no answer. Somewhere inside the bathroom, drops of water fell on the rim of a plastic bucket. The soundless room shook with every drop. Avi was not in the room, nor was he out on the balcony. Jeet stood up suddenly and rushed to the door. He yanked it open. A shocked Avi stood with his hand raised to knock.

"Where were you?" Jeet shouted.

"I saw him, Jeet," Avi said entering the room.

"You…What? What the hell were you doing?"

"Calm down. I could not sleep and went downstairs."

"Don't do that again. We must stay together. Remember?"

"Yes."

"What did you see?"

"I'm not so sure. I don't know if I saw him or not. I thought I saw someone standing outside the hotel across the street. I think he nodded at me once and then disappeared." Avi's trembling hands were witness–he had seen the man. "What does the fucker want? Why doesn't he just ask for money?"

The little rabbit jumped in his throat, startling Jeet. Till then, it had been invisible, caged. The town was its old, familiar territory. It had broken through the shackles of Avi's cultivated ruthlessness, doing a little dance of victory.

"Jeet, I hate this town. You know that, don't you?" Avi said with his hand over his eyes. His voice had dropped to a whisper. Jeet said nothing. "I hate the people here. I hate the stupid small-town politics. I cannot stay here and wait for the town to get back at me. I know what to do. I will not let this bastard blackmail us. If it comes to… if it comes to… some tough choices, I will make them."

"Like what? Kill again?"

"Fuck you! Don't you ever use that condescending tone with me."

"You make that choice, Avi. I hope you get a chance."

Avi stared at the wall for a long time.

"We made a choice then, didn't we?" Avi asked, his voice suddenly calm.

"Yes, we did."

Bhoite Wada had always been a symbol of Amrapur's splendour, even when the long-forgotten rulers were replaced by those elected democratically. The Bhoites, who once wore crowns and jewellery, now wore Gandhi caps and spotless white clothes. Bhausaheb Bhoite, the big-moustached ruler and the father of Bappa and Jagan, was a despised but feared man. An independent candidate for the State Legislative Assembly, his support in forming a government had always been crucial. The national political parties and governments indulged him, just as they had indulged his father. The little people of the town, as Bhausaheb called them, never dared to stray. They relinquished their ambitions, happiness and wealth for one family's greater prosperity. The kingdom had collapsed twenty years ago. Bappa died, and with him died the future of the Bhoite family.

"I can't believe that this is the Bhoite Wada," Avi said as they stood outside the once-palatial building.

The front yard was covered with a thick canopy of leaves shed by the giant moss-covered *gulmohur* and peepul trees. The outer walls of the palace were dusty and unkempt. Silence reigned, where once the bustle of countless people had reverberated. It was evening, but there seemed to be no light in the bleak ruin.

"It looks as though nobody lives here," Anita said.

Jeet pointed towards a little lamp visible from a window pane and said, "There seems to be some light."

"Let's knock on the door and see," Avi said and walked up to the door.

An old woman with heavily lined skin opened it.

"Jagan used to live here," Avi said. It was not a question but a statement.

The old woman stared at him, as though he had said something unpleasant. "He is gone," she said. Her voice was gravelly.

Shaking his head impatiently Avi said, "Gone? Gone where, old lady?"

Anita pushed him aside. *"Mai?* You are *Mai,* aren't you?" she said. Anita could not believe that she was looking at Jagan's mother.

The woman peered at Anita with narrowed eyes. "Who are you?"

"It's Anita, *Mai,"* Anita said, holding out her hand.

"Anita? My God, you look so beautiful!" the woman said and smiled.

"Thank you *Mai.* We need to find Jagan."

"He is gone."

"Gone where?"

"To a place from where he will not come back," she said and two large tears dropped from her eyes.

"What place is this?"

"Amarnath Mental Asylum."

There were many ghost stories in the town, some centuries old, some new. Every story involved Amarnath Mental Asylum. That was where the ghosts rested in the day after their escapades at night. It was a three-storeyed building on the outskirts of town, painted a cheery white.

"Shit. I never thought I would have to step inside this place," Avi said.

It was not true. The two old friends, Avi and Dev, had once decided to venture into the asylum at night, to finish off all the ghosts. They wanted to become heroes and write comics based on their adventures. They had never come within a kilometre of the asylum in the daytime.

Avi's forehead was a terrain of angry lines. His lips were twisted in a scowl. This seemed to be the constant alignment of his features. Dev wondered how easy it was to get used to the new habits of old friends, and how difficult to listen to their denouncements of little memories.

They entered the asylum.

"Jagan Bhoite," the middle-aged, shifty-eyed doctor repeated. "Why do you want to see him?"

"We need to talk to him," Dev said.

The doctor laughed as though it was the best joke he had heard in ages. He slapped his left knee repeatedly.

"Was that funny?" Anita asked.

Dev looked at her, frowning, and then shook his head. She crossed her hands. The doctor kept laughing for a long time.

"We really need to talk to him," Dev said again after he stopped.

"That man hasn't spoken to anyone for years. And you come out of nowhere wanting to talk to him," he said, shrugging in disbelief.

They stared at each other. Maybe Jagan had not spoken but written to someone, Dev thought. But he had a deep sense of foreboding. He ran his hand through his wild hair, trying to wipe away that feeling.

"Can you please take us to him?"

"You see, this is a government hospital and the rules are strict," the doctor said, with a flourish of his hand.

Old, rotting files were stacked in rusting cabinets. Broken instruments were lying all around. There was a moss-covered sink in which a steady stream of water fell from a deformed tap. A sickening smell of strong antiseptic hung in the air.

Dev nodded at Avi. Avi pulled out his wallet and took out a five hundred rupee note. The doctor's eyes bulged with greed.

"Now, can we?" Dev said.

The doctor took the money from Avi.

"We need to know everything about Jagan Bhoite, doctor," Anita said.

"Come with me," the doctor's demeanour seemed to have changed completely.

***

They stood before a manacled skeleton on a bed. His hands and feet were limp inside the rings of the shackles, feeble and defeated. The skin was stretched on his bones. His face was not visible as he had buried his chin deep inside his neck.

"What happened to him?" Dev asked.

"It was his older brother Bappa's death."

"Bappa's death," Anita said and stared at the doctor.

"I think he worshipped his older brother. He cried for three months after his dead body was found. And then he went berserk. He attacked a boy in his school with a knife. The boy almost died. His family locked him up for three years inside the house. But after Bhausaheb Bhoite died, they brought him here. For ten years after that, he kept repeating 'I will kill them all. I will kill them all'. He has not uttered a word in the last few years."

Dev desperately wanted to look into the eyes of the man whose life they had unknowingly destroyed. The strange noises in the mental asylum fell shrill in his ears. The ghosts of their terrible sin did reside here.

"Why the shackles?" he asked.

"We don't know how he will react. We did remove the chains once, but he almost suffocated the man next to him in the middle of the night," the doctor said with a sigh.

"My God," Avi said and looked away. After a few moments, he walked out of the hospital ward.

"Has he been released in the last few days?" Jeet asked the doctor.

"No," the doctor said, his eyes tinged with suspicion. "Why do you ask?"

"Nothing," Dev said and walked out. Avi and Anita followed him.

***

"That rules him out, doesn't it?" Avi asked as they stood outside the mental asylum.

Nobody replied.

"Now what do we do?" Avi wondered aloud. "Who else could it be, if not him?"

Nobody had an answer to that either.

"What have we done?" Anita asked. Her voice was hoarse.

"You think this is our fault?" His face contorted in anger.

"Yes," she said.

"Oh don't give me that shit, Anita," he hissed. "That bastard inside, he tormented so many of us. I would have gladly killed him then."

Placing a placating hand on Avi's shoulder, Dev said, "No, you wouldn't have."

Avi shrugged his hand off. "Listen to me, you guys, and listen to me very carefully. I have not come to this town to relive my guilt. I am here to find the bastard who called me back," he said and waved his forefinger at them as though trying to hammer in the words. He suddenly stopped waving his finger, shocked at hearing his own words. "I have built something wonderful out there." His voice was that of a defeated man who realised that he would never be able to go back to his life in Bangalore. The red and blue billboard of his company flashed in front of his eyes. The exact shape of the logo was already fading in his memory.

Dev put a hand on his shoulder again and this time he didn't shrug it off.

"A lot of people depend on me, Dev," he said. Dev nodded. "You remember the time when all of us used to depend on you? Especially me? Everything I did, I did after I asked you. You know what I have done in the last twenty years? I have tried to become like you. I have succeeded, Dev. I really have. This thing... I know it will make me go back to what I was. I cannot do that to myself," he said. Avi's voice was filled with the tears that he tried not to shed. But they fell out, even as he spoke.

"Let's go back to the hotel," Dev said.

The second night in Amrapur was hotter. The sweltering wind blazed through the town, burning the air. Jeet could no longer bear the combined assault of the heat and the sight of the relentlessly pacing Avi. He walked out to the balcony and closed the door behind him.

Would he ever see Maggie again? What must she be thinking? He pulled out his mobile and dialled her number, but disconnected before the call could be completed. She would want answers and he had none to give. He gripped the phone tightly, almost on the verge of smashing it on the ground. It suddenly started to vibrate in his hand. The little blue screen flashed a number that was unrecognisable. He pressed the green button.

"Are you thinking about your little girlfriend, fatty?" the voice asked.

Jeet started to shiver. He could not utter a word.

"What happened fatty? Did she bite off your tongue?" the caller asked and laughed.

Jeet rummaged through his memory to find a face to associate with the voice, but came up with nothing. The man's voice sounded slurred.

"I have waited for a long time for you. Look at you now. Not an inch of fat on you. Where did it all go? Oh yes. Now I remember. Perhaps you repented what you did twenty years ago. Killing can do that to you."

Jeet felt naked and threatened. Was the man watching him? There was darkness all around. Jeet walked back to the door and leaned on it for support, distrustful of his shaking knees.

"Who are you?" he rasped.

"Later. First, I want you to answer one question," the man said, his voice morbidly mischievous.

"What?"

"I want to know, who would you choose—your girlfriend or your childhood friends?"

Jeet pressed the phone so hard against his ear that it hurt. His throat went dry.

Laughing hysterically, the man said, "What actually happened, Jeet?"

Clenching his teeth with impotent rage, Jeet hissed, "What do you want?"

"I am just an agent of your choice. You tell me what you want. You will have to make that choice soon."

The man ended the call. Jeet held the phone to his ear for a long time, fearing that the man would call back, but the phone remained lifeless.

Dripping with sweat, he walked back in. Avi was lying on the bed with his arm over his eyes. The urge to wake him up and tell him about the phone call was overpowering. *You will make that choice soon.* His knees felt weak and he flopped onto a chair.

He speed-dialled her number. She picked it up on the second ring.

"Jeet! Are you all right?"

He wanted to laugh when he heard her voice. Her voice was frayed, deeply worried. Surely, the man would not travel all the way to London to harm her. Or would he?

"Yes I am," he said, laughing silently.

"You sound strange. What's happening there? I've called you a million times!" she said, her voice quivering.

"Don't worry. I'm fine. Just wanted to check if you were okay," he said and regretted it immediately.

"What do you mean? Jeet, are you in any kind of danger? I haven't slept since you left. I am travelling to India tonight."

"No!" he shouted so loudly that Avi woke up.

"No. Don't do that. You promised, remember?" he said lowering his voice.

"But…"

"Maggie, listen to me. I am not in any danger, okay? It's just that this town is making me sick. There are some very bad memories here. But I will be back soon. You believe me, don't you?" he said, naked desperation in his voice.

She was silent for a long time, then said, "Okay."

"I promise I will be back. I love you," he said and switched off the phone before she could say anything more.

"Who was that?" Avi asked, with a yawn.

"Maggie. Maggie Girard," he said.

"Your fiancée?"

Jeet nodded. He had never called her that, not even in his heart, but it sounded right. Maggie Girard, his fiancée, his wife. This was Maggie, who wrapped herself around him when he was sad, who rejoiced more than he did on the rare occasions when he was happy, who never asked him about Mr and Mrs Mehra, who didn't want to know anything about his past and its sins, and who was in danger because of his terrible secret.

"I am going to marry her," he said.

Avi had gone back to sleep, tired and disinterested.

Jeet walked out to the balcony and raised his hand to the sky. "I am coming back, baby," he said softly.

He would answer to God for his sin, but not to a man. Maggie deserved her happiness. He closed his eyes and saw Bappa's floating body. He wanted to forget that image until he died, after spending a lifetime with Maggie. And then he would wait for God's judgement.

Dev stood near the window as dawn broke. They had survived another night. Anita lay on the bed.

"One more night," she said.

"Yes," he said, looking outside the window.

"We all lived our lives, did we not?" she asked in a hollow voice.

"Was there an option?"

"Jagan didn't."

He said nothing.

"I don't know what I should feel. He made our lives miserable when we were kids. But after looking at him, I felt like crying," she said. "Imagine that, crying for Jagan Bhoite." She laughed instead and stopped abruptly.

"We have cried a lot for ourselves," he said.

"We wanted to do it, didn't we?"

He did. Some part, some horrifying vicious part of him, had liked the sensation of the thrashing, dying Bappa. And that vicious part had swallowed his entire personality for those few moments, shouting somewhere deep inside him to squeeze, squeeze harder.

"I cried for many days. But somehow I also wanted to laugh. Laugh as if I had done the greatest thing in my life," he said.

Admitting it to her suddenly made him feel weightless. He walked up to her and kissed her lips. She kissed him back with sudden force. His hammering heart was on hers, both beating together. She held him, breathing in his smell, her every hungry inhalation something to wallow in later. He slowly unbuttoned her clothes, revealing her body. She tore his clothes off and caressed the countless bruises on his taut skin. He touched her gently, afraid of the damage his callused, hard hands could inflict on her unblemished skin. Her skin rose in goose bumps, yearning for his touch. He kissed her neck, her collarbone and her breasts. He explored her navel and the creases of her thighs, making her cry out for what she wanted. She breathed in sharply and exhaled deeply, her legs wrapped around him. He took his time, tormenting her, making her thrash about, listening to her cries. After a long time, her legs became slowly slack, and he entered her in one hard motion. She gasped with sudden pain, but her hips moved hungrily towards his. He arched back to meet her manic thrusts. They seemed to move like that for an eternity. At last, he slumped over her, spent and knowing that she was, too. He heard her murmuring, as though his ears had just regained their sense of hearing.

"I have waited a long time," she said.

"So have I."

"Abbas Haq zindabad! Abbas Haq zindabad!"

Avi bolted up in his bed when he heard the cries. Sunshine suffused the room. He had not been able to sleep, floating in and out of consciousness the whole night. There was still no power. Wiping the drops of sweat on his face, he scanned the room. There was no sign of Jeet. The crowd was becoming noisier outside. Avi walked up to the window, perplexed. A man, buried under numerous thick garlands, stood in an open jeep, waving with both hands. The people were delirious seeing the man wave at them.

"Abbas Haq zindabad!"

The words hit him like a blow. He reeled, looking at the giant photograph of the man in the jeep.

"Sorry, Avi. I had gone down to get a telephone directory…" Jeet stopped mid-sentence as he looked at Avi.

Avi wordlessly pointed below.

The last time they had seen him, Sarafa Bazaar's ashes and Sharif Miyan's blood were smeared on his snarling face. Now, flowers of different hues jostled for proximity to his clown-like grin.

"My God. It can't be. It can't be," Jeet whispered.

"Abbas. That bastard! He is a member of the Legislative Assembly," Avi said.

Jeet ran out and banged on the door of Dev and Anita's room. Anita opened the door, perspiring.

"You need to come to our room," he said and then walked away.

A few moments later, Dev and Anita had reached the balcony.

"What?" Dev asked.

Avi pointed at the tall hoarding mounted on the open jeep. "Abbas Haq, forge ahead, we are behind you," it said.

Dev clenched the balcony railing, fearing he would fall if he didn't. The giant face of Abbas Haq on the hoarding was his worst nightmare brought to life. Anita held Dev's hand. She remembered Sharif Miyan's flowing henna-coloured beard, soaked in blood, his eyes frozen in anguished disbelief, his white sherwani crimson with his blood. She had crawled up to the still body. Lifting his large lifeless hand, she had rubbed it, comforting him after his death. And the man who had killed the soul of the town was staring at them from the hoarding, grinning deviously.

"We need to do something about this," Dev said as the procession wound its way through the street.

"What?" Avi said.

"Confront that bastard..." Dev realised mid-sentence that Avi's question was not about what he thought they should be doing, but an expression of incredulity.

"You think you can suddenly wear your superman cape and go save this town?" Avi said.

"Listen Avi," Dev said, trying to control his anger.

"No, *you* listen, Dev. We are here because a man has threatened us. We tackle this bastard and get out of this town. We are not going to do anything else," Avi said, jerking his head.

"Avi, this man killed the one person we all loved," Anita said.

"Is he going to come back to life if we do something to Abbas?" Avi asked.

"You find the man who asked us to come here, Avi. And I will do something about Abbas Haq," Dev said and walked out of the room.

Dev stood in front of the mirror in the bathroom and splashed water on his face. The murderous cacophony of the mob that had burnt the Sarafa Bazaar echoed in his ears. Every scream was deafeningly loud, as though the carnage had taken place only a few moments ago.

The reflection in the mirror was that of a coward who had witnessed a crime and had actually concealed it for the last twenty years.

He had been selfish then, for the lives of his friends and his own.

What was the excuse now?

Should he continue to live a life of guilt and repentance, or follow his newfound love? He felt like smashing the mirror. The face in it mocked him, laughed at him.

Closing his eyes for a moment, he made a decision.

Dr Joshi wondered what he was going to do with the five hundred rupees the four strangers had given him. Should he buy a sari for his wife? No, that would make her expect it every time he got some extra money. Maybe a bottle of something stronger than the cheap, pathetic whisky he had every Saturday? Yes, that would be a good idea. A bottle of the red wine he so desperately desired every time he saw it in the display shelves of the wine shop. It made him smile.

There was a sudden commotion that broke his reverie. He cursed the insane bastards. Their only purpose in life was to make him miserable.

"Dr Joshi! It's Jagan Bhoite," the ward boy came into his cabin, panting with fear.

"What?" Joshi stood up.

"Please come at once!" the ward boy said quickly and ran away.

Joshi went to the medicine rack and picked up a shot of morphine. He ran to the ward. What he saw stunned him. Jagan Bhoite had dragged the heavy iron bed almost to the entrance of the ward. Holding a ward boy's neck in the crook of his arm, he was growling. His eyes were bloodshot. The long matted hair added to his fearsome aspect.

"Grab him!" Joshi shouted but none of the ward boys moved. They all had bruised faces and were huddled in a corner, whimpering. The ward boy whom Jagan was strangling was dying a slow death. His bulging eyes were turning white. He didn't have much time before Jagan crushed his neck.

Joshi jumped in front of Jagan and tried to jab the syringe somewhere in his body. Jagan released the ward boy who collapsed on the ground, and clutched Joshi's hand. Joshi cried in pain as the lunatic's nails tore into his soft flesh. He dropped the syringe. Jagan kicked him between his legs.

He could not breathe and pain exploded through his entire body. Jagan grabbed Joshi's hair and tripped him. He raised his right foot high in the air and brought it down on Joshi's throat. It made a crunching sound.

He raised his foot and stamped again. Then he pulled out the bunch of keys from Joshi's pocket and opened his handcuffs. He spat on Joshi's face and fled the hospital.

Dev picked up the receiver of the public phone and dialled a number he thought he never would. It was picked up after five rings. After every ring, Dev had the uncontrollable urge to put the receiver down.

"Hello?" he heard the gruff voice of the man he loathed.

"Jeevan, it's Dev," he said.

There was a long silence.

"What does Mr Peace want from me now?" Jeevan said. The sarcasm was infuriating. Dev fought hard to swallow the acidic retort. He needed Jeevan's help.

"I need a gun," Dev said, his mouth bitter, as though full of vomit.

"Well, well, well! I cannot believe what I'm hearing."

"Jeevan, I just want an answer. Are you going to give it to me or not? I really have no time to put up with your sarcasm."

"Yes. I am going to give it to you. I'm glad that you have learnt the truth. Without the gun, you cannot fight, can you Dev?"

"Where can I get it? I am in Amrapur," Dev said and hoped that Jeevan would not be too keen to know why he was there.

"There is a man who owns a liquor shop in Amrapur. Note down his number," Jeevan said and gave him the number. "He is a supporter of our cause. You will get what you want from him."

Two hours later, Dev had the pistol in his left pocket. The *ghoda,* as the liquor shop owner called the gun, was sticking in his hip. Every speech he had made in the ravaged villages echoed in his ears. He had pleaded with the people to shun violence. The Adivasis had endured exploitation by the land-grabbers. Every once in a while, a young man, angered by the atrocities, would take the extreme step of attacking the oppressors. The retaliation from the land-grabbers was always swift and brutal. Hamlets were burnt down in a matter of minutes. Men were tied to trees and rabid dogs were unleashed on them. Women were viciously raped, their breasts were slashed and they bled to death. Children were burnt alive.

All those speeches were made pointless by the black, shiny gun he now possessed. But there was no other way.

Abbas Haq would pay for his sins, and so would Dev.

Inspector Kamble was about to start his motorcycle and head home, when a *havaldar* rushed out of the police station calling his name.

"Why the hell are you shouting? Are red ants biting your arse?" Kamble asked irritably.

"Just got a call from the *pagalkhana,* sahib," the *havaldar* said breathlessly. "It seems one of those madmen went berserk and killed two people—a doctor and a ward boy."

"Tell Sub-Inspector Mhatre to look into it," Kamble said and kick-started his motorcycle.

"Sahib, Mhatre sahib asked me to report to you," the *havaldar* said. "Apparently, the killer is Jagan Bhoite."

"What?" Kamble was stunned.

"Yes sahib. Jagan Bhoite."

Kamble turned the ignition key to switch off his motorcycle. It would be a long time before he could go home riding his shiny new bike.

Kamble entered the *pagalkhana,* as the havildar called the mental asylum. He looked at the scared bunch of ward boys dressed in dirty white uniforms and motioned to one of them to come closer.

"Take me to where it happened," he said. "Jagan Bhoite did this?"

"Yes sahib," the ward boy said.

The dead bodies were lying on the ward floor. Dr Joshi's throat was mashed like a watermelon. The ward boy's tongue was hanging out from his mouth with his neck twisted at an impossible angle.

"Shende," Kamble said to the havildar. "Get the forensic people on this. I want a complete report as soon as possible."

The havildar nodded and then started talking on his walkie-talkie.

"Mhatre, get everyone in the headquarters to hunt down Jagan Bhoite. Get him alive. Nobody harms him. Is that clear?" he said to the Sub-Inspector.

"Yes sahib," Mhatre said and rushed out of the hospital.

Kamble rubbed his eyes with his palms, warming them for the many sleepless nights ahead. It was a political minefield. Bhausaheb Bhoite's eldest son had been killed during the riots of 1989. The family had degenerated rapidly after lighting the elder son's pyre. Bhausaheb started drinking and forgot to rule the town. It was just the opportunity Sanjay Sawant, Bhausaheb's brother-in-law, had been waiting for. He quickly assumed control of the Bhoite family. There were rumours that Sawant had a key role in turning Bhausaheb into an alcoholic. Bhausaheb died a broken man, just six months after his son's death. Sawant was not a patch on Bhausaheb and promptly lost the next elections. Since then, the Bhoite family had faded from the people's consciousness. Sanjay Sawant still fancied himself as the king of the town and maintained a ragtag army of misguided young men. But the advent of Abbas Haq and his vitriolic speeches had elevated him to the Legislative Assembly and had relegated Sanjay Sawant to political obscurity. Jagan Bhoite's sudden escape from the asylum might just fan Sawant's lost hopes. Kamble felt a deep sense of foreboding looking at the hideously sprawled bodies on the hospital floor.

"Are there any other doctors around here?" he asked the ward boy.

"Dr Chaudhari comes for the day shift," the ward boy said.

"So where is he?"

"His shift is yet to start, sahib," the ward boy said

Kamble glared at him and the ward boy flinched. At six feet two and a hundred-and-twenty kilograms, Kamble could cast his shadow on most people. His dark complexion and thick moustache made him look perpetually angry.

"Get Dr Chaudhari to report here before his shift today," he said and the ward boy scurried away.

⁂

"What happened in the last few days with Jagan Bhoite?" he asked Dr Chaudhari, an old man, well into his sixties and conspicuously suffering from Parkinson's. His inexorable shaking had deepened as he sat in front of Kamble.

"Nothing sahib. He never showed any kind of abnormal behaviour." His words were interspersed with the chattering of his teeth. Kamble wondered what constituted abnormal behaviour according to Dr Chaudhari. A man not talking for decades, lying on a hospital bed? Or his sudden, violent killing of two people? Kamble kept looking at Dr Chaudhari as though he didn't believe anything he had said. Many people told him their life stories when he gave them that disbelieving look.

"But sahib, something happened yesterday…I am not sure if it has any relevance here," Chaudhari said, trying to please him.

"Doctor, why don't you tell me what happened, and I will decide if it is relevant or not," Kamble said.

"Sure sahib," Chaudhari said, with a violent spike in his shaking. "Yesterday, four people had come to meet Jagan Bhoite."

Kamble bent forward. "Who were they?" he asked.

"Don't know sahib," Chaudhari replied. He recoiled as though he feared Kamble was going to shoot him for not knowing.

"His family?" Kamble prodded.

"No sahib. I know his family well. None of them have visited him for the last fifteen years."

"Do you have any record of who visits the patients?" Kamble asked but, looking at the terrible condition of the so-called hospital, he already knew the answer.

"No sahib," Chaudhari stuttered.

Kamble thought about it for a few moments. "Was there any immediate reaction from Jagan?"

"Don't know sahib. Dr Joshi should be...," Chaudhari said and stopped mid-sentence, suddenly remembering that Dr Joshi was dead.

Kamble took a deep breath and dismissed Chaudhari.

"Did any of you see the four people?" he asked the dazed ward boys.

"They were young, sahib. Three men and a woman. One of the men had a long unkempt beard."

Kamble nodded and noted it down. He dismissed the ward boys and called Mhatre on his mobile.

"Nothing to update, sahib. We have searched the Bhoite Wada. He has not reached here. His mother is crying non-stop and says she doesn't know where he is. We have posted plainclothes havildars near the house. We are also checking the nearby houses, but I don't have any hope there," Mhatre said.

Kamble switched off the phone. That was when he heard a commotion outside the hospital. He pressed his fingers on his temples to quell the impending headache. The commotion was caused by Sanjay Sawant's cavalcade.

"My nephew can't do this," Sawant said. He spat betel juice on the hospital wall, leaving a red stain. Kamble said nothing. Sawant continued, "How can he do anything? He has been a mental patient for the last so many years."

"I have witnesses who say that he did it," Kamble said.

"Fuck those witnesses! I am telling you he has done nothing," Sawant bellowed, spraying Kamble's face with red spittle. "I will have to talk to the Superintendent of Police about this. But I am warning you. Don't you even think of hurting my nephew! I am so happy that he has overcome his terrible illness," he said and walked out of the hospital.

Kamble knew what would happen. He would get a call from his superiors, who would agree with what Sawant had said. He lit a cigarette and took a deep cancerous drag.

Anita saw the little blue rectangle mounted on an iron pole with 'Mehrab Road' written on it. The words were barely visible through decades of caked dirt and bird shit. Shambhoo's paan stall was still next to it. The fat, gnome-like Shambhoo had not aged a day. He even had a paan in his mouth, like always. "Shambhoo chews a paan even in his sleep," Dev used say. A steady stream of saliva trickled from the corner of his mouth, soaking the cloth on his shoulder.

This was where she had stared down Bappa and his friends so many times. All of them undressed her savagely with their eyes, while she dared them to do it for real. There was a longer route to her home, but she never took it. She wondered what would have happened if she had taken that longer route. Maybe Bappa and his friends would have left her alone. Maybe she would not have hated Bappa. Maybe she would not have dreamt of seeing him die. Maybe she would not have seen him die...

Shambhoo saw her as she stared at his paan stall. There was a flash of recognition in his eyes. He smiled a red, toothy smile, as though he suddenly remembered the event that used to be the highlight of his day—Bappa teasing that beautiful girl. And now that beautiful girl was all grown up. How could he not mentally undress her? She felt like burning down the paan stall.

Walking ahead, she didn't look down, just as she used to twenty years ago. The road had not changed. Old potholes were cured, like acne, only to spawn new ones. The dingy bars on either side of the road looked vapid in the searing sun. A few drunks were sprawled next to the bars, their heads caked in dried vomit. This part of the town had given her bad memories forever.

She reached the place where she had survived for twelve years. It had not changed, either. There was the little gate that opened inwards, the small patch of scruffy grass with a few colourless flowers peering out like shy children, and the muddy path through the grass leading to the entrance. She touched the door and thought that the ancient scratches on it had become a little more pronounced.

She knocked on the door and waited, all the while wondering what she was thinking—that she could just walk up to her house and everything would be all right?

The door opened with a familiar reluctance. An old man wearing large glasses stood at the entrance—he had cataract and looked at her as though he was peering through a dense fog. She thought of turning back and running away.

"Yes?" the man said.

"I am Anita," she blurted out. "I used to live here many years ago."

The man said nothing. He kept staring at her as though it still didn't make any sense to him.

"I am Sharad Kulkarni's daughter," she said.

The man removed his glasses and wiped them on his food-stained vest.

"I know Sharad Kulkarni. Or knew him," he said. "He died seven years ago, didn't he?"

"Yes he did," she said.

She had escaped from Amrapur, holding her mother's wet, shaking hand, wading through the water-clogged road as the rain pelted down. The belching, beating, cursing, vomiting monster was left behind. Two years before that rainy night, her mother had received a letter from her sister. The postman had given a blue inland letter to Anita on a dull Saturday afternoon, not realising the pivotal role he played in the escape. What if he had not delivered the letter? What if he had delivered the letter on any other day but Saturday, when the monster worked in the afternoon shift? What if he had just dropped it at the door instead of handing it to her? Any of those possibilities would have made the escape impossible.

Her mother read the letter with a panic that surfaced slowly, like mercury in a thermometer. She crumpled the soft paper in her hand. Anita, stunned by the savage treatment of the letter from *Akka,* her mother's sister whom they both revered and adored, had stopped her mother from tearing it up. That letter formed the blueprint of their escape two years later.

Akka, who was the greatest exponent of Kathak in India, implored her mother to grab as many clothes as possible, catch a bus and come to her in Pune. She had started an academy where she trained rich women and their daughters in dance. She wanted her mother to leave that monster behind and run to her. Anita laughed at the word monster. Seeing it written in *Akka's* beautiful handwriting somehow made it real. Her father, as she had always known, *was* a monster.

Her mother lit the stove and held the pale blue letter on the bright blue flame, turning it into black ash. *Akka* never wrote again, as though aware of the miraculous journey of her only letter. Her mother had clutched Anita's shoulders, pressing them so hard that they hurt, and extracted a promise of silence from her. The monster had boundless power over her. Her choices were a subset of his, her wishes were at the mercy of his whims. It took her mother two years to dig a tunnel through the prison of her marriage, and scatter aside the mud of her married life. Two days before the escape, one of the monster's drunkard friends had grabbed Anita. Her mother threw burning oil on his face. Some of the oil had splashed on her mother's hand, giving her big pus-filled boils. The monster had beaten her for hours. That day, the tunnel was complete. They escaped that night.

The monster had come to Pune the next day. One of the women to whom *Akka* taught Kathak was the wife of an Assistant Commissioner of Police. The policemen had grabbed the abuse-hurling, door-banging, drunken man and systematically beaten him for two hours. The monster died, and what remained of her father was the drunkard, who returned to Amrapur. He died twenty years ago, and died again thirteen years later.

Anita learned Kathak while teaching the obese, disinterested and snobbish daughters of the countless madams and *tais* in

Pune. *Akka's* business grew with the addition of two new pairs of legs.

***

"How did he die?" she asked.

"Don't you know?" the man responded. He stopped wiping his glasses and stared at her through narrowed eyes, as though he didn't believe his old ears. Anita shook her head in a silent "no". She bit her lower lip to stop herself from crying. The house had had more than its share of tears.

"Why don't you come in?" the old man said and walked inside. She held the door frame to steady herself and took a step inside—a step she had vowed never to take in her life.

"Sit down," the man pointed to a white plastic chair. He went inside the house and returned with a glass of water from a black earthen pot. It was the same spot her mother had chosen. "This is where the water becomes coldest," her mother had said after trying out many places.

She gulped the water as though she had been thirsty for days. "How did he die?" she repeated.

"The doctor said he died of suffocation. He drowned in his own vomit. Perhaps he was too drunk to even realise that," he said.

Anita thought that it was a fitting death. For the years of suffocation she and her mother had suffered in this house, it was good to know that he had died of suffocation. She hated herself for thinking that.

"Nobody discovered his body for seven days. I smelled a faint unpleasant smell for four days and it only grew worse. On the seventh day, we knew something had happened to your father," he said.

She knew how he must have smelled the first couple of days after his death. He would have smelt of urine and cheap liquor. She sat there on the white chair for a long time. She had always thought that if she ever went inside her house, she would hear her father beating her mother and yelling vicious curses in his slurred voice. But she heard nothing. It was as though all the noises had died with her father.

"Oh yes," he said and got up. He rummaged through a stack of books kept on a rack and pulled out an old envelope. "Your father asked me to give this to you, if you ever returned," he said.

She took the envelope with her name written in Marathi on it with shaking hands, and got up. "Thank you. I will leave now," she said and walked towards the door.

"He was a terrible man to live with," the old man said.

Nodding, she walked out of the house for the last time.

She walked away with steady steps, fearing her stoic façade would collapse soon and she would wail like the little girl she once was. She stopped and opened the envelope. There was a piece of paper in it, with just one word: "Sorry."

She stared at the piece of paper for a long time. Her vision blurred. Two large tears fell and slid down the paper, dissolving the old ink, wiping out the word. It was meaningless, it was offensive—to the memory of her mother who had died a sad broken woman, and to the years of her childhood destroyed by fear. One word was the length of his remorse? She crumpled the piece of paper and threw it away.

"Sorry Father, I can never forgive you," she whispered.

He watched her as she walked away from her old home, drinking in the sight of her every movement: the forlorn furrowing of her forehead, her rapidly blinking eyelids, like the wings of a little bird trying to wipe away the tears, and the shape of her beautiful body hidden under the salwar kameez. He thought he had come alive again. How could he have survived all these years without her? She stopped abruptly in the middle of the street. The people walking on the street somehow deviated from their path after seeing her, as if she was the source of some immense aura. She read something on the piece of paper in the envelope and cried a few precious tears.

He remembered her smile. It was as though she knew some deep secret. A secret so profound, it made her glow from inside. He had not seen that smile for the last two days. But she would smile soon, after she saw him and knew what he had done for her, the sacrifice that he had made.

She would smile and tell him the secret. And then, she would be his forever.

"Where the hell were you?" Jeet asked her as he opened the door.

She didn't say anything and entered the room. Jeet grabbed her shoulders so hard they hurt. His fingers almost dug into her flesh.

"Answer me, dammit!" he said and shook her violently.

She could not control it any longer. A sob escaped her lips, spawning a torrent of sobs and tears. She put her head on his chest and cried—for her childhood, for her dead mother. Her tears drenched his chest.

"Where is Dev?" Avi asked Anita.

Jeet gently pushed Anita away.

"What do you mean?"

"He is missing too," Jeet said. "We thought he was with you."

Avi's phone started to ring. There was no number on the screen. He shrugged, and was about to switch off the phone when he realised that the caller could be the man who had called them to Amrapur. He looked at Anita and Jeet. "I think it's him," he said.

"Oh my God," Anita said.

Avi's breathing was uneven, as though the asthma that he had almost conquered had suddenly come alive. He picked up the phone.

"Hello," he wheezed.

"Hello Avi. I am sure Jeet and Anita are with you," the man said.

"Yes."

"So why don't you put it on speakerphone?"

Avi pressed the speaker button.

"Jeet and Anita," the man said. "You are all wondering why I have not contacted you yet, aren't you?"

"What do you want?" Avi screamed.

"I enjoy your fear. That was what I wanted, to start with. How does it feel to live a life that is filled with fear, you fucking murderers?"

Avi flinched.

"I want all four of you to be at the place where you murdered Bappa Bhoite tomorrow night," he said. "Especially that bastard, Dev."

"Who are you?" Anita asked.

"Tomorrow," the man said and switched off the phone.

They were silent for a long time, afraid to say anything. The hum of the overhead fan was deafening.

"Do you know this voice?" Avi asked finally.

Jeet shook his head.

"No," Anita said.

There was a knock on the door.

"It's me."

It was Dev's voice. Jeet opened the door.

"Look, I'm sorry. I shouldn't…" Dev stopped mid-sentence when he saw the expressions on their faces.

"Did he contact you?" he said.

"Yes," Avi said and told him what had happened.

"We will not do what he says," Dev said.

"What do you mean?"

"I know he will kill us all if we do as he says."

"Dev, I have had enough of listening to you. I have listened to you for far too long, even when you were not there. There was this little man in my head for many years, who had your voice. He was always telling me what to do. But not anymore."

Dev felt a deep sense of loss that he had never felt before, even when he had lost his father to the revolution, or his mother to melancholy. Avi's friendship was always inviolable.

"I have a plan to catch this bastard, and that includes going to meet him tomorrow at the riverside. If that does not include you, or any of you," Avi said, looking at the three of them, "I don't care."

"What is your plan, Avi?" Dev asked. His voice was steady, devoid of any emotion.

"I intend to talk to my cousin, who is a local politician. He would know someone who would do it for me."

"Do what?" Anita asked.

Avi's eyes were unfocussed. Dev knew his friend was frightened of his own thoughts. "When we, or I, meet this bastard tomorrow, this man will kill him and take care of the body," he said. His mouth stayed open for a few moments.

"Are you with me Jeet?" Avi asked.

Jeet shook his head.

"Why?"

"I wouldn't be able to live through another twenty years with a new guilt, Avi."

"Don't give me this shit, Jeet. What do you think this man wants? He is some scumbag who will torment us for the rest of our lives—*if* we have a life after he is through with us. I don't want to give him that chance."

"Do we give him the same treatment as Bappa?" Jeet asked.

"Shut up! It was a terrible mistake. I have paid the price for it. So have you. All of you."

"I can't kill again, Avi," Jeet said.

"Why are you saying that?" Avi shouted. "It was a mistake, you know that, dammit!"

"No it was not," Dev said, with tears in his eyes. "I always wanted to kill him. I could have stopped. If I had, maybe you would've too. Maybe he wouldn't have died."

"And then he would have killed me," Avi said. It stunned Dev. "Maybe you should have let him kill me, Dev. He would've, if you hadn't attacked him."

"Avi, wait!" Dev said, but Avi didn't. He walked out of the hotel room. "Don't worry, my friend. I will be there for you," Dev whispered. Then he said to Jeet and Anita, "There is something I need to tell you. I have some unfinished business with Abbas. Don't interfere. I wanted all of you to leave town, but you didn't. We are in great danger now. But I have to confront Abbas one last time before we face this danger."

He walked out, took three stairs at a time and disappeared into the crowded street.

There were many things Manoj Jadhav regretted in his life. Like his puppy's death, due to gangrene in its hind leg. When the leg broke for the sixth time, his father refused to take it to the vet. Spending his hard-earned money on repeatedly healing a dog was beyond him. Manoj's mother, suspicious as always, had asked him what was happening. He had shrugged. The nagging witch knew something. After all, she was his mother. Manoj regretted that the puppy died after he broke its leg for the sixth time. He wanted it to survive till he had broken the leg ten times. He also regretted his brother's moving out of the house after he got married. One night, his sister-in-law told his brother that she was losing her underwear almost every week. She suspected that Manoj was stealing it. There was silence from his brother. Manoj knew all his dirty secrets. His brother feared him.

Her bras smelled of talcum powder. Manoj had never imagined that the florid powder would smell so good after a few hours in her underwear. His brother moved out of the house in two weeks. His mother had asked him why he kept his study table cupboard locked all the time. He gave her his familiar shrug. What was he going to tell her? That he hid all those wonderful smelling souvenirs in it?

He regretted succumbing to his father's relentless blackmail. He had threatened to throw Manoj out of the house if he refused to get married. He heard his parents talking one night—that perhaps marriage would make him normal. What the hell was wrong with him? They treated him as though he was a retard who needed fixing.

Almost every girl rejected him—he was too short, too ugly, too fat, too dark. The reasons were many. Everyone found a new one. Then, one day, a family said yes because the woman was shorter, uglier, fatter and darker than him. He tried to explain to his parents that a clerk's salary was not enough to run a household.

They told him he need not worry as his father would take care of that. He argued that he was too young to get married. They told him his father had two kids when he was Manoj's age. He could never tell them the real reason. There was just one girl that he wanted to marry, and he could not find her. He went to the riverside that evening and cried. Promising to meet her one day, he told her he was sorry for not waiting. His parents married him off within a month.

There were two events he never regretted, though. One of them gave him great joy and the other gave him great hope. The death of his mother was the most joyous moment. She died after a short but excruciating battle with throat cancer. The old hag knew all his secrets. It was good that she died with them unrevealed. The second was the death he had witnessed—the murder of a fifteen-year-old boy by four twelve-year-olds. One of them was Anita. She would one day be his when he told her about that death.

One day, he learned about the lunatic, and he knew what he had to do. It was so simple, he almost wanted to beat himself for not thinking of it earlier. He would soon embrace her. He would make sure that the three bastards would pay for the crime they committed, for dragging her into their terrible act, and for making her disappear from his life for twenty long years.

He tried talking to the madman. They said he had not spoken for years. But he had persevered and was rewarded. He told the man what he saw twenty years ago—the secret that he had so desperately wanted to hear. Manoj smiled at the memory of how the fool had believed every word that he said. He knew the only thing that had tormented the monster for the last twenty years was the thought of revenge. All he needed was a little prodding. The crazy bastard had laughed when he told him what he had seen. He had asked him why he hadn't told him for so long. Wasn't it obvious to the fool that he was scared of him?

Gazing at the balcony of her room, he took a deep breath, as though the air carried her smell. He had done all of it to get her back to town. He knew she would be grateful to him for hiding her secret. She would fall in love with him the moment he told her about the enormity of his sacrifice. He would forgive her. For that's what soul mates do, don't they? They forgive.

It had taken him two years to find them all. He had imagined the sight of each one of them reading the little messages he had sent. How scared they must have felt! Just like that flailing puppy. They must have made little whining sounds. They must have cried like that puppy did when it hit the ground. How he wished he could have seen it. He intended to apologise to her for making her go through it. She would be so relieved and happy that it was not meant for her. He just had to do it to get her back. She would understand.

He had told the madman that she should not be touched. He could hardly wait to gather her in his arms after the lunatic had killed those three bastards. They were the wall between him and Anita twenty years ago. But now he would use the vengeful monster to break that wall.

Two days had passed since they came back to town. Every minute that she lived with them made him feel like killing them himself. What the hell was the madman waiting for? Why did he not finish the job? How difficult would it be for him to get his revenge? Just get the three bastards in one place and kill them with the gun he'd provided. Why wait so long? He shivered. His mind wrestled with doubts.

Would the lunatic keep his promise?

Avi punched in the ten digits on his cell to call Shah Sadan. Staring at the number on the screen for a long time, he gingerly touched the call button. It needed only a little pressure, and he would return to the place he hated most. The screen light of the phone dimmed slowly, and the numbers were engulfed by the darkness in that little space. He pressed the green button before they disappeared completely, uncertain whether he would be able to type them again.

The phone rang.

"Hello." It was the voice of his eldest aunt, a big fat woman who smelled of *Dalda vanaspati* all the time and had called his mother barren, as though she were some piece of land that his father had acquired. After sixteen years of pillaging, all she had yielded was a frail son.

"Hello?" Her voice ratcheted up with irritation. This was the same tone that she used to talk to her husband, his father's younger brother.

"It's me. Avinash," he said softly, his tongue unwilling to give any emotion to the words.

"Avinash?" she said, perhaps not believing what she had heard. "Avi! How are you my son? It is so wonderful to hear your voice."

Clenching his teeth Avi managed to ask, "May I speak to Jayant, please?"

"Of course! Where are you?"

"I am in Amrapur."

"Sorry?" This was her perverse habit of making people repeat everything unpleasant, which she used to practise with great regularity on his mother. *"How many acres of land does your father own in the village, Sejal?" "None." "Sorry?" "None".*

"I...am...in...Amrapur," he said slowly, pausing after every word.

"So when are you coming home, Avi? You must come home right now. Everyone will be so happy to see you. Most of all, Rasikbhai."

He wondered if they actually thought he carried millions of dollars in his pockets, and was the same naïve, timid, twelve-year-old kid who could be sweet-talked or bullied into complying with their foul plans.

"I have no intention of coming..."

"Your uncle is here!" she said, interrupting him. He heard her calling his uncle's name. Then a loud murmur, as though they were deciding on what to say to Rasiklal's son so that he would bring his millions to them.

"Hello," he said impatiently.

He was about to switch off the phone when his uncle brayed, "Avi, my son! How are you? Rasiklal!" He shouted in the phone as if his father was somewhere in the network. "We have been trying to reach you for a long time son. Where have you been? You never came home for Diwali either."

Avi said nothing. There were some more loud murmurings, and then his father came on the phone. "Did you call to check whether I am dead or alive?"

Avi felt like laughing—this, coming from the man who had disowned him when he was born.

"I don't care either way. Just give the damned phone to Jayant," he said coldly, but the line had been cut. He held the soundless phone at his ear till his fingers hurt. There was no other option but to go home. He smiled bitterly at the thought of that word. Home.

As he stood outside Shah Sadan, his old feelings returned to haunt him. Gleaming cars were in the garage. There were Marutis and Fiats, as well as a Ford Ikon. The little path from the large, noisy, iron gate to the entrance of the house was, as before, littered with bicycles and toys.

He walked up to the door and rang the bell. It was opened by a plump sixteen-year-old girl in impossibly tight clothes.

She was wearing garish makeup. She raised a heavily painted eyebrow askance.

"Who are you?" he asked.

"Oh my God, you are uncle Avi, right?"

He nodded.

"Daddy!" she shouted and ran inside.

The house had not changed—the same old bricks coated with the same old paint, the gaudy chandeliers, the blood red curtains. In no time, the news spread that Avi was back in the house. The one who has a big company in Bangalore? Yes, the same. The one who has crores of rupees? Yes, yes! The one whom we keep seeing in the newspapers? Yes, he is here!

He sat in the middle of a sofa, surrounded by people, of whom he only knew half. They had aged, and their expressions had changed. The others looked at him with amazement, as though he were a God who had acquiesced to visit them.

"You are returning after twenty years! Here, do have some sweets!"

"You have to stay with us."

"How many crores do you have?"

"Shut up! Don't you have any manners?"

"Have you got married?"

"My sister's sister-in-law's cousin would be best suited to you."

"Have you brought gifts for us?"

Avi wanted to shrug violently. "I need to meet Jayant," he said above the din.

"He should be coming home very soon. Here, have some laddoos."

He got up without saying a word and went up to confront the patriarch, hoping his father had not changed his room. The family were stunned by the suddenness of it. They didn't follow him. He walked inside the room and saw his father sitting on a reclining chair facing the window.

"I turned out all right without running a damned sari shop, didn't I Baba?" he said.

His father didn't say anything. Rocking in his chair without making any sound, he didn't even look at his son.

"Say something, dammit!" he shouted. "You ignored me when I was nothing in your eyes."

His father wore thick, black-framed glasses, magnifying the rejection in his eyes many times over. "You think you have achieved everything now?" he said in his gruff, aged voice.

"Yes. I have. More than you could ever imagine in your life! And I did it without any help from all of you. Especially you, father."

"Then why are you here?"

Avi was shocked by the question.

"You need something, don't you?" his father said with a sarcastic smile. "We all need the family, Avi, whether you agree or not." The patriarch looked out of the window, his turning away an act of finality.

Shaking uncontrollably, Avi wanted to say many things, but he just could not. The anger made his vision red. He walked back down. The family stood there with their mouths open.

"Where is Jayant? Ask him to meet me immediately," he said and walked out.

"What have you gotten yourself into?" Jayant asked.

"That is none of your business."

"Who is this man?"

"I don't know."

"You don't know? And what is the reason for him to be blackmailing you?"

"Again, you don't need to know that. Now, are you going to do it or not?"

"What do I get?"

"I thought you agreed with my father. That the family is there to help."

Jayant laughed. "Your father is a…" He stopped mid-sentence when he saw the expression on Avi's face.

"You get five crores. It should be enough to fund your next election."

"Ten."

"Five is all I have Jayant. You can take it or I can find someone else."

Jayant craned his neck and scratched his chin thoughtfully, as though he was making a very difficult decision. Then he nodded. "Okay. I want half now."

Avi smiled and pulled out a huge bundle of thousand rupee notes.

"One lakh is all I have right now, Jayant. You will have to just trust me," he said.

Jayant took it.

"Who is going to do it?" Avi asked.

"I know the perfect man for this job. Don't worry."

"He will know what to do?"

"Shoot the man troubling you and take care of the body. I guess it should not be too difficult."

Jayant Shah, who had been a member of Bhausaheb Bhoite's goon squad, was now a rising star in small-town politics. Avi looked at the man who had shared the same house with him for most of his first twelve years. He wondered if the air that he breathed was somehow different. How could he turn out to be like that? And was there really any difference between him and Jayant? He shook his head. All these thoughts were pointless now. He had made his decision the moment he had walked out on his friends.

"Jayant, I need to know who is going to do it," he said in his coldest voice.

"His name is Janardan Mhatre. He is a Sub-Inspector."

Abbas put a garland atop the memorial stone where Sharif Miyan's teastall used to be. The ground was still ash-coloured and reminded people of the inferno that had once raged there. The people in his convoy clapped, prompting the spectators to applaud wildly. The thundering noise made Abbas jump a little. He took a couple of steps back from the garland. He closed his eyes and saw the blazing fire once more—bright orange, the smoke blackening the sky and the bodies charring. He opened his eyes and saw the people surrounding him. They were smiling, laughing and cheering him on. Nobody had applauded when he killed his uncle. It was a death that gave him a new life, away from the ratty two-room family home.

Abbas had cried the most during Sharif Miyan's funeral. He wept tears of happiness, for a beautiful future in the Foreign, with all those beautiful women and crores of rupees. The entire town, liberated from the suffocating curfew following the riots, poured out on the streets for the funeral. The number of policemen had been reduced by the government, as though they thought that riots would not strike the same town again. They watched in disbelief as hundreds of people, Hindus and Muslims, converged on the streets to grieve Sharif Miyan's death. The people wore stunned expressions, as though shocked by their own barbarity. Abbas was sure none of the people on the street were part of the mob that murdered their neighbours. The two were distinct animals—the hunters and the hunted, the killers and the mourners.

Within a few days, he had convinced his mother to mortgage the little house. He had raised a princely sum of twenty thousand rupees and almost flew to meet Sadiqbhai. There was a silent admiration on Sadiqbhai's face. If he knew, or suspected Abbas of Sharif Miyan's murder, he never mentioned it. Abbas also sensed awe in the way Sadiqbhai spoke to him. When he said that he had enough money to fund his trip to the Foreign, Sadiqbhai nodded his head and answered that he could have all the riches of the Foreign in India itself. Would he be interested? Abbas stared hard at Sadiqbhai, unsure of what he meant and, for a maddening moment, remembered what his dead uncle had said. "Sadiq is a crook. He is a poisonous spider who will trap you in his web of lies."

Sadiqbhai took him to meet the president of a political party that was trying to establish itself in the town. The president of the party and Sadiqbhai had a long whispered conversation, after which the president had looked at him as though he were evil. They told him there was no need to go to the Foreign. He could have everything here. He was the nephew of Sharif Miyan, the dead saint of the town. All he needed to do was to join the party and never let the people of Amrapur forget the life and death of Sharif Miyan. And they would ensure he got what he had always dreamt of. As a measure of good faith, they gave him ten thousand rupees.

Abbas didn't sleep that night. He returned the mortgage of the home, telling his family that he would not go to the Foreign after all. They were happy, but they were mortified when he told them he was joining a political party. They tried everything but were not able to dissuade him.

From that day onwards, Abbas never looked back. The things he had wanted from the Foreign—money and women—became irrelevant after he had lots of both.

Smiling at the people, he waved. They were his people. He ruled them. And they were hailing a killer who had murdered the soul of the town. He felt like crying, running up to the place where he had killed his uncle and smashing his head on the memorial stone. Why was Sharif Miyan's dying, blood-soaked face becoming clearer with each passing day? And how would Allah punish him for his act?

Dev wanted to kill the grinning, waving Abbas in front of the people. He put his hand in his pocket and gripped the smooth butt of the gun. The gun felt strange in his hand, as though it were a living being, squirming to break free, to do what it was built to do. Dev wondered about his purpose in life—he thought it might be to help the gun achieve its purpose. He removed his hand from the butt of the gun and watched Abbas Haq.

He would find time when Abbas was alone and, then, he would tell Abbas what he had seen all those years ago.

"What do you mean, escaped?" Jeet shouted at the ward boy in the Amarnath Mental Asylum.

Anita put a calming hand on his shoulder.

"Don't you understand what I'm saying?" the ward boy said with an exaggerated movement of his hand. "Does he not understand?" he asked Anita. "He killed Dr Joshi and Atmaram. The police are chasing him."

Jeet felt the blood drain from his face. He looked at Anita. Her face was ashen.

"Dev and Avi..." she said instantly. Her voice was like cracking glass.

She dialled Avi's number. It rang five times and then she was on his voicemail. She redialled many times. The same metallic voice came on every single time.

The ward boy dialled the number that had been given to him by Inspector Kamble.

"Sahib, two of the four people who visited Jagan two days ago are here. A woman and a man," he whispered into the phone.

"Hold them! I'm coming to the asylum," Kamble shouted so loudly that the ward boy jerked the phone away from his ear. He ran to the asylum office to stop them, but they were gone.

Dev stood in front of the Party building. He had been following Abbas for the last two hours, but had found no opportunity to take the gun out of his pocket. And now the bastard had disappeared inside his party office. He was getting frustrated and his hands were beginning to shake.

The office was in the middle of the crowded Budhawar Market. The market streets were filled with vegetable and fruit carts. People were busy haggling over prices. Bikers had taken over the rest of the street, with their thumbs on the horn, adding their screeching notes to the cacophony.

A little girl tapped him on the back. She was holding *gajras* in her frail hands.

"Do you want a *gajra* for your wife?" she asked in a smart, coached manner.

Wife. He closed his eyes and breathed in the intoxicating fragrance. A *gajra,* a wife, a little house, laughter and peace—these were things he had never known. After spending just two days with Anita, those things sounded so beautiful. The gun was a constant reminder of the choices he had made. Abbas could not be pardoned, even for a beautiful dream. He shook his head at the girl and she moved on.

The entrance of the office was guarded by two bearded men. The bulge of the guns tucked in their waistbands was very obvious. Dev took a deep breath. A brew of smells—ripe fruits, mouldy vegetables and hot dust—hit him. It was the smell of his childhood, spent in roaming through areas like the Budhawar Market with his friends. He wondered if he would survive the next few minutes. Would that smell be his last memory? Would he ever meet his friends again? Would they forgive him for doing it? He knew he had no answers to those questions. Not all questions are answered, are they? Just like the question papers of countless exams he had written in school—you could pass even if you did not answer all the questions. Life is not like that. You fail a few questions and you fail in life. Why did he not remove his hand from Bappa's throat? Why did he not do something to help Sharif Miyan? But he knew the answer to one question: What would he do if he met Abbas again? He walked towards the office door.

There was a rule in the Party—no tea inside the office. Abbas had been unable to hold a cup of tea for the last twenty years. His nightmares always included boiling tea, with the little brick-coloured bubbles exploding on the surface. Sometimes the tea boiled over. Those were the times when Abbas woke up crying. His wife Shabnam asked him about it a few times after their marriage, and he had reacted so violently that she never dared to ask him again.

He could not help but admire his posters every time he saw them—the son of a rickshaw puller, now the chief of a prominent political party in this town, who was expected to win by an unprecedented margin of votes in the coming elections. There were many people in the party who begrudged his presence, his power, but they could do nothing. The people of Amrapur loved him and his speeches. Some people called them inflammatory, divisive and harmful to the peace and harmony of the town. A smile spread on his face every time he heard that word. Has anything ever been achieved by harmony? What would the leaders do with harmony? Why would people come to listen to his speeches in droves if they wanted harmony? Elections can never be won by harmony.

He wondered what his long-dead father would think of him now. And what would that bastard Sharif Miyan think? All they had wanted him to become was a teastall owner, as though that stupid teastall was some Hotel Taj Mahal.

But there was something he could never understand. There was always a dull ache in his heart every time he thought about Sharif Miyan. There was the overpowering guilt he felt every time he saw the spot where he had killed him. And that nightmare about boiling tea. Why?

Dev walked up to the guards and they all scrutinised him very carefully.

"I need to meet Abbas bhai," he said, hoping his voice was not shaky.

"What for?" a guard said, flashing his paan-red teeth.

"I am a reporter and need to cover his story for the upcoming elections."

"You don't look like a reporter," the other guard said.

"What does a reporter look like?"

"Get out. Abbas bhai is busy right now."

"I'll go. But you can tell your boss that you shooed away a reporter who wanted to write a lot of good stuff about him. I'm not sure what I will write in the article now," he said and made to walk away.

"Wait," the paan-chewing man said. He glanced at the other man for a brief moment. "Wait here. Let me ask Abbas bhai," he said and walked inside.

The other man stared at Dev as though he was devising ways of torturing him. Dev smiled.

"Abbas bhai?"

"What is it, Qutub?" Abbas said. A big glass, brimming with his favourite whisky nestled in his hand. He was sprawled on a diwan, lost in thought, his eyes red. His close confidantes, silent and waiting for their leader to come out of his melancholy, were nursing their drinks.

"There is a reporter outside who wants to meet you," Qutub said.

He regretted interrupting Abbas bhai. Abbas was already irritated with him for being a little less intelligent. He always called him monkey-man. And now he had given him one more opportunity to get mad.

"Ask him to go fuck his own sister!" Abbas said loudly.

Qutub flinched. He stood outside the room for a moment, with the words of the reporter buzzing in his head. Abbas bhai always lamented that nobody wrote good things about him in the newspapers. He was known to have harmed reporters who had said a few nasty things about him. This reporter was promising to write something good about him. If only he could summon the courage to talk to Abbas bhai once more.

Abbas solved his problem by walking out. "You're still here? Is your penis caught in the door?"

"No Abbas bhai," Qutub said sheepishly.

"Then?"

"This reporter said that he admires you a lot. And that he wants to write some very good things about you," he said and swallowed hard. He suddenly realised that he had insinuated that nothing good was written about Abbas bhai. It was true, but it would cause him serious trouble if Abbas bhai took offence. He took heart when Abbas bhai stood with his head down, patting his long beard.

"Okay. Send him in," he said.

Qutub ran outside before Abbas bhai could change his mind. "You!" Qutub pointed a finger at Dev. "Come in."

Dev entered the Party office. Once a murderer, always a murderer. He smiled bitterly.

"Why are you smiling?" Qutub asked him.

"Meeting Abbas bhai has been a long cherished wish," he said.

"You are lucky to meet him," Qutub said, his chest swelling with pride. "Very soon he will become the chief minister of the state. And I know he will become the prime minister one day."

"I am sure of that," Dev said.

Would Abbas recognise him? He felt like laughing at the thought. He didn't recognise himself anymore. The twelve-year-old boy who had witnessed Abbas murder Sharif Miyan was long gone.

The nauseating smell of paan, *gutka,* cigarettes and alcohol had settled in the dank, musty rooms of the office. The walls were covered with colourful posters of Abbas in various poses.

Dev desperately tried to trace the way towards the backdoor, in case his plan didn't work smoothly. He saw none, but knew that he had to pull it off anyway—just one-and-a-half-hours remained before Avi fell in his own trap.

Avi was shivering slightly and tried to control it. There was no going back now. This was the time to relax, to be in control. He had done all the planning—just the execution remained. It had worked every single time since that train journey, this never-ending cycle of planning and execution. He had created a business empire based on it. He could certainly eradicate his past. In the next few hours, he would end the nightmare forever.

The ties of blood had not worked, but the lure of money had. He had learned that a long time back. You stand in the middle of the road shouting for help and no one even comes close to you. You shout words like lakhs and crores, and everyone lines up, even family. He wanted to stand outside Shah Sadan and shout that the family was nothing but a bunch of slimy, greedy arseholes. He felt like laughing at the reaction his father would have—he had always sided with the family in their relentless humiliation of his mother and his dreams. He hoped that Dev would not put a spanner in the works. What could he be thinking—the eternal saviour? Thanks Dev, but I can take care of myself now. I can take care of you too. I don't need rescuing anymore. Not after you said that you regretted it.

His phone chirped, perhaps for the millionth time. Anita's number blinked on the screen. He pushed the green button.

"Avi, you are absolutely wrong in assuming that we regret saving you." She sounded breathless and relieved at the same time.

"Anita, I never had any regrets. And I had assumed that all of you didn't have any either. All I had were nightmares of that day. But not because of regret," he said softly.

"We all had our nightmares Avi. And I am so happy that we were there for you that day. I would do it again, even now. If someone tried to harm you, I would kill him," she said.

"Then why the regret? Why the guilt?"

She was silent for a while, then said, "The regret was for the loss of our childhood. The day we killed Bappa, we were damned. Did you ever have a moment of true happiness or peace?"

"What I'm doing is to eradicate the memory of it, once and for all."

"No, Avi. What you're doing is giving yourself another lifetime of guilt. We had no choice twenty years ago. You have it now."

"So what do you want?" he shouted. "That this man should kill us all?"

"No. All I want you to do is be here with us. We committed that crime together. We stay together and confront this man. We don't do what he wants us to do, Avi. That includes setting up this trap. We play his game and we lose."

"Now you're talking like him," he said and switched off the phone.

The plan had been set in motion. It was pointless to change it now.

Anita, stunned by Avi's impassive, cold voice screamed, "Avi. Please! Come back! Jagan has escaped…" but the line had been cut. She frantically dialled Avi's number again and got the message that the phone was switched off. "God! I should have told him earlier."

Jeet had no idea why he did it, but he dialled Maggie's number. Her picture flashed on his mobile screen. She was smiling in that photograph. It was a smile that could light up a bleak day, a smile that he fell in love with, twice. There were no traces of that smile on Anita's face. It had deserted her long ago.

After the fifth ring, he heard her voice. "Hi. I had to leave for India in a hurry. Please leave a message."

A cold dread spread all over his body. "Oh my God," he whispered.

She shrank back at the wretchedness in his voice. She had seen him like that once before, when they were hiding behind the counter of Sharif Miyan's teastall. His chubby cheeks were trembling with fear and helplessness, and his eyes were glazed over like shattered marbles.

"I have to stop her!" he said.

She took the phone from his hand. The screen had the photograph of a woman. She had blue eyes and a familiar smile. Anita redialled the number and heard the voicemail message.

She grabbed his shoulders and shook him. "Jeet! She must be airborne right now."

Like an automaton, he dialled the airport. The flight had departed three hours ago. Three hours more to go.

"We cannot stop it, can we?" he said.

"No," Anita replied softly.

He staggered a little. She held him.

Abbas was sprawled on a stained, red sofa. There were three other men in the room who stood still, as though part of the furniture. They all looked like the men standing at the door.

"What do you want?" Abbas growled.

Dev let out a tiny sigh of relief. Abbas had not recognised him. Abbas himself was unrecognisable. The scrawny young man, who had the diffident manner of a petty thief, had grown into a rotund, hairy man. His loose kurta failed to hide his huge belly. The beard was prematurely white. He had a conical head and short tapering legs.

Taking a deep breath to calm the buzzing in his head, Dev said, "I am here for a story for the *Times of India*."

"Where is your identity card?" Abbas said. There was a black birthmark on his right cheek that had sprouted hair. It was perhaps the only feature he had carried through the twenty years. He used to scratch it like an insect bite.

"I am a freelancer. If the editors like my articles, they pay me money," Dev said and removed a pad from his cloth bag as a distraction. "I really admire what you have done for this town, Abbas bhai. I intend to write a very good article."

Abbas grunted. He patted his beard, wondering why this reporter would write a good story about him. Most journalists were hostile towards him ever since he had beaten up a local reporter—which was fine by him. The sister-fucking reporters could write whatever they wanted, as long as the people were with him.

"How do you plan to go about improving the condition of the town once elected? The current MLA has virtually destroyed everything."

Abbas sat up on the sofa. He liked the tone of this reporter. He launched into a hateful tirade against the incumbent MLA.

Dev saw him gesticulating theatrically and understood what people liked about Abbas. It was his naked hatred that fanned their deepest feelings of anger. Dev tuned him out. After several minutes of Abbas's monologue, Dev decided that it was time.

"Abbas bhai, I know quite a few things about your opponent that could be very useful to you," he said in a hushed tone.

Abbas peered at him with narrowed eyes. "What is it?"

Dev looked around the room eyeing the men. "Can I talk to you in private?" he whispered.

Abbas patted his beard. Cold sweat erupted all over Dev's body. An imperceptible shiver ran down his spine.

"Why not say in front of my men?"

"I have told my source in your opposition camp that only you would hear it," he said, pursing his lips in a thin, determined line.

"What makes you think that I can't ask these men to extract it from you?" Abbas said with his palms on his knees.

"That's possible. But then, you are a smart man, Abbas bhai. A great man, actually. A visionary who knows it is important to have followers like me."

Abbas stared at him with his red, hooded eyes. The men began to fidget, but nobody spoke. The clammy, suffocating room suddenly became hotter. The angry breaths of Abbas's men seemed deafening. Every line on Abbas's face could be clearly seen.

Abbas finally nodded at his men and they walked out of the room. The last man closed the door behind him.

"Now," Abbas said, bending towards him as though indulging a child, "what is it that you have to tell me?"

"I have to show you something," Dev said and put his hand in the cloth bag. He clasped the butt of the gun and hoped that it would not slip out of his sweaty palm. "Listen very carefully, Abbas," he said.

Abbas recoiled at the change in tone. His face contorted in anger. His mouth opened to say something nasty.

"I have a gun in my hand, inside this bag," Dev said and brought the pistol out.

Abbas stared at it as though he was seeing one for the first time. He began to shake. "What…What do you want?" he said, glancing at the door.

"Abbas, look at me," Dev said.

Sensing that Abbas was going to bolt from the divan and make a run for the door, Dev stood up and pointed the gun at him. His hand was steady, his voice cold.

"You take one step towards that door and you will die," he said.

The strength went out of Abbas's body. His taut shoulders went limp.

"You didn't recognise me, you bastard?" Dev said. "You killed Sharif Miyan."

A faint realisation flickered in Abbas's eyes. He chewed his lips savagely.

"Abbas, it's me—Dev."

"I am sorry," Abbas sobbed.

"No you're not. Not yet," Dev said through clenched teeth. "We walk out of this door, like long lost friends. I will have the gun in your back. I don't want to use it."

Abbas looked at him as though he was too shocked to understand.

"Get up," Dev said quickly. There was very little time before the men outside lost their patience. "Let's go." Dev put his arm over Abbas's shoulder. "You tell your men that we have to meet someone very important. And you don't want any of them escorting you. Just ask for the keys to your jeep."

Abbas didn't move.

"Do you hear me, you bastard?" Dev buried the barrel of the gun in his ribs.

"I'm going to get you. You are a dead man already," Abbas stammered.

"I don't want to splatter your brains here. But if you talk once more, I will do it."

Abbas looked panic-stricken. He opened his mouth in a silent cry. His lips pulled back on his teeth.

"You make one tiny noise and I pull the trigger," Dev said, stunned by the viciousness in his own voice. He tapped Abbas's shoulder, motioning him to walk.

"What are you going to do?"

"Just get out of here for now."

"My men will sense something's wrong."

"That would be too bad for you," he said and cocked the hammer.

They walked out of the room. The men, standing in a ring outside, waiting to be called back, were surprised to see them. Dev gave a tiny jerk to the gun barrel.

"This man has something that I need badly. I will be back in a while. Don't follow me," Abbas said, his voice breaking.

The men looked at each other as they spread out to let them go.

"Give me the keys of the jeep."

A man handed him the keys. Dev then prodded Abbas towards the jeep. His hand was slick with sweat. The butt of the gun was hot. It was almost over. It would be impossible for Abbas's men to follow them once they were inside that jeep. Nudging the gun in Abbas's ribs, he whispered, "Walk faster."

Qutub hero-worshipped Abbas bhai. The fire in his words gave a meaning to Qutub's life. Like a pet dog, he just wanted to be near Abbas bhai, ignoring the ridicule from everyone about his lack of intelligence. And like a dog, he had an instinct for his master's safety. Qutub saw Abbas bhai's face and knew there was something very wrong with him. He was sweating like never before. He thought about asking Abbas bhai if he was all right, but was mortally afraid of his anger. Nobody dared to question Abbas bhai. He had once cut Shafiq's lip for questioning what he was doing. But Qutub knew something was very wrong. He decided to take the risk. If Abbas bhai got angry later, he would gladly cut his own face.

"Abbas bhai!"

Dev clenched his teeth as he heard the shout. He looked behind and saw the man who had stopped him at the door running towards them. He had a paan box in his hand.

"Abbas bhai, you forgot your paan box," the man said as he reached them.

In one hand, Abbas had the jeep's keys and the other hand was across Dev's shoulder.

Qutub looked at Dev. Something passed between their eyes—a flash of realisation.

Dev pulled out the gun. He grabbed Abbas's throat and shielded himself with his body.

"Get back!" he shouted at Qutub who stood with his mouth agape. "You move, and Abbas dies!" Dev screamed and dragged Abbas.

The men stood rooted to their places, as though the sight of Abbas bhai being dragged away was something that was beyond their comprehension.

Dev got into the driver's seat and slid to the passenger seat, the gun barrel glued to Abbas's head.

"Tell them not to follow us," he said to Abbas.

Abbas nodded at his men.

"Get in the driver's seat."

Abbas did.

"Drive."

The crowded Budhawar Market street was still buzzing with frenetic activity. All of it had happened in barely a few seconds. People were yet to fathom the enormity of what was happening.

Dev lowered the gun to hide from the crowd and pointed it at Abbas's heart. "Drive!" he shouted.

Abbas put the jeep in gear. It lurched ahead.

It took them almost half-an-hour to leave the Budhawar Market street. All the while, Dev looked behind to check if Abbas's men were following them.

"What do you want?" Abbas asked, finally summoning the courage to speak. His voice was quivering so badly that Dev almost laughed.

"You are going to confess to all your crimes, Abbas," he said.

Abbas stared at him.

"You thought I was going to kill you, didn't you?"

Abbas said nothing. The man held a gun a few inches from his heart and didn't want to kill him. It was unbelievable. Abbas could barely see, as sweat poured down his face. He wiped it with his sleeve. His hand brushed the barrel of the gun.

"I have repented," Abbas moaned.

Dev laughed till the tears came to his eyes. "You bastard! I saw you at the spot where you killed Sharif Miyan, fooling all the people. You had that stupid grin on your face. Some joke, eh Abbas?"

Abbas was quiet for a few minutes. The gun brushed him every now and then.

"I... I am sorry Dev," he said, swallowing loudly.

Dev said nothing and peered through the windshield of the jeep, as though reliving a terrible memory. He felt very tired, suddenly. His grip on the gun loosened. He looked at the man who was responsible for his nightmares and wondered if he should shoot him and just get it over with.

"Go to the *Janmat* office," Dev said.

All this while, Abbas had been thinking that they would go to the police station. He had a chance to escape there. Surely, the mother-fucker would get shot by the policemen. But now the bastard wanted him to go to the local newspaper. The reporter whom he'd had beaten up was from *Janmat*. They would gladly record his confession. He chewed his lips furiously. Once they reached the newspaper office, he would have no chance. The man would extract the confession from him. And then, perhaps, he would let him go. The newspaper would publish his past. There was no proof against him, but the newspapers would lap it up and publish it with added masala. Nobody would vote for him. People would hate him.

The same people who cheered for him just a few hours ago. He had to escape.

That was when the motorcycles rammed into the jeep, on Dev's side.

The rickety jeep shuddered at the impact. Dev saw that Abbas's men were sprawled on the bonnet. Abbas braked hard. Dev's head crashed against the low top of the jeep and, for a few moments, everything blacked out.

Qutub lunged at Dev and caught his hand holding the gun. Qutub was a big man with big hands, and Dev winced from the pain. The gun was no longer pointing at Abbas.

"Jump, Abbas bhai!" Qutub shouted

Abbas, who till then had been sitting in the driver's seat paralysed, suddenly jumped out of the jeep.

Dev fired.

The people on the street, who were watching the jeep as though it were some kind of entertainment, ran at the sound of gunshot.

The windshield of the jeep cracked, with a round hole in the middle.

Dev raised his left hand high and, summoning all his energy, crashed his fist into Qutub's nose and felt it crunch. Qutub moaned and loosened his grip on Dev's hand. Dev raised his hand again and smashed it on the busted nose. Blood spurted out and Qutub released Dev's hand.

The other man who had crashed into the jeep grabbed Dev's neck from the back and pulled him out. Dev thrust his elbow into the man's ribs as he fell out. Then he lowered his head and whipped it into the man's face. Howling, the man released Dev's neck. Dev quickly turned back and kicked him in his crotch with all his might. The man slumped to the ground.

Dev looked all around, but could not see Abbas. He screamed in rage. He felt like shooting the two men writhing on the ground. He held the gun between the eyes of the man who was thrashing about, cupping his genitals. The man suddenly went still, his eyes bulging. Dev cocked the hammer and pressed his finger on the trigger.

The urge to pull the trigger was all consuming. Dev was shocked that his hand was absolutely steady. The man let out a low moan. More men were running towards the jeep. The man looked at them with hope in his eyes. It would be so easy to just wipe that hope—all Dev had to do was move his finger.

But the man was not Abbas. He had not killed Sharif Miyan.

Dev's hand shook.

Dev kicked the man in his stomach and, shoving the gun in his pocket, ran.

The road curving along the hillock was freshly tarred. The light was feeble and partially illuminated the school perched atop the hillock. The giant clock-tower had stopped working years ago, and time was frozen. Along that road was the little path that led to the riverside—a path they had all walked with happy hearts, a path they could be walking for the last time. Fear was a living thing, wrapping Anita in its slick embrace. She looked at Jeet who had a faraway look in his eyes, perhaps searching for an airplane in the sky.

"Are we ready?" she asked

"Yeah," he said.

They walked down the curving road. The sky was darkening and rubbing out the horizon. The birds sounded irritated. Anita had never gone to the riverside at night. She wondered if Dev and Avi ever had. A heart-wrenching sadness engulfed her. Would they ever be happy again? As they were when they made that little fort? She remembered how immersed Jeet was when making that fort, as though it was to be his greatest creation. And perhaps it was. Everything else that he made since was an echo of that destroyed fort.

"Will you take me to one of your exhibitions, Jeet?" she said. She felt like hugging him.

"Yes," he said and smiled. The smile didn't reach his eyes. "I need to tell you something Anita."

She stopped and looked at him. She had always known this time would come, when the chubby boy from her childhood would confess to her what she always knew.

"I loved you from the day I first saw you," he lowered his eyes as though ashamed of what he had said. "We may not survive this. I don't know if I should have said this. But it sort of felt like the right thing to say." He looked at her. She was staring into the distance as though she had not heard what he had said. They stood there for a long time, the darkness engulfing them.

She nodded. "I saw it a long time ago. You used to look at me so many times. So many people stared at me, Jeet. But I never felt the weight of your eyes," she said and smiled.

"I love Maggie. I will always love her."

"I know you do," she said and hugged him fiercely.

⁂

This time, Avi found the road that led to the riverside. He looked behind to ascertain whether Inspector Mhatre was around, but he never saw him. He wondered if he had made a mistake by relying on Jayant. The trees looked skeletal. The night creatures were noisy. He looked all around many times, wondering where the attack would come from. But the woods were directionless and engulfed him.

That was when he saw the outline of a man, or he thought he saw it. It was like a flash of memory. One moment it was there, and the very next it had disappeared. Perhaps it was the same man he saw three days ago in front of the hotel. He quickly pulled out the gun he was carrying. That gun was the reason he had travelled by train. He knew he might have to use it. Planning is everything. But he did not see the man again. He searched around the patch where he thought he'd seen him. He cursed Jayant.

The blow landed on the back of his head. Avi was airborne for a fraction of a second, and then he was floating up, leaving his body behind. His vision was blurred and he fell face down. The ground smelled of rotting grass and animal shit. The pain exploded in his head. He screamed but no sound came out. He tried to turn to look at the man who had hit him but could not. His body was paralysed, incapable of obeying his brain. He heard a voice. It sounded as though someone was talking to him with a loudspeaker inside his head. The sound was deafening and incomprehensible. A toe crashed into his ribs. He clearly heard the crack of the breaking rib. He yelped like a dog. Another kick. Another crack.

Then there was darkness.

⁂

Jeet heard his friend cry out.

"Avi!" he shouted and ran. Anita ran behind him.

A few seconds later a shriek echoed in the jungle. Unable to discern where it was coming from, he ran and called Avi's name. Coming out of the thick overgrowth of the bushes, he saw Avi sprawled on the ground. There was a man with a raised club-like object about to land a blow on Avi.

"No!" Jeet shouted and ran towards him.

The man turned towards Jeet and Anita. His face was covered with a black and white cloth. His eyes shone like an animal's. He turned and disappeared into the jungle. Jeet ran up to the bloody heap that was his friend. "Avi!"

"Oh My God!" Anita screamed.

Jeet turned Avi over and felt his pulse. It was unsteady. His breathing was fitful. The back of his head was soaked in blood.

Manoj was furious. Every moment away from Anita was a lifetime. She was his purpose, his reason for existence, and she didn't even know it. What was his life without her? He had a soul-destroying clerk's job in an obscure government department. Every day spent in the company of musty files, corpse-like co-workers and overbearing, subservience-demanding superiors. Nobody's secrets were worth knowing there. The only reason for their existence was to make him like them—a walking, talking, file-handling carcass. Along the way, the wife had popped out two children, his contribution to the worthless continuation of his lineage. Why did everyone celebrate their births? They called them miracles, those little shitting, bawling creatures spawned by him.

Two years ago, when the memory of Anita had returned to rescue him from the morass of existence, he had felt liberated. There were so many secrets to know. How did she look now? How had she lived away from him? Did she remember him? The end of his quest to know more was near. He couldn't wait any longer.

The lunatic had a chance to eliminate three of them and he didn't do it. He had disappeared.

"Aho! What are you thinking again? Always lost in your daydreams," his wife brayed. She wore a purple sari, discoloured in many places. She was on her haunches, sweeping the biscuit crumbs that their son had dropped off the floor. Her hair was thin and straggly.

"Leave me alone."

"I wish I had. My biggest mistake in life was marrying you," she said. "What are you dreaming of anyway? Some naked girls?"

"None of your business."

"Everything is my business!" she yelled in anger. "Your pathetic little clerk's salary is just not enough to feed these children anymore."

He ignored her. She stood two inches from him with her hands on her hips, her corpulent body stinking.

"You cannot ignore me, you little bastard."

He lunged at her and grabbed her hair. "You bitch! You motherfucking bitch!" he said and slapped her hard.

She slapped him back. He kicked her in the stomach. She cried out in pain, her misshapen yellow teeth and black gums a stomach-churning sight. The first memory of kissing that mouth suddenly came alive. It had tasted of stale tea and onions.

"I will kill you!" he shouted and hit her again.

She laughed hysterically, mocking him, "You can't even kill a fly, you bastard."

Her terrible smell, her fetid mouth, her deformed face—all created to ridicule him—had to be obliterated. He kicked her so hard that she collapsed on the floor, clutching her stomach. He grabbed her throat and sat on top of her.

He squeezed.

"Baba, no!" his children screamed. His older son, who was eight years old, rushed to him and tried to prise his hands. Manoj pushed him back so hard that his head banged against the wall and he passed out. His daughter stood in the doorway crying. Manoj squeezed harder. Her tongue jutted out of her mouth. A beautiful, heart-warming sight. Her eyes bulged, brimming with the naked realisation of an imminent death. He laughed. "You thought I was joking?" he shouted and squeezed harder. Anita was waiting for him to get rid of his past and be with her. He would not let her down. She came back for him because he had wanted her to. He squeezed.

He opened his eyes and saw his wife's grotesque face. "Ugly bitch. Can't even die gracefully." The soft flesh of her throat had yielded. His fingers had dug into her throat. Plucked the life right out of her. He laughed. He released her neck. Her head plopped down with a little thump. He got up and spat on her. "Bitch," he said. His daughter's whimpering was the only sound in the house.

"Shut up!" he shouted at his daughter. She ran off.

"Blood-sucking vermin," he said and walked to the sink in the kitchen. He washed his hands and wiped them on his pants.

Walking out of the house, into a beautiful future with the woman who was his destiny, he decided to finish the work the lunatic should have done.

Jeet touched a sticky drop of blood that had remained on his hand even after washing. Avi's blood. His friend, perhaps, wouldn't need that little drop. Jeet's clothes were covered in dried blood. Anita sat next to him, her eyes closed, her head leaning on the back of the wooden chair.

Jeet had had to call Mr Mehra, who, incidentally, was the Finance Secretary, to get the complete attention of the doctors in the Amrapur General Hospital. The doctors had told Jeet that Avi's vital signs were very weak. That it was going to be a difficult journey to consciousness for his friend.

He wondered where Dev was. All of this would not have happened if Dev had been with them. He would have done something. Jeet felt like laughing at that. It was as if he was a twelve-year-old again, and Dev was the do-all, know-all superman they worshipped.

"Why are you smiling?" Anita said, her eyes still closed, mysteriously aware of his smile.

"You know what I was thinking? That if Dev was here, he would not have let it happen," he said, shaking his head a little.

She pressed his hand, looking straight at him with her dimpled smile.

"We were so great together, weren't we?" he said.

"Yes, we were."

Suddenly feeling cold, Jeet hugged himself. At any moment, the medical staff could come and inform them that Avi was dead. Avi with his little rabbit. The school topper who called him fatty with no malice. Who diligently built the fort wall, when he actually wanted to build the fort entrance, or the watch-tower, because fatty wanted him to. Who threw the stone, shattering Bappa's eye, because Bappa had hit fatty. And fatty had let him walk into the trap, because he thought of him as a conceited, unrecognisable man—not the twelve-year-old owl.

"You know, he called me," he said.

"Who?"

"The man who did this to Avi."

She turned him towards herself. "What did you say?"

"You heard it, Anita. He called me yesterday," he said without looking at her.

"Why the hell did you not tell us?"

"He told me I would have to make a choice." Tears welled up in his eyes.

"What are you saying?"

"He knows about Maggie. He said she would come for me. And I will have to choose between one of you and her."

She was silent for a long time. "You don't have to beat yourself over it. I would have done the same thing if I were in your place," she said, finally.

Dev touched the memorial stone where Sharif Miyan served his tea to the town. It was warm, slowly getting cooled by the night, after another day in the town's heat.

"I am sorry, Sharif Miyan," he said, "There is no justice for you."

He had abandoned his friends. Avi was in terrible danger, but he was blinded by rage. Revenge. He laughed. That's what it was. And now Abbas had escaped. His friends were dragged into it. He was responsible for dragging them everywhere with him, wasn't he?

Dev dialled Anita's mobile number from a public telephone booth in one of the countless dark alleys of the town.

"It's me," Dev said. "What happened?"

Sobbing, she said, "He tried to kill Avi."

Dev closed his eyes. He had lost the most precious thing. The town had extracted its revenge. All his feeble attempts to escape the town were a mirage. It had systematically torn his little world apart—his father, his mother, his friends, his love.

"He is in the hospital. In the trauma centre," Anita said. "The doctors say he may not live through it."

"Leave this town immediately, Anita. Please," he said softly.

"No. We stay. We face the consequences of what we did. All of us."

What they did in a different life. Why are sins carried over from a past life? Why should punishment be delayed? Why did he ask them twenty years ago to run, to hide?

"I can't come anywhere near you," he said. "I have done something that I thought was right, but it has gone horribly wrong."

"What have you done?"

"I wanted Abbas to confess. But he escaped. It is going to end very badly, Anita."

"I know," she said.

"I'll be watching you two. I will not let this man get to you," he said and disconnected the phone.

Inspector Kamble was in a rage. He stood next to the dead body of Sub-Inspector Mhatre. Someone had attacked and killed one of his men. It had never happened before.

"I am going to find out who did this to you, Mhatre," he said. His eyes were blood-shot. "Someone, clean him up!" he shouted at the morgue staff. They cowered at the sight of him.

He stormed out of the morgue and lit a cigarette. "Bhute, take me to the hospital where that other man is admitted," he said.

"Did you see that man?" Kamble asked Jeet and Anita.

"No," Jeet said.

"Why did he attack your friend?"

"Don't know," Jeet said.

Kamble thought something passed between the man and the woman sitting in front of him. They knew why their friend had been attacked. And it scared them.

"You do not have to hide from me. The way I see it, you two were at the spot and it could have been done by you," Kamble said and stared at them.

They said nothing.

"Jeet Mehra, your father is a big bureaucrat, right?" Kamble asked in a low and vicious voice.

Jeet said nothing.

"You think I will not hesitate to arrest you?"

"I don't know who did this, Kamble sahib," Jeet said slowly, as though chewing each word.

Kamble felt a sickening anger. How many times would he have to bow down to these big officials and their kin? Even when one of his own lay dead in the morgue. With great difficulty, he stopped himself from jumping at the smug son of a bitch sitting in front of him.

"You two cannot leave the town till this matter is resolved. A man was killed. My man. I am going to find who did it," Kamble said and rose. He tapped his baton on Jeet's shoulder once and left.

Jagan stood inside the palatial Wada that lay in ruins, its splendour a dimming memory. There were no more vehicles parked in the front yard. No multitudes of people coming and going and waiting. His father was gone, and so was Bappa. With him, the pride of the Bhoite Wada was gone too.

He cried. He was the coward, the weakling who should have died—not Bappa. He was a brother who had protected him until his last breath.

He ran up the stairs to the terrace. The unused tank was forever hidden from the world. Jagan's sanctuary. Unknown to everyone, he hid there. The sun rose and set many times. The dampness was comforting, familiar. The darkness was his long lost friend. Not even Bappa could find him there, so what chance did the pesky policemen have? When he was sure no one was looking for him, he stepped out from his hiding place.

The four people who had visited him—ghosts from his past—were somehow linked to Bappa's death. They knew how he died, how the river became his grave. Dev, Anita, Jeet, Avi. They were all grown up, but they would still be scared of him. Especially, Jeet. He would find them and ask them about his brother. The old gun, once proudly owned by his father, would help him.

He was alive again, with anticipation running through him like a giant wave. It would be just like the old days, and this time he would do all the work, guided by the spirit of his dead brother. He gazed up at the sky.

"I will find out what happened, Bappa," he said. "Just be with me, okay?"

Anita's phone rang. It was an unknown number.

"You have to come to the school, you bitch. Bring your friends too," the man said. His voice was a vicious whisper, hurting her ear. She could not speak.

"You know something, bitch? All that you and your friends are going through is just because of you. Now how do you feel about that? All of you in the same classroom, in the next one hour," the man said and the call ended.

She kept staring at the phone, not knowing what to make of it. She was responsible for everything?

"It was him?" Jeet asked.

"Yes."

"What does he want?"

"He wants us all to come to the school and go to exactly the same classroom."

Jeet nodded. "So it is time to end this, isn't it?" he said.

"Yes. It is."

The man switched off the phone and smiled. A toothy smile ringed by a white beard. The four bastards would pay for ruining his life. They were all back where he wanted them. And now he would be very slow with them. He would make them beg for their lives. And then he would laugh at them. Laugh till tears of joy came to his eyes.

Manoj dialled Bokade's phone number, wondering whether the bastard would pick it up. Surprisingly, he did.

"We have to finish this off tonight. I have done what you wanted me to," Manoj whispered. His fear of the class teacher was still alive.

"Come to the school—the same class where I taught you."

The memory of breathless fear, strangely, gave him comfort.

Inspector Kamble was stunned by what he saw. The woman was not murdered, she was butchered. Blood slowly oozed out of her throat.

"Who is her husband?"

"Manoj Jadhav, sahib. The neighbours saw him running out of the house."

Kamble had four deaths in the last three days. One of them was his own man. The town was small. It didn't deserve so many deaths. Could all of them be related? He had a deep, gnawing feeling that they were.

"Jeet Mehra and Anita Kulkarni, what the hell are you hiding?"

Kamble followed Anita and Jeet as they walked up the hillock to the school. There were no lights on the path and the overgrowth of the trees gave him ample cover. He had never done surveillance like that. That kind of stupidity was for the police in bigger cities like Mumbai. He always wondered why his friends in Mumbai did that. If you are suspicious about someone, you just ask him. Everyone talks after a few hours in the darkness of the special rooms in the police station. He couldn't do that to the only son of the top bureaucrat of India, though. He had agonised over informing his superiors that Ramashankar Mehra's son was involved in something murky, but decided that it was better to keep it hidden. He would love to get his fingers around the throat of the man who killed Mhatre.

Three months was all that Jeet had spent in the school, but its every detail was etched in his memory. The buildings had not changed. There were the same six buildings covered in green paint, standing in a semicircle. There was the rocky playground, where many games of football and cricket were played. The noise of the day was a faint echo. Stillness had settled on the school.

Jeet looked at Anita. Her lips were drawn in a thin line, the way they used to be when she was either terribly frightened or angry. He held her hand—it was clammy and cold. They took the coiling stairs to the second floor of one of the buildings. Their old classroom was situated at the end of the aisle.

"Don't worry. One way or another, this ends tonight," he whispered.

They walked inside the darkened classroom.

A harsh yellow light from a big torch fell on their faces.

"I have been waiting for you," a voice from their childhood said. It was the voice that taught them hatred. A voice they had always associated with the most dreaded moments of their lives. Bokade's voice.

Bokade laughed. In the stillness of the classroom, they were back to being twelve-year-olds, with their tormentor laughing at their terror.

"Bokade!" Jeet said in a whisper.

"You four bastards destroyed my life. All I wanted was to teach you." His voice reverberated in the hollowness of the empty school.

Jeet looked at Bokade with horrified fascination as he raised his hand. He was holding a gun. Anita stared at it with her mouth open, but the scream refused to come out.

"You…You sent us those messages?" Jeet said.

"No. That was me."

Anita knew that voice—the high-pitched voice of the boy who used to follow her like a smitten dog. The creep. His voice had not changed at all.

"Who...?" Jeet said.

"Shut your fucking mouth Mehra!" Manoj screamed. "She has recognised me."

"Manoj? You did this to us?" Anita whispered.

"Yes, Anita. I love you. These three bastards must have told you so many lies about me. Bokade, shoot him now," Manoj said and took a step towards Anita.

"Not yet," Bokade said.

Manoj stopped. He gaped at Bokade. "What?"

Bokade had a steel cylinder in his hand. He pulled the little knob at the top and it extended to four times its length.

"I have been waiting for a long time for this," Bokade said and whipped the air with the antenna. It made a sound like a viper's hiss.

"Kill him, you fucking retard!" Manoj shouted. His well-laid plan was falling apart at the last moment. Bokade kicked him hard between the legs. He collapsed on the ground, clutching his crotch and howling.

"Don't you talk back to me," Bokade said and kicked him on his head. Manoj's head snapped back and he lay still.

"Now, the two of you. Sit on the front bench, will you?"

Jeet couldn't move.

"Now!" Bokade shouted. Spit flew out of his mouth. His lips were pulled back against his teeth.

They numbly walked to the bench and sat down.

"You two have been very bad of late," Bokade said as though he was a little disappointed with them.

A shiver of terror ran through Jeet's body. Bokade shook his hands the way he used to twenty years ago, as though he was totally unaware of the gun.

"Raise your hand," he said to Jeet.

Jeet didn't.

Bokade fired.

Anita shrieked and turned to look at Jeet. He was still sitting next to her. The bullet had missed him, but his cheek was singed. Jeet felt as though his face had touched a burning piece of metal. He smelt his burnt skin.

"Raise your hand," Bokade said in the same disappointed tone, as though he was not even aware he had fired a shot.

Jeet raised his right hand.

Bokade smiled and hit his hand with vicious force. Jeet had not expected the TV antenna to hurt so badly. A thick red line rose on his palm. Jeet clenched his fist.

"Will you raise your voice when talking to me, boy?"

"No," Jeet said, biting his lips.

"Just no? Am I not your sir anymore?"

"Sorry, sir."

"Sorry won't do," Bokade said, shaking his head in mild disapproval. "Raise your other hand."

Jeet knew Bokade had gone insane and his brain blamed the four of them for it. He glanced at the door with sweat pouring all over his face.

Bokade didn't wait for him to raise his other hand. He went for the face. Jeet raised his hands to shield himself, but he was late. The antenna hit him on the forehead. He felt tears sprouting in his eyes.

"Now we are getting somewhere. The little boy is crying. That's good. It means you are sorry for what you did," Bokade said, smiling hideously.

"Now, it's your turn, girl," he said to Anita.

She raised her hand.

That was when Manoj lunged at Bokade with an ululating cry.

"Run, Anita!" Jeet shouted.

Bokade grappled with Manoj who had grabbed him at the waist. Bokade struggled for a little while and then shot Manoj in the face. The blood splashed on the gun. Manoj collapsed on the ground with a soft thud that was buried in the echo of the gunshot. Jeet flung himself at Bokade and grabbed his right hand, which held the gun. Bokade slammed his left fist on Jeet's throat. He couldn't breathe. Bokade raised his fist again. Jeet twisted his neck to avoid the blow. It landed on the back of his neck. He felt his neck go numb with pain, but he didn't release his two-handed grip on the gun. The next blow landed on Jeet's nose. There was a soft crunching sound and blood erupted from his nose. He felt dizzy and knew he only had a few seconds before his grip on the gun came off. He pulled his head back like a whip and slammed it with all his might into Bokade's face. He felt the tender parts of Bokade's face yielding under the blow. Jeet realised that he had managed to weaken Bokade, that he was now one blow away from incapacitating him. Bokade's fist landed on his already shattered nose. Jeet felt his grip go limp, a deep dread rising up like vomit in his throat. He slumped to the floor wordlessly. All it took was a few seconds. Anita watched it in a trance. Jeet collapsed on the floor. Bokade had an irritated expression on his face, as though he had been interrupted by a little gnat. Jeet would be dead if she didn't do something.

Bokade pushed Jeet's limp form and raised his hand to shoot. Suddenly, the classroom was engulfed in darkness. His eyes were blinded momentarily by the sudden loss of light. Anita hurled the big torch at him with all her force. It hit him on his head, but the impact was nothing. She stood still, shocked by the impotence of her blow. He laughed and aimed the gun at her.

"Drop the gun Bokade!" He heard the voice of the man he had dreamt of torturing forever. Dev Gokhale.

"I have been waiting for you for a long time, you bastard," he said.

Dev shot him. The bullet entered his left shoulder, exited it and embedded itself into the wall behind. Bokade shrieked and fired at Dev. The bullet missed Dev by inches. He ran out of the class. Bokade staggered before running after him.

Inspector Kamble heard the first gunshot and felt every hair on his body stand on end. He ran up the road leading to the school building when he saw a man with a big flowing beard running ahead of him. The man was so fast that he disappeared into the darkness. Kamble cursed the thousands of cigarettes that he had smoked. He pulled out his gun, held his aching back and ran towards the school. He swore loudly when he heard two more gunshots, and tried to run harder.

The loud sound of a vehicle stopped him in his tracks. He quickly hid behind a tree. It was Abbas Haq's jeep. There were three men in the jeep, armed with hockey sticks. Abbas was driving. Kamble loathed the man. He hated every single minute of the time he had spent protecting the venom-spewing politician during his countless speeches and rallies. Abbas Haq's presence changed everything. This was much bigger than he had thought.

Bokade looked around in the darkness of the school ground but could not see Dev.

"Gokhale! You bastard!" he shouted.

Hiding behind a pillar on the ground floor aisle, Dev saw the frightening fury in Bokade's eyes. Once a killer, always a killer, isn't that so? He felt a sudden calm take over his body. He stepped out from the shadow of the pillar and pointed the gun at Bokade.

Before he could pull the trigger, a shot was fired.

It was Abbas's gun, spouting smoke.

"Stand where you are, Dev," Abbas shouted. His men rushed towards Dev.

Bokade reeled like a drunkard and fell on the ground. He writhed violently for a long time.

Dev pointed the gun at Abbas's men and walked up to the sprawled form of Bokade. Blood was spurting out of his stomach. His mouth was covered with red bubbles.

"Ba...bastard," Bokade said and lay still.

Dev kneeled down. He felt nothing–there was a numbness that made time stand still. He had expected a sense of deep relief. A death had wrecked their lives twenty years ago. Another death did nothing to mend it.

Anita came out, shouting Dev's name, and ran straight into Abbas. He grabbed her by the neck and she cried out in pain. Dev stood up with the gun pointing at them.

"Drop the gun right now, Dev." Abbas tightened his grip on Anita's throat.

Dev's hand wavered as Abbas held the gun to Anita's head. He dropped his gun.

"Now, kick it away," Abbas said.

Dev kicked it. It was gobbled up by the darkness.

Abbas nodded at his men and they launched into Dev. The first blow hit him on his knee and he collapsed. The second blow landed on his ribs and he heard them crack. The men started beating him up methodically.

"Yes, I killed that senile bastard Sharif Miyan! *You hear me?"* Abbas screamed.

Dev curled up into a foetal position and waited for the blows. With every blow his consciousness was deserting him. He could faintly hear Anita's shrieks. He hoped they would spare her. One kick landed on his head. Then everything was dark.

"Stop!" Kamble shouted.

The men stopped abruptly, surprised by the intrusion.

"I have radioed the headquarters and the police will be here in a few moments," he said. "Drop the gun, Abbas."

"Kamble, you dare to interrupt me?" Abbas said, trying to rein in Anita who was savagely twisting in his arms.

Grinding his teeth, Kamble said, "I heard what you just said.'

"You fucking maggot! You survive on the crumbs I throw and you dare talk to me like that?" Abbas barked at his men, "What are you waiting for? Kill the bastard!"

Qutub raised his hockey stick high in the air. Kamble fired. The bullet hit Qutub in his thigh and he collapsed, whimpering and cursing.

"I have had enough of you politicians," Kamble said pointing the gun back at Abbas.

Abbas was incredulous at the lowly policeman's temerity. "You…you…" he said, anger making his vision blurry. Cocking the hammer of the gun, he pulled back Anita's head.

Kamble fired.

"How will you manage the political storm?" Anita asked Kamble as she sat in front of him in the police headquarters.

Kamble sighed deeply. He hadn't slept since killing Abbas Haq. He hadn't gone home for the last three days. His clothes reeked of sweat and the countless cigarettes he had smoked.

"I will have to live through it."

"Thank you," Jeet said quietly. It hurt when he said those words. His jaw was fractured and his throat had suffered damage. The lacerations on his face would leave scars for life.

"How is Dev Gokhale recovering?" Kamble asked.

"He is all right. Getting discharged today," Anita said.

"And Shah?"

"He will be there for some more time."

Leaning back on his wooden chair, Kamble said, "You see, I don't really know what happened that night. The man Abbas killed was a convict. He was your teacher twenty years ago?"

Jeet nodded.

"I don't believe any of the things that you told the police," Kamble said and looked at both of them.

They said nothing.

"Why did you all come back?"

"This place is where we have our roots. We came back for a small reunion."

Kamble snorted. He lit up a cigarette and stared at them through the smoke. "I think there are some things that I will never know. I don't want to. But let me tell you this," he said and leaned forward. "I want you to leave this town as soon as possible. The case will take its own time and all of you will be required but, till then, I don't want you in this town. Bad things have happened since you have come back. I don't care if your father is the Prime Minister of India."

Jeet nodded. He wondered if the town would ever let them go. He looked out of the door and saw Maggie sitting on the wooden bench outside. There was intense worry in her eyes. He smiled at her, and she smiled back with trembling lips. He had to get away from Amrapur.

"Yes. I think this town has had its fill of us, Inspector," Anita said and stood up. "No words can ever express our gratitude. You could have so easily walked away from it all."

Kamble took a deep drag from the cigarette. After a few moments he smiled. They smiled back.

"We are leaving tomorrow, babe," Jeet said to Maggie.

She put her head on his shoulder and cried. Seven days ago, lying on the hospital bed, speaking through his broken jaw, he told her everything. She had held his hand throughout, gripping it fiercely when he told her about Bappa's death.

"So you are in love with a murderer," he said.

"No, I'm not," she said with a finality that startled him. "You are not a murderer, Jeet. That twelve-year-old boy is long gone. He is just a bad memory, a bad dream. You woke up from that dream after twenty years. I never asked you about your past. I knew…I sensed that you were running away from it every single minute. But it never let you. I knew there was something terrible hidden in that past. I feared that it would consume you if I called it out. It would consume your art."

He had tears in his eyes. They seeped into the bandage that covered his jaw.

"But today you have called that terrible thing out, and you have buried it forever. It is not coming back, Jeet. It is gone now. You are not that twelve-year-old boy anymore."

She kissed his hand and then pressed it against her wet cheek.

Dev touched Anita's face. She had a bruise running from below the eye to the chin. "I will be leaving tomorrow," he said. His hand shook as it gingerly touched the bruise.

She said nothing.

"People need me."

"Just like your father," she said and took his hand.

He smiled. "I saw a dream when I was in the hospital. It was not a dream, really. It was just this one image. When we were building that fort, you had asked Jeet whether there would be any living quarters in it. He had asked why. And you'd asked, what if the King and the Queen wanted some time away from the world?"

She nodded slowly, recalling the moment. She had never forgotten it.

"Jeet and Avi had laughed. But you…you had looked at me. And we had looked into each other's eyes. In that moment, you were the most beautiful thing I had ever seen. I have never seen anything that was as beautiful. It was the last thing I saw before passing out," he said.

She kissed him fleetingly on his swollen lips. His lips were torn by one of the blows. Two of his ribs had cracked. His knee cap was dislocated. He had bruises that were turning a hideous shade of purple.

"Why did it have to happen, Dev?"

"Because a boy always thought of himself as someone who had to protect his friends. Because his father never taught him that, but he learned it from him anyway."

"Can I come with you?"

"No," he said, calmly. He had battled with that question and made peace with the inevitable answer. "I love you. I always have. I always will. And that is the reason why I cannot take you with me."

She put her head on his chest, feeling his deep, rhythmic heartbeat. "What will I do now?" she said.

"You will fulfil your promise to your mother."

His breath fell on her bruised cheek, soothing it.

"Will we meet again?" she whispered.

He was silent. She closed her eyes and breathed in his skin and his breath. She knew they would never meet again.

"Don't forget me, Dev."

Maggie couldn't help crying for all the terrible nights Jeet had endured as she watched him sleep on the hotel bed. There was no tormented look on his serene face. His brow was without a furrow. His breathing was not the familiar laboured heaving. She had not called her boss in the art magazine for the last seven days. Wondering if she still had a job, she pulled out her mobile. Its battery was dead. She picked up the phone and dialled the reception.

"I need to charge my mobile phone."

"The power will be back in three hours, madam," the man said.

She looked at the watch. The work day would end an hour later in London.

"Can you please connect me to a number in the UK?" she said.

The man was silent for a few moments.

"Hello?"

"Sorry madam. We don't do that," he said.

"Why?"

"Well, I am sorry madam, but our telephone operator is not here right now."

"Okay, please call me when he is back."

He coughed a little. "Uhh…Madam, he won't be back tonight. There is a telephone booth just outside the hotel. You can make an ISD call from there."

She banged the phone down. Not wanting to leave Jeet alone even for a moment, she desperately paced the room. The editorship at the art magazine was her only source of income while she completed her work for the exhibition. She needed the job.

"I'll be back in a minute," she whispered in his ear.

She walked out of the hotel after asking the receptionist for the directions to the telephone booth. Night had engulfed the sleepy town in its cold embrace. She saw the yellow booth and walked towards it.

The white woman walked out of the hotel. Now, he would know what happened to his brother. The four of them would beg him to spare her life, but he wouldn't. The things that he had thought of doing to Bappa's killers! They would cry for her life, for forgiveness.

But he would get his revenge—for Bappa, and also for his family.

The phone rang like a terrible shriek. Anita grabbed it. She had slept in Dev's warm embrace, but a deeply unnerving feeling had remained.

"Madam, you are with the people in the room number two hundred five, right?"

"Yes," she said, her heart hammering uncontrollably. The town was still not done with them.

"There is a call for Mr Jeet Mehra. But nobody is picking it up. Would you like to take it?"

"Yes," she said, quivering.

The receptionist connected the call.

She dropped the phone the moment she heard the voice.

Dev woke up and picked up the phone.

"Dev Gokhale. You bastard! Come to the bridge now. You thought it was all over, didn't you? Well it's not!"

Dev heard Maggie's voice. She was hysterical. He heard a slap. He held the phone tightly, blood draining from his fingers.

"Jagan, listen. Please don't harm her. I'm coming," he said.

Wiping the sweat from his brow, he hobbled out of the room.

Anita ran to Jeet's room. Jeet couldn't speak when she told him after waking him up. He ran out of the room, she followed. They ran down the stairs of the hotel, behind Dev.

"Take this gun. I will confront him. You two come from over the bridge. He won't be able to see you," Dev said and handed the gun to Jeet as they reached the bridge. Twenty years ago, Bappa's body had gotten wedged on the exposed metal truss under the bridge.

"No," Jeet whispered.

"You want her to die?" Dev shouted in his ear. "Take it. I will face him. You get a chance, you shoot him."

"Dev, listen…" Anita said.

"No! This is not going to end like it did twenty years ago," he said and limped ahead.

"I'm here, Jagan," Dev said as he shuffled down the embankment of the weak stream.

Jagan had tied Maggie to the same truss on which Bappa had once been impaled. There was a rag in her mouth. Her eyes were bulging out.

"What did you do to my brother?" Jagan asked. His voice was soft; it was almost as though they were having an everyday conversation.

"He drowned in this water. I killed him," Dev said.

"Why?" Jagan screamed. "Why? Why? Why?"

"Jagan, listen to me! He was trying to kill me. I had no choice."

Jagan started laughing.

Dev knew it was going to end very badly for both of them. Jagan was standing on the precipice of insanity, from which there was no return. They had both endured twenty years of solitude. He looked from the corner of his eyes and saw the shadows of Jeet and Anita moving on the bridge.

"What choice do I have today, Dev?"

"You have the choice of forgiving me or killing me. But leave the girl out of this," Dev said. He was surprised at the calmness with which he spoke.

"How can I leave her out of it? Did you leave me out of it when you made that choice? You didn't. She will pay for it too," Jagan said and put the gun to Maggie's head.

Maggie started making retching sounds. Dev closed his eyes, praying for Jeet to shoot.

Jeet saw the gun pointed at Maggie's head. He fired.

The bullet missed Jagan by a foot. He shrieked with rage. He fired at the wooden bridge, where Jeet and Anita were hiding.

When he was twelve years old, Dev Gokhale was the fastest runner in school. He could run the hundred meters in eighteen seconds. It was a record that had stood forever. Dev flew at Jagan who was merely twenty feet away, but the bullet was much faster. It plunged into his body, passing cleanly through his heart. Dev crashed headlong into Jagan's emaciated chest. Jagan caved in and Dev fell on him. The gun flew out of his hand. Jeet screamed and ran to them. He hit Jagan on his head with a log of wood. Jagan lay unconscious.

"Dev!" Anita screamed.

"God no! God no!" Jeet pulled Dev away from Jagan.

Blood was spurting out of his mouth. He coughed. Frothy blood erupted from his heart.

"It's over," he said.

Epilogue

It would be the last journey Avi would embark on from Amrapur railway station.

"You sure you want to take the train?" Anita asked.

"Yes," Avi said. He could've so easily asked one of his drivers to get his Mercedes. "This is the only way I can leave this town behind."

They all waited till the train arrived at the platform. No words were necessary.

Avi hefted his bag when the train halted. "Goodbye," he said and boarded the train. He raised his hand and waved as it pulled out of the station. He kept watching them until they were out of sight, walked into the first class compartment and sat staring out of the window. Within minutes, Amrapur was far behind.

"We will never meet each other again, will we?" Jeet said to Anita as they walked out of the railway station.

She was silent for a long time, then said, "I hope we do, Jeet." Her car was waiting. She opened the door. "I hope we do," she said again.

The car moved ahead. She leaned back on the seat and closed her eyes.

Jeet watched the car till it disappeared. He walked up to Maggie who had waited for him outside the station.

"She will never get over losing Dev," she said.

"I hope she does," Jeet said. "I hope we all do."

Maggie held his hand.

"It is time to go back," he said.

She smiled.

Acknowledgements

My wife Pranita for her encouragement and support.

My agent and friend Kanishka Gupta from Writer's Side Literary Agency. A special gratitude is due for Devaki Khanna and Rahul Soni for improving this novel immensely.

I am indebted to Lekshmy Rajeev from Niyogi Books for believing in this novel, and my editor Gita Rajan for her patient and inspired editing.

Special thanks to friends who beta read my writing—Deepa Aithal, Alexandra Stopford, Abhijit Kothiwale, Shalabh Maloo and Shruthi Krishnamoorthi.